CRIME
IN THE
ALLOTMENT

A fiercely addictive mystery

CATHERINE
MOLONEY

Detective Markham Mystery Book 20

Joffe Books, London
www.joffebooks.com

First published in Great Britain in 2023

Cover art by Dee Dee Book Covers

ISBN: 978-1-83526-227-6

For Neil

PROLOGUE

Ninian Creech was in a foul mood as he stomped along one of two parallel grass avenues that ran between the plots of Beauclair Drive Allotment Association at the edge of Hollingrove Park.

It was a grey, dank New Year's Day, the cold, overcast sky and dreary weather matching his disgust with the world in general. Thank God he was at least able to escape the cramped little terraced house on Bromgrove Rise to his care-taker's shed where he was free from his wife's interminable reproaches.

The shed was initially a cold, dark space when Ninian took it over, but over time he had made it quite cosy with a second-hand rattan armchair, along with odds and ends from home that he had managed to smuggle out without his better half noticing. He had introduced a little heater and primus stove too, though technically people weren't supposed to cook on site and no doubt that almighty busy-body Mrs Margaret Cresswell would have something to say about it when she chaired the next meeting of the allotment committee.

Well the old bat can stick her objections where the sun don't shine, Ninian thought crossly as he unlocked the shed and hung up his coat on one of the pegs he had fixed between two narrow Perspex windows positioned at right angles to the left of the door. He was pleased to see that the winter jasmine he had put in a jam jar on the little fold up table was still looking fairly jaunty, like a burst of sunshine in his cramped little den.

Ninian did not exactly resemble a poetic soul, being a prematurely aged man who had a bald pate with a fringe of white hair and drooping beard of the same colour. Wrinkled, stooped and weather-beaten, he wore the air of one who had always worn a domestic yoke, but even a yoked creature can have its own whims and fancies.

Flipping the convector heater on, he set about making tea and then, with his well-sugared beverage and a short-bread biscuit from the tin he had got for his birthday, he sank into the rattan armchair with a sigh of satisfaction and some amelioration of his previous grumpiness. Eyeing a pad-locked cupboard under the sink (for the shed benefited from running water), he debated adding a nip of Scotch before deciding against it. While not exactly subscribing to poncey notions about 'Dry January', he could do with cutting back a bit.

Mind you, he hardly knew how he would have survived the festive season without illicit stiffeners. It had been their turn to host his know-all brother-in-law Steve, who the wife persisted in saying worked 'in oil' when he was nothing more than the owner of a garage in Birmingham. Those solar-powered fairy lights Steve had brought for the bushes in their front garden were a bleeding nuisance. Not only did they give up the ghost at the first sign of rain, but he had been endlessly criticised for 'doing it wrong', to the point where he fantasised about wrapping them round the throats of his nearest and dearest. Bad enough that the neighbours had a ringside seat as he stumbled about in the pitch dark alternately jabbing at useless rinky-dinky remotes and repositioning those poxy panels every which way in the boggy flowerbeds, but Steve giving himself airs when any fool could see the decorations were duds was the giddy limit. Needless to say, *he'd* copped the blame for the whole fiasco. Steve could do no wrong and that was that. The only blessing being that there weren't a wife and kids in tow . . . a battalion of monstrous Mini-Mes would have been pretty much the last straw. As it was, they were stuck with golden boy till the sixth, which meant he would have to be pretty inventive with excuses for dodging his obligations as host. The missus had been downright suspicious when he said there was stuff he had to check out, but she was distracted by having their guest to fuss over and coddle.

He didn't think much of the hideous garden gnome which was Steve's Christmas present to him ('I know how you green-fingered types like to put on a show', *Ho Ho*), leaving the ceramic figurine shrouded in its carrier bag. There was something creepy about the goblin's leering expression, as though it knew something to his disadvantage. And the garish colours offended his eye. It looked like something Steve had picked up at a car boot sale, whereas his hostess hit the jackpot with what looked like a bloody *flask* of Chanel No. 5. Oh yeah, Stevie Boy knew which side his bread was buttered all right.

Christmas was a right pain in the backside when all was said and done. All the fake jollity and feeling you had to join in for fear of being called a Grinch. That Secret Santa bollocks the allotmenteers insisted on was one big cringe. He was almost certain whoever had got him that stupid whoopee cushion did it out of spite. Like they didn't know he was hoping for a new tool bin!

Ninian's thoughts turned to the allotments.

All in all, it wasn't a bad place to have ended up after those years as a school caretaker. No more shrieking hooligans to contend with, for one thing. Though there was no escaping teachers, with a few of the Hope Academy crowd being conscientious horticulturalists and proud possessors of various greenhouses, huts and polytunnels scattered round the site.

What was it Hope's deputy head Elsie Parker was always saying? Oh yeah, all that about having an allotment being great for *mindfulness* and *mental equilibrium*, or Yin and Yang as youth worker Hilary Probert called it.

He supposed there was something in it . . . having green space where you could breathe and engage with nature, especially if you lived in a flat and didn't have your own garden. Mind you, it didn't mean you got away from all the aggro of folk not getting on and bitching about each other, seeing as the allotments were a kind of miniature society with factions and rivalries, gossip and rumours to beat all get out. Plus, people could get pretty steamed up about their radishes and runner beans, especially if they thought someone was stealing a march or nicking stuff.

The allotmenteers themselves were fairly possessive about the place, turning down the council's invitation to host 'allotment therapy' programmes in conjunction with Bromgrove Mental Health Services. Ninian kind of understood where they were coming from. You didn't necessarily want some nutjob with God knows what mental issues waving a hoe around and only a very small path between you . . . it just wouldn't feel *safe*.

Speaking of safety, he supposed he ought to give things the once-over. It was only a small site, with thirty full and ten half-plots, but the proximity of Hollingrove Park meant there was a waiting list. At this time of year, he had the place all to himself, given the miserable weather and the fact that even the most diehard fresh-air fiends were probably too stuffed or hungover to wield a spade.

Sighing virtuously, he retrieved his coat and headed out, passing the grey concrete hut where the committee held its meetings and kept the communal lawnmower along with assorted communal odds and ends.

The majority of plots at this time of year comprised freshly tilled patches of brown soil, with overwintering vegetables covered by layers of newspaper or protective fleece and little heaps of compost and manure dotted around. Mostly the place looked neat and well-maintained, the sheds and greenhouses securely padlocked and equipment stowed tidily away. Trellises and canes stood stiffly to attention, looking bare and forlorn after their winter pruning, but he spied the odd splash of colour here and there where allotmenteers had opted for winter-flowering clematis, hellebores, honeysuckle and pansies.

Ninian gave the new waterless compost toilet a wide berth. Nothing wrong with the old septic tank set-up in his opinion, but these trendy eco-warriors had to have it their own way. Well you wouldn't catch *him* using it. This was one issue where he and Margaret Cresswell were in complete agreement. He grinned at the recollection of her expression when that bloke from the council gave them his spiel on how to keep the rats out . . . looked like she was going to *puke* when he talked about them liking human waste so you had to get out the old chicken wire and sawdust. But hippy-dippy Hilary Probert had *loved* it. Ninian snorted, reflecting that if that one got her own way, they'd be overrun with ponds and frogs and God knows what else . . . chickens most like . . . As it was, her plot was starting to look a tad overgrown with those brambles, untamed blackberry bushes and overhanging fruit trees. Madam Cresswell was sure to be on Hilary's case about it, not to mention her 'rustic' shed which looked as though it was about to fall down.

Catherine Leckie, headteacher at Hope Academy (popularly known as Hopeless), was another one keen on wildlife and all that environmental jazz. Even wanted them to keep bees and run 'nature detective' programmes for local kids. But the association shot her down in flames. Valerie Shipley had been particularly snotty about it. Not surprising really seeing as it was Leckie who got Valerie's brother chucked off the allotment for being a peeping Tom. It had all been hushed up pretty quickly, so Ninian never got to find out exactly what had happened or who it was Dave Shipley was supposed to have been spying on. He couldn't imagine anyone looking for action amongst the beets and pumpkins — not exactly a turn-on in his book — but he remembered watching that *Lady Chatterley* series on telly, the one with Sean Bean and some posh blonde bird . . . there was that scene with them chasing each other starkers in the rain and doing it up against a tree, so maybe there was some sort of Adam and

Eve vibe going on. The wife had pronounced it 'disgusting', but then she would . . .

Reluctantly pushing away thoughts of pulchritudinous Joely Richardson, Ninian continued on his rounds.

It was such a compact site, there wasn't really all that much for a caretaker to do. But Cresswell and the rest of them no doubt figured having a salaried 'supervisor' gave the association more of an exclusive cachet than if they used a rota of volunteers. He had the feeling that for most of this lot, having an allotment was something of a status symbol. And now they had plans for expansion and an eye on the redundant kitchen garden (relic of the old Hollingrove estate) that adjoined their acreage. With such a prize in prospect, it made sense to talk up their security consciousness.

Despite the fading light and increasing chill, he lingered, feeling for some reason impelled to do another circuit.

He frowned as he passed Donald Kemp's patch. Just because the bloke was the son of Councillor Frank Kemp, he seemed to think it gave him the right to carry on like he was on the set of *Steptoe and Son* . . . that grotty, rain-damaged sofa with springs sticking out, for God's sake . . . and those rickety chairs . . . plus the broken windowpanes in his shed. At this rate, he'd be another one for Cresswell's shit list. The thought gave the caretaker no small satisfaction, as he cordially disliked Kemp's arrogant manner. The jumped-up so-and-so couldn't even keep a civil tongue in his head, invariably referring to Ninian as 'Wossname'. That lad's comeuppance was *well* overdue.

Ninian's expression cleared as he contemplated Catherine Leckie's pristine plot, reflecting that her stylish shed, with its red pine cladding and the little lean-to for coats and muddy boots, looked like something straight out of *Grand Designs*.

He was about to pass by when something caught his eye.

Her garden shed padlock was off and the door of the shed slightly ajar. He'd been so lost in his own reflections, that he hadn't noticed the first time around.

Ninian felt the first stirrings of uneasiness. That wasn't like Catherine Leckie, he thought. She was one of those who never lost her keys to the site and was meticulous about everything to do with security, even kicking up a fuss about needing to open and close locks with clean hands because particles of soil had a propensity for jamming them.

She would never have left her shed unsecured.

Suddenly he was struck by the murkiness of the twilight and the loneliness of the place, his previous feeling of wellbeing snuffed out as though by an invisible hand. Nonetheless, the caretaker reluctantly made his way to the shed by a little path that ran down the side of the plot.

Feeling foolish and self-conscious, he knocked hesitantly on the door and called out, 'Miss Leckie . . . Er, anyone at home?'

No answer.

He felt an overpowering repugnance to push the door open . . . The sensation was so strong, his arms hung like lead weights at his side. And now the blood was singing in his ears so that he was momentarily dizzy and lightheaded.

Almost as though he knew what awaited him . . .

Catherine Leckie lay curled on her side like a child asleep.

But this was no natural slumber, and death had not come to the allotmenteer as a kindly friend, the flex knotted tightly round her neck and eyes bulging out of their sockets telling their own pitiless story.

Ninian shrank back and, blindly, drunkenly, staggered away to raise the alarm.

What became known in Bromgrove as the allotment murders had begun.

CHAPTER 1

Monday 2 January found DI Gilbert 'Gil' Markham deep in thought on his favourite bench in the terraced graveyard of St Chad's Parish Church round the back of Bromgrove Police Station. He always felt it was crucial to have this time of reflection at the start of a major investigation before being plunged into the hubbub of CID.

The weather was unusually mild and clear, in contrast with the murky drizzle of the previous day, and he allowed himself to savour the tranquillity of the Victorian cemetery with its soft vernal tints of lichen and cypresses amidst serried ranks of blackened headstones, vaults and monuments. The grey squirrels were out in force, frisking around with a vigour that suggested *they* were strangers to any sort of festive slump or sluggishness.

There was always something vaguely penitential about the New Year, Markham thought wryly, as though the hedonism of Christmas somehow had to be expiated via endless 'health targets' and 'wellness goals'. *Just another commercial racket*, was his partner Olivia Mullen's conclusion, though she had been pleased with the Fitbit Smartwatch he had given her for Christmas.

Markham's feisty red-haired partner, who taught at Hope Academy ('Head of English as a second language', as she sarcastically put it) had broken up with him the previous year and subsequently become involved with a colleague at the school. However, it appeared that Mathew Sullivan ultimately preferred men to women, though he and Olivia remained friends. Markham was never sure exactly how deeply Olivia had committed herself or how far she had gone with the other man, but the break-up with Sullivan resulted in her returning to their apartment at the Sweepstakes, a complex of ultra-modern apartments off Bromgrove Avenue. Things had undoubtedly shifted between them; certainly, on his side, some of the trust had gone. The sex was passionate — as good as ever — but he could not shake off the sense of being a *shelter* for his clever, highly strung lover, though from what exactly he could hardly say . . . He knew he could not pin all the blame for his romantic difficulties on Sullivan. Markham's caseload and habit of withdrawing into himself during investigations had also played their part.

Part of the problem was his closeness to DI Kate Burton, second in command in the tight little unit that waspish colleagues had christened 'Markham's Gang'. The earnest psychology graduate was engaged to Professor Nathan Finlayson of Bromgrove University's criminal profiling department but showed no particular haste to get her fiancé to the altar. This procrastination did nothing to allay Olivia's jealous suspicion that the DI held a candle for Markham, despite Noakes insisting 'her and Shippers' — the nickname having been bestowed on account of Finalyson's startling resemblance to serial killer Harold Shipman — 'were bound to get hitched in the end, even if it turned out to be the longest engagement on record.'

Noakes.

Markham's haughty aquiline features broke into a smile at the recollection of his former sergeant. On retiring from CID, Noakes had taken the job of security manager at

Rosemount Retirement Home only to embroil himself more thoroughly than ever in the affairs of his former colleagues, wangling a role as occasional civilian consultant much to the ill-concealed chagrin of DCI Sidney ('Slimy Sid' to the troops) who abhorred the Yorkshireman's appalling dress sense, resolutely un-PC approach to life and general uncouthness. It had passed into CID legend how the portly sergeant, well-refreshed at his leaving do, had nudged rubicund Chief Superintendent Ebury-Clarke in the ribs and declared, 'Life depends on the liver' before demanding a pint of Drambuie Shandy. Even worse was when he declined an invitation to become an Honorary Life Tangent of Bromgrove Police Club on the grounds that with his luck it was probably a secret society for elderly transvestites 'like the one Prince Philip belonged to'. DCI Sidney, an ardent fan of the royals, was outraged, even after Markham had explained that his friend was thinking of the Freemasons.

Noakes's detractors found Markham's 'bromance' with the pug-featured, jowly veteran unfathomable, but the DI valued his friend's disdain for station politics, sympathy for the underdog and a strangely poetical strain in his make-up which was markedly at odds with his slobbish exterior. Noakes was the only one apart from Olivia who knew that Markham was a survivor of childhood abuse by a stepfather and had lost his brother Jonathan to drink and drugs. He was doggedly loyal to his former boss and cared nothing for the baleful resentment of Bromgrove's high command, a quality which had endeared him to Olivia. He and Olivia, indeed, formed something of a mutual admiration society. Noakes regarded her with a chivalrous devotion that was decidedly aggravating to Muriel, his bossy social-climbing wife and former shining light of the amateur ballroom dancing circuit where they had (somewhat incredibly) first met.

Back in the day, when Noakes was still in CID, he had enjoyed chewing the cud with Markham in St Chad's cemetery, awakening much trepidation in the soul of the Reverend Simon Duthie (a late recruit to the priesthood after a career with Lloyds Bank) who simply did not know how to take this bizarre relic of an earlier era. Theological sallies, in particular, caused much consternation, since Noakes always threw them out with a perfectly straight face. Markham had long cherished the memory of Duthie's poleaxed expression when his friend enquired 'where the vicar stood on having the theme from *Star Wars* as a tune cos his daughter fancied it for her wedding.' Buxom, permatanned Natalie Noakes was no nearer making it up the aisle than Kate Burton, but it was an excuse for her father to badger the priest about 'pop in the pews' until the poor man didn't know where to put himself. Continuing with the nuptial theme, Noakes had proceeded to regale Duthie with the one about an elderly Mancunian who said, 'I grew up in a two-bedroomed terrace with twelve brothers and sisters. I didn't know what it was like to sleep in a bed all by myself until I got married.' Noakes chortled happily over the punchline, however the clergyman — founder of the *Bromgrove Marriage Encounter* movement — was less convulsed. Unsurprisingly, the incumbent of St Chad's now gave the graveyard a wide berth lest he should be ambushed by the Incorrigible One, so Markham knew he was guaranteed a peaceful interlude.

At least the other two members of his team were thoroughly unexceptionable, he thought with satisfaction. DS Doyle, a gangling easy-going young detective whose auburn hair and freckles had earned him the sobriquet the Ginger Ninja, had been Noakes's protégé and the two men were still close, not least on account of their shared passion for the Beautiful Game. There had been a time when Doyle was distracted by his somewhat tempestuous love life, but he was in calmer waters now that he had settled down with teacher girlfriend Kelly. Ambitious and the proud possessor of a degree in criminal law, Markham had no doubt the youngster would one day make inspector.

Roger Carruthers, the other DS, had taken longer to bed in. Strangely anaemic looking, with his prissy horn-rimmed specs, sibilant speech and penchant for black leather trench coats, there was something of the Gestapo officer about his appearance. Noakes, predictably, initially failed to warm to the Oxbridge graduate (like Burton, a fast-track detective) whom he called 'Roger the Dodger'. The fact that Carruthers was the nephew of Superintendent 'Blithering' Bretherton and initially rumoured to be DCI Sidney's spy didn't exactly help matters. However, over time he had somehow gelled with the team, sharing Burton's fascination with psychology and the others' fanatical devotion to Bromgrove Rovers. More importantly, in the long run he had proved himself to be no snitch and well able to give as good as he got, with a wry sense of humour that served him in good stead. Twitted by Noakes about his decision to take up golf, he had replied deadpan that he wasn't sure of the rules and didn't even know how many bats he was allowed to carry in his case. The day they were in their favourite pub the Grapes squabbling amicably over the menu and Markham heard Carruthers wisecrack, 'If you can't pronounce it, we can't afford it!', he somehow knew everything would be all right and the newbie was going to fit in just fine. Even Noakes had come round in the end, once he realised that Carruthers admired Markham and intended to remain loyal no matter what blandishments were held out by the top brass. For his part, Carruthers gradually got used to Noakes's unusual role and now called him 'Sarge' like the rest.

It was pleasurable to ponder the merits of his team, Markham thought.

Unlike the ghastly discovery to which he had been called out the previous day.

But now it was time to do a quick mental recap before heading in to CID, so he cast his mind back to the scene . . .

He had been quite taken with the Beauclair Drive allotments which, even on a drear January day with the plots stripped back to their essentials and SOCOs swarming over the site, possessed a peaceful charm as of somewhere secret and inviolate.

Once he had donned his paper suit, the police pathologist Doug 'Dimples' Davidson, back from his sabbatical, was waiting for him at Catherine Leckie's shed. Davidson, a bluff countryman with the air of a rural vet (the spit of Siegfried Farnon in the classic BBC series *All Creatures Great And Small*) looked grave as he greeted Markham.

'Our victim's the headteacher from Hope,' he said without preamble. 'Quite young to have snagged the job, but very capable and a real dynamo . . . I remember being impressed by her during the interview process.'

Recalling that Dimples was a school governor, Markham now understood the medic's unusually serious mien. He remembered too that Olivia had spoken warmly of the new broom, though in truth she was so relieved to see the back of ultra-PC Tony Brighouse ('Call Me Tony') that just about anybody would have ranked as an improvement in her book.

Catherine Leckie must have been an attractive woman, he thought, looking down at the slim form and the long chestnut hair that partially obscured her features. But there was no escaping that ugly garotte, darkened complexion and glazed protruding eyes. At least there was nothing equivocal about cause of death.

'I've done the preliminaries, Inspector,' the pathologist said gesturing towards two paramedics who waited discreetly with their gurney. 'I'll put a rush on the PM and give you a call as soon as we're finished. As to time of death, judging by rigor I'd say around nine or ten o'clock last night.'

Since the tweedy medic could be miserly with such information, he was clearly keen to catch the perpetrator.

'What the hell was she doing out here so late?' he muttered. 'Some kind of romantic assignation or what?' He gestured towards the shed's interior. 'She's got strip lighting in there and it's nicely kitted out . . . quite the home from home . . . but even so . . .' There was bewilderment in his tone and Markham suppressed a smile at the thought that Mrs Davidson was not the kind of woman for al fresco high jinks.

'New Year's Eve and all that,' he murmured.

'I suppose so.' Davidson shook himself. 'Right,' he said briskly as the paramedics came forward. 'Time to move her.'

The DI bowed his head respectfully as Catherine Leckie left her little earthly paradise for the last time. He tried to think of an appropriate prayer, but somehow the words just wouldn't come. Then, clear as a bell, he heard Olivia's voice quoting Francis Bacon. '"God Almighty first planted a garden and it is the purest of human pleasures",' she had recited teasingly when he baulked at getting window boxes for their apartment.

So now he prayed that the murdered headteacher's soul had been transplanted to a realm untroubled by winter rain and storms where seeds of love would flower again. And he vowed that he would call her killer to account.

A raucous burst of hilarity on the far side of the allotment made the DI's head shoot up.

The laughter died abruptly as though cut off by some invisible signal, Markham being known to lash out at subordinates who were so ill-advised as to attempt anything approaching gallows humour. Legendarily chilly, austere and quietly spoken (which inspired the nickname 'Lord Snooty'), he rarely showed what he was feeling, but respect for the dead was one of his red lines no one cared to cross. Noticing a young constable go scuttling down one of the grassy avenues, clearly bent on a hasty exit, Markham was satisfied he'd got the message across.

Aware that Forensics were impatient to process the scene, he contented himself with a brief survey of the shed. It was high-spec and indeed quite the home from home, he thought sadly, being furnished with quiet, good taste that spoke of a gentle and cultured character. Botanical prints and engravings adored the walls, while the simple rustic furniture — including a wooden rocking chair, dining table and chairs, bookshelves (several Jane Austens, he noted) and vibrant braided mat — was harmoniously arranged to soothe the eye. A little home office squeezed beneath one of two double-glazed windows showed that the dead woman used her shed for work, while a full-length potting bench with sink bore a watering can, seedlings and garden implements all meticulously arranged and spotlessly clean. There was a pleasant woody smell which awoke nostalgic memories of trips to the garden centre with his flower-loving mother as a small child. The shed felt warm and cosy too with no hint of damp or mustiness, no doubt thanks to a slimline space heater in the corner. Altogether, it was a delightful retreat.

There was no sign of any disturbance or struggle, which suggested the allotmenteer was taken by surprise . . . had maybe welcomed someone she knew without realising that she was in mortal danger . . .

Could it have been, as Dimples suggested, a romantic assignation? A huge chrysanthemum plant, all russet and golden blooms, wrapped in cellophane, stood on the floor next to the door. There was no card with the flowers, but the bouquet could be some sort of gift — though nothing to say it couldn't have come from school governors or a professional contact as opposed to some admirer. There were tealights and candles on one of the shelves along with a bottle of red wine. So perhaps this was all about a lovers' rendezvous that went tragically wrong. Or maybe Catherine Leckie simply fancied seeing in the New Year by herself in this little sanctuary that clearly meant so much to her.

With one final look, Markham left the SOCOs to their work . . .

Now reluctantly, he got up from his bench in St Chad's cemetery, squaring his shoulders as he wended his way down through the picturesque terraces towards the gate at the bottom. The sky suddenly darkened as though to reflect the enormity of his mission.

Time to put the investigation in motion.

* * *

CID always looked stale and forlorn in the New Year, with tatty tinsel and bedraggled decorations trailing from the ceiling and across workstations. But from tomorrow, when the cleaners were back at work after the bank holiday, all traces of frivolity would be eradicated.

It was high time the department had a refurb, he thought with mild irritation as he settled himself in his small office with its unrivalled view of the car park. Something high-tech and *Line of Duty* with lots of chrome and plate glass . . .

In his dreams.

'Happy New Year, sir,' DI Kate Burton greeted him softly from the doorway.

He wondered if he would ever be able to cure her of deferring to him like this, seeing as they were now the same rank. But part of him (the misogynist part, no doubt!) appreciated the courtesy.

Once upon a time Burton had favoured neutral-coloured Chairman Mao trouser suits that swamped her curvy frame, but today she was wearing a charcoal-grey jersey dress that clung in all the right places. The severe schoolmarmish bob was a distant memory, superseded by a layered hairdo with blonde streaks à la Emily Maitlis. But the intelligent, shyly eager eyes that glowed like enormous brown lollipops, until she whipped on her glasses, were the same as ever.

As they chatted lightly about the holidays, Markham detected a reticence regarding her home life. Ostensibly she and Nathan Finlayson, after going through a rocky patch, were 'back on', having reconciled over the festive season, but he sensed a strained wariness that belied her account of domestic bliss. The DI liked Finlayson, with his self-deprecating manner, lack of pomposity and dry wit, and hoped they could sort it out. In the final analysis, whatever the affinity with his colleague, he felt that he was bound to Olivia. And although, with a certain dog-in-the-manger contrariness, a part of him resented another man attracting Burton's devotion, he knew in his heart that the situation was best left as it was.

After some five minutes, Doyle and Carruthers arrived, in high spirits at the prospect of being part of a murder investigation. Doyle had brought brownies from home, while Carruthers carried almond croissants and a tray of hot drinks from the neighbouring Costa, it being something of a

(Noakesian) tradition that meetings should feature eats and treats. DCI Sidney had more than once commented acidly on their preoccupation with 'provisioning', but it made no difference to the team's rituals and Markham secretly liked the sense of homely camaraderie that characterised their briefings. Burton's preference for wholefood was not forgotten ('Are vegans the ones with the pointy ears?' Doyle had asked mischievously the first time she held forth about the health benefits of clean eating, in an echo of Noakes's insistence that he had never met a sane vegetarian). Carruthers dutifully produced a granola bar and soy macchiato for her while the rest of them enjoyed their daily sugar rush.

'Right,' Markham said finally when they had fuelled up and swapped anecdotes about their festive experiences, 'let's see what we've got.'

Burton needed no further prompting, crib sheet and glasses at the ready.

'Our victim is Catherine Leckie, headteacher at Hope,' the DI commenced. 'She was found in her garden shed at Beauclair Drive allotments by the caretaker Ninian Creech around four in the afternoon on New Year's Day—'

'What do we reckon to the caretaker then?' Doyle interrupted eagerly, mindful that the discoverer of a homicide victim always merited close examination.

'According to uniforms at the scene, he's an unlikely contender . . . seemed a bit decrepit and genuinely shocked,' Markham replied, 'but of course, it could've been an act.' They knew only too well that appearances could be deceptive. 'He used to work at Hope, so that's a connection to the victim.'

Burton frowned slightly before continuing with her recital.

'It's a small site over by Hollingrove Park,' she said. 'No CCTV.' Her colleagues groaned at this. 'The place is leased from the council by Beauclair Drive Allotment Association. The Chair is one Margaret Creswell . . . she's a governor at Hope, so that's another connection. A couple of the teachers from Hope have plots there.' She checked her list. 'Elsie Parker, one of the deputy heads, and Rebecca Atherton who runs the Pupil Referral Unit, or "sin bin" . . . There's a youth worker name of Hilary Probert and some local business people . . . Raymond Cotter, he owns a couple of fashion outlets over in Old Carton and there's a rumour that Catherine was seeing him—'

'As in romantically?' Carruthers cut in.

'It's not clear how far it had gone, but it seems they were pretty friendly,' came the careful reply. 'Moving on, there's Donald Kemp,' she cleared her throat, 'as in *Councillor* Kemp's son.' Cue more groans. 'Then we've got a brother and sister, Valerie and Dave Shipley. Some bad blood there apparently . . . he was chucked out of the association after a complaint by Catherine, so that needs checking out . . . Oh, and there's a Michael Oddie who paid her quite a bit of attention . . . In terms of the allotment, those are the names that cropped up, but obviously there are a number of other members. As I say, it's a small site and several people were travelling or away for the holidays, which narrows down the pool of suspects.'

'You've done well in such a short time, Kate,' Markham said approvingly, causing her to flush with pleasure and her male colleagues to exchange knowing glances. 'Do we know anything about folk who might have grudges against Ms Leckie?'

'There was some sort of family feud with her brother Greville, guv. Something to do with their mum's funeral and will.' Anticipating his concern for the next-of-kin, she went on, 'FLOs are with him and I've arranged for us to see him tomorrow.'

'Excellent. Anyone else with a potential motive?'

'A troublemaking sixth-former called James Daly . . . Catherine expelled him last year after claims about bullying and sexual harassment. And apparently Raymond Cotter's ex-wife Bernadette Farrelly wasn't a fan.' Folding her crib sheet, she concluded, 'So there's a dozen or so who look promising one way or another . . . something to work with at any rate.'

'I'd like to take another look at the site, Kate,' Markham said. 'Soak up the vibes, so to speak . . . We can do that this afternoon while Doyle and Carruthers get everything set up here and coordinate the house-to-house enquiries. Church Avenue and Rockbourne Close are nearest to the park, so it's possible the locals noticed something unusual.'

'What about interviews, guv?' Doyle enquired.

'You can get started chasing folk up right away. I want to see as many members as possible tomorrow evening in St Bruno's Parish Hall,' Markham instructed. 'The church is practically next door to the allotments, so that might help to jog memories.' He paused. 'George Noakes used to have an allotment at Beauclair.' The others grinned as though to say, *Wouldn't you just know it!* 'I'll swing by Rosemount in the morning and see what he can add.'

'Is Sarge coming on board then, guv?' Doyle asked innocently.

'I believe there's a good case for saying Noakesy's insights will prove invaluable,' the DI replied smoothly, not without an inward qualm at the prospect of broaching this with Sidney. He would have to choose the right moment . . . and bring Burton along for the ride, since she was a dab hand at dealing with the DCI, distracting him with news of the latest developments in psychological profiling and the like. Somehow she managed to do with his without coming across as either sycophantic or insincere, which only increased Markham's regard for her.

* * *

'Have you heard much from Noakesy then?' he asked Burton as she drove them out to the allotments with her usual scrupulous attention to the speed limit.

'Last time we spoke, he was sounding off about Morrisons putting Easter eggs out on Boxing Day. It really got his goat. He was muttering about kids having no clue about religion . . . thinking it's the feast of the Easter Bunny and that kind of thing.'

Markham chuckled, recognising one of his friend's perennial hobby horses.

'And he was grousing about the services at St Mary's Cathedral. Said he can't stand the new Dean or Archdeacon or whoever he is . . . Apparently last Sunday he started out by telling the congregation what the gospel was going to be. Then he read the gospel. Then, for the sermon, he told everyone what the gospel had been.'

'I believe they call it reinforcement learning.'

'Well, whatever it is, Noakesy was fed up . . . Apparently, Muriel thinks this bloke is the bee's knees, but Sarge thinks he's patronising . . . like when it comes to the Last Judgement, instead of all that about sheep and goats, Jesus is going to say, "Right, I want you all to break up into small discussion groups and report back after purgatory."'

'Sounds somewhat reminiscent of our Diversity and Inclusion training sessions.' And he knew just what Noakes thought of *those*.

Burton smiled. 'He likes the clergy to give it to him straight . . . Be loyal to the Church. Stick to tradition. Keep the Commandments, otherwise you'll be cut off and might end up being burned.'

'Yes, it's that Methodist upbringing and Sunday School indoctrination.' And a sort of Englishness, Markham supposed . . . If cycling from the pub to Evensong, past the cricketers on the village green, had passed into folklore and the old customs were no longer what they were, there were still certain enduring signs of what it meant to be *Made in England*. And George Noakes was just one such example.

'I didn't know Sarge used to have an allotment,' his colleague interrupted his thoughts.

'Oh, that's way back in the mists of time . . . but it should play well with Sidney,' he added cynically.

'Noakesy'll definitely want to be in on this case.' Burton hesitated. 'I don't want to speak out of turn, boss, but I got the feeling something's wrong at home.'

Markham's antennae twitched. '*Oh?*'

'More than his usual Anti-Christmas Syndrome kicking in or anything like that,' Burton observed wryly. 'Something else . . . but I didn't want to push.'

'Perish the thought, Kate.' Markham knew his fellow DI was the last person to try and force confidences. 'I'll try and winkle it out of him tomorrow,' he reassured her.

The allotments, cordoned off with police tape, were deserted save for the uniform posted at the gate who saluted smartly as they passed through.

Markham hadn't expected anything to jump out at him, but he was curious to see how his fellow DI responded to the place.

'My dad would have liked this,' she said wistfully as they surveyed the various plots. 'He had his hen house, of course . . . but the local allotments didn't let people keep poultry back then. I think these days it depends on the council or the committee, so it's not a no-no anymore.'

Markham knew that his colleague had struggled badly when her father died.

'He was green fingered then?'

'Oh yes,' she said with an effort at lightness. 'A bit like King Charles . . . was convinced you just have to talk to plants and they respond.'

They paced up and down in companionable silence, totally at ease with each other. Privately, Burton felt absurdly happy as she stole sidelong looks at her colleague's chiselled profile, but her demeanour was phlegmatic as usual.

'There's some sort of legend attached to this place,' she remembered suddenly.

'Really?'

'Yes . . . something about the ghost of a dead baby . . . they found the body in an old glasshouse.'

'When was this?'

'Oh, it was the nineteen-sixties . . . Someone at the council mentioned the story when I was checking out the background. It happened at Christmas . . . the parents were never found.'

'Any signs of foul play?'

'Bruising, but the autopsy was inconclusive.' She shivered. 'Poor little thing, dumped out here like rubbish.'

Markham detected an unusual intensity in Burton's tone. For some reason, it looked like the fate of that abandoned infant had got under her skin, the pert features looking quite forlorn.

'One more circuit and a quick look at Catherine Leckie's shed,' he said briskly, 'and then it's back to base.' He smiled at her. 'I know you'll want to check that the tasks have been divvied up properly and chase up Dimples.'

'D'you think we could be looking at a crime of passion, guv?'

A one-off, was what she meant, as opposed to something more sinister.

The dread possibility of a serial murderer hung in the air between them.

'I don't want to rule anything out at this stage,' Markham said slowly. 'It could be random . . . unpremeditated.'

But they both knew that nothing about the scene was a fit. Not for a crime of passion. Nor for some opportunistic, spur-of-the-moment attack. The undisturbed shed. The chilling efficiency of the killer's chosen weapon, whatever it turned out to be . . .

If this was Eden, a serpent lurked in the undergrowth.

And he had the feeling its poison was not yet spent.

CHAPTER 2

Everywhere was dripping and dank when Markham called on Noakes the following morning, even the flowers in Rosemount's immaculately tended beds looking dejected and flattened by sporadic gusts of rain. The tall pines and cypresses which lined the winding driveway reared up bravely against a leaden sky, while a lone gardener toiled up and down pathways as he diligently cleared mulch and soggy leaves that had drifted down. Rosemount's brochure boasted that its landscaped grounds, including a knot garden and lake, 'held the suspended stillness of a Constable landscape'. But today it felt more like being in a gloomy Rembrandt, Markham thought as he crunched across the gravelled forecourt to the porticoed front door.

Inside the white stucco Georgian mansion, however, all was warmth and comfort, with the delightful subtle scents of an old country house and none of the antiseptic ambience one traditionally associated with nursing homes.

The personable young clinical supervisor greeted Markham like an old friend (given the frequency of his visits to Noakes, the DI supposed that's what he was fast becoming). 'You'll find Mr Noakes in the residents' lounge, Inspector,' she said. 'He wasn't sure the painting of Nelson was hanging straight.'

Markham smiled as he made his way across the hall to the right-hand side of the house.

Noakes was very keen on patriotic art (the more un-PC the better). General Charles Gordon, the defender of Khartoum, had previously held pride of place in his pantheon of warriors, but it sounded like naval heroes were now in the ascendant. Despite being troubled by the whole 'Kiss me, Hardy' story, he had settled it in his mind that this legend definitely *didn't* mean there was 'anything dodgy going on' and chosen a striking reproduction of Turner's *The Battle of Trafalgar* to adorn the lounge, much to the satisfaction of his new assistant, a cheery eighteen-year-old called Kevin who belonged to the Bromgrove Sea Cadets. Rosemount's Board readily allocated funds for such 'beautification' on the grounds that it not only enhanced the building's impressive interior but formed a striking backdrop to meetings of Bromgrove History Society and other local groups which held cultural gatherings on the premises.

Of course, Noakes's freelance curatorship was hardly part of his job description, but the old villain had somehow carved out a unique role for himself at Rosemount in much the same way as he had insinuated himself back into CID after collecting his carriage clock.

It amused Markham how his friend's sartorial eccentricities were far better suited to his new environment than to the world of policing, though what the staff and residents made of today's startling combo — baggy turquoise chinos, striped shirt topped with a red Pringle sweater, and his beloved George boots (the only footwear an alumnus of 2 Para would countenance) — was anyone's guess. As usual, his regimental tie was skew-whiff as though it was strangling him, and a tweed jacket heavily patched at the elbows hung discarded from the back of a Chippendale chair. As the DI watched from the doorway of the lounge, Noakes stood in front of his new acquisition squinting furiously with a spirit level clutched in his right hand.

'Looks straight to me, Noakesy,' Markham said advancing further into the room.

The lounge was a gracious space, even if it contained far too many poufs for Noakes's liking.

There were comfortable furnishings with deep seat armchairs and rolling vintage bookshelves, along with strategically placed coffee tables and charming engravings on the walls. Pastel blue painted walls were offset by rich crimson upholstery and cushions, so that the overall effect was one of understated luxury — unsurprising given that Rosemount's intake consisted primarily of well-heeled private patients, though the home also took some NHS overflow by way of a nod to ethical nostrums. The room, together with a little annexe used as a writing room, was agreeably scented by pots of winter honeysuckle and its bay windows looked out onto an enclosed courtyard that might have graced the pages of *Country Life*, with trailing ivy and delightful stone sculptures of pouting cherubs that made the DI suddenly think of that tiny abandoned corpse found at Beauclair Drive allotments. It was an uncomfortable memory.

Forcing down thoughts of the dead baby, he crossed the deep pile carpet to join his friend.

'Very impressive,' he observed appreciatively.

'It ain't bad,' Noakes replied with elaborate casualness, as befitted a connoisseur.

'Is General Gordon going to join him in here?' Markham enquired with a gleam of mischief. 'Or are you keeping him in the staff room to put the fear of God into any slackers.'

'Reckon it's all about getting the balance right,' his friend said with dignified complacency. 'The old folk might freak out a bit seeing Gordon in his fez an' the natives ready to chop him into bits.' Which was one way of putting it. 'Whereas with this one, there's nowt to make 'em fret about voodoo an' cannibalism an' stuff . . . They c'n jus' imagine old Horatio on deck doing his heroic bit.' Bleeding to death from a sharpshooter, thought Markham wryly, but each to his own.

'Excellent,' he said heartily. 'Are we going to use your office or what?'

'Let's stay here, it's nice an' cosy,' the other replied. 'No one'll be along for a bit cos it stands to reason they like their lie-ins. I'll have a word with Kev about the elevenses.' *Nothing like getting your priorities right.*

Noakes promptly disappeared on his errand, leaving Markham to sink into a red velvet wingback. The peace and comfort were so seductive, that he momentarily closed his eyes.

With a clatter and bustle, Noakes reappeared trailed by his ruddy-cheeked subordinate who was carrying a tray and looked comically out of place in these plush clubroom surroundings. It was obvious the two of them got on, the older man adopting a fatherly tone that indicated he was well pleased with his apprentice. After an exchange of pleasantries, the youngster departed, leaving them to their excellent coffee and shortbread.

'No need to ask if it's going well for you here, Noakesy,' Markham commented, eying his friend shrewdly.

'Yeah well, they're nice folk an' the boss man don' interfere too much.' High praise in Noakes's book. With self-conscious pride he added, 'Asked if I wanted to live in . . . there's a flat going if we fancied it.'

'What does Muriel say?' Markham could imagine Mrs Noakes being tempted by the chatelaine-like possibilities. Whereas Olivia found the woman's snobbery and social pretentions exasperating to the nth degree, *he* empathised with the insecurity that he sensed was at the root of her posturing. The psychologists would probably label it a type of Imposter Syndrome . . . whatever the cause, he found it poignant more than anything else. In fact, it had struck him that the same was true of DCI Sidney who was mellower these days, as though the prospect of his own retirement in the not-too-distant future was slowly releasing him from the straitjacket of corporate ambition and professional jealousy of Markham . . .

Noakes's voice cut across his thoughts.

'Well, the missus *thought* about it . . . executive perks an' all that. But in the end she decided it wouldn't be fair on the community, seeing as she's so . . . *involved* with lots of local stuff . . . Then there's the neighbours an' everyone to think of . . .' Proudly, he added, 'I'm always telling her, "You're so busy coming an' going that one day you'll meet yourself coming back!" But she just says, "If you want something done, ask a busy person"!'

Markham felt a lump in his throat as he contemplated his friend's beaming expression, the pouchy, jowly features creased with admiration for his formidable spouse. And if Muriel *did* have a finger in every pie, who was to say she wasn't a force for good? He stifled a grin at the thought of Natalie's likely impact on the sedate environs of Rosemount. While Noakes's daughter was these days less inclined to rock the mini-skirts and leather trousers that she sported during her reign as the doyenne of Bromgrove's less salubrious nightclubs, her brassy charms would undoubtedly have sent residents' collective blood pressure skyrocketing (to say nothing of her effect on impressionable Kevin).

As Noakes's face suddenly clouded over, Markham had the conviction that Kate Burton was right and something *was* bothering his former wingman. Best to come at it circuitously once they'd had a chat about the latest investigation.

Noakes, predictably, was fascinated by details of the allotment murder and listened attentively as Markham ran through the details.

'I've heard the missus talk about Margaret Cresswell,' he said. 'Widowed for yonks, but Muriel reckons she might be on the prowl.'

It sounded like this was a case of 'frenemies', the DI thought sardonically. Surface friendship concealing a rich seam of cattiness. No wonder Oscar Wilde had it that true friends stabbed you in the front!

Aloud, he said, 'What makes Muriel think that?'

'Jus' a glint in Cresswell's eye kind of thing,' Noakes said vaguely. 'Plus she's got cosy with some old boy who lost his wife a few years back.' He scratched his head. 'Think he's got an allotment at Beauclair . . .' His face cleared. 'Yeah, Peter Barlow . . . seventy odd if he's a day. His wife was a teacher before she ended up in a wheelchair when she got . . . MS,' he declared.

'What was it like at Beauclair when *you* had your patch there, Noakesy?'

'Oh dead relaxed,' Noakes replied. 'But the missus heard that nowadays they're all properly up thesselves . . . there's a bossy-boots committee always banging on about rules an' regs an' all that.' He scowled. 'It's meant to be somewhere you can potter around an' *chill* . . . But now there's lots of nit-picking an' the eco-mob getting steamed up about all sorts . . . Swampy types,' he added darkly. 'I'm glad I got out before any of that palaver.'

'*Hmm*, that's interesting . . . So people can get quite territorial and obsessive?'

'You better believe it. Yeah, I'm well out of the whole she-bang,' Noakes repeated emphatically. 'Besides,' with marked complacency and an expansive gesture, 'I've got the grounds here for when I want to do a bit of digging.' A pause and then, 'How's Slimy Sid with all of this . . . got his twisters in a nick in case some nice respectable customers involved.

'I'll be seeing the DCI later today,' Markham said evenly.

'Will he let you bring me in on this one?'

'If you behave yourself, I'm sure I can swing it, Noakesy.'

Had the other been a cat, he would have purred. As it was, meaty hands cradling his paunch, he contemplated his old boss with ineffable satisfaction.

'How was your Crimbo?' he said at last.

'Quiet . . . We enjoyed Midnight Mass at the Cathedral.'

'Oh aye, us an' all . . . But I didn't like the way that fella quoted Latin in his sermon . . . a bit Papist if you ask me.'

As one whose Latin scholarship doubtless consisted of 'Amo, Amas, Amatitagain,' Noakes clearly resented such imprecations.

Trying not to laugh, Markham changed the subject.

'Ebury-Clarke will be looking over my shoulder on this one, Noakesy, so we need to be careful . . . *tact and discretion* our watchword.' Neither of which had ever much troubled his former sergeant.

'Sure thing, guv. *Hey,*' with an evil grin, 'd'you remember when he did that speech to the council an' I joshed him about it afterwards . . . said he was applauded in an' then at the end clapped-out, *geddit?*'

'Indeed.' Markham prayed the Chief Superintendent had a short memory for such delightful banter.

'It was Chris Carstairs's joke but I nicked it.'

DI Chris Carstairs in Vice was generally regarded as the station wit, his deft word-mongery much admired by Noakes.

'Let's hope Ebury-Clarke appreciated the, er, subtlety,' the DI replied faintly.

Seeing that his friend was now in high good humour, he felt he could risk an enquiry about Natalie.

Noakes was a doting father, albeit he was not in fact Natalie's biological parent. Discovering this during a previous investigation had sent Noakes temporarily off the rails — so much so, that he had nearly committed professional hara-kiri as a result, in addition to endangering his relationship with Markham. But he had weathered the storm, being a man who, no matter how many times he was knocked down, always got up again (not the least of the attributes that had won Markham's esteem).

'She's in the family way,' was the completely unexpected reply.

Markham was startled. 'Are you sure?' he asked, though Noakes's glum face was all the confirmation he needed.

'Yeah, she took the test last week an' the GP's confirmed it. Six weeks gone . . . due in the summer.'

'I assume it's Rick's,' Markham continued hesitantly, referring to Natalie's on-again, off-again fiancé, the highly eligible heir to a fitness empire whose hard-as-nails mother made no secret of the fact that she thought he could do better.

'Yeah,' though the piggy eyes slid away from Markham's.

The DI cleared his throat.

'How does she feel about it?'

'It ain't the right time,' Noakes said unhappily. 'They hadn't planned on starting a family till *later*, see . . . once they were *established* with their careers an' all that.'

Markham heard an echo of Mrs Noakes.

'What does Muriel think?'

'Well now that Nat's just started on her part-time degree, it's a bit of a bummer really.'

The DI was reasonably sure Muriel would have expressed it differently, but got the drift. The Noakeses had been inordinately proud when their 'late developer' offspring — a beautician and 'holistic practitioner' — retook her A levels before signing up to do a part-time degree in History at Bromgrove University where she was now in her second year. Muriel in particular derived considerable kudos from what Olivia termed the rebranding of Natalie. No doubt the idea of her daughter's upwardly mobile trajectory being thrown into jeopardy was pretty much intolerable.

'Of course, she's going to have the baby, no question about that,' Noakes said stoutly. 'We've been pro-life in our family from time immoral.'

Markham bit his lip, unable to smile even at one of Noakes's notorious malapropisms.

The whole subject was somewhat fraught for the DI, owing to the fact that a botched abortion Olivia had undergone meant she could never have children of her own. But he didn't betray his discomfiture by even a flicker.

'An unplanned pregnancy isn't the end of the world, Noakesy,' he said gently. 'Not these days.'

'I quite fancy being a granddad,' the other said wistfully, as the DI recalled his friend's invariable clumsy gentleness whenever confronted with juveniles in past investigations. 'But it's the wrong time,' he repeated sadly. 'Nat's looking at adoption an' that side of things.'

'You and Muriel wouldn't feel able to . . .' Markham's voice trailed off. *What was he thinking of?* Muriel would metaphorically clutch her pearls and run for the hills at the bare idea of late-night feeds and puke down the front of her Ted Baker dresses, quite apart from distaste at the prospect of her daughter having a shotgun wedding.

'Nat don' want us stepping in . . . she thinks it'd cramp our style,' Noakes said loyally.

Hmm, Markham thought. *Muriel's* maybe, but Noakes and style didn't belong in the same sentence!

'Things will sort themselves out,' he reassured his friend, aware that it was a weak platitude in the circumstances.

'Oh aye.' Noakes sighed gustily before asking, 'Whass your plan for today then, guv . . . in terms of the green-fingered brigade?'

'I'm taking Burton to see Catherine Leckie's brother Greville,' he said. 'Out in Old Carton . . . They had a quarrel when their widowed mum died . . . some sort of row about the funeral and her will.'

Noakes nodded sagaciously. 'Families often fall out over the loot.' He wrinkled his nose. 'I heard the poor lass were doing well at Hope . . . didn't put folks' noses out of joint like "Call Me Tony".' He and Olivia were united in their scorn for the former headteacher. 'I mean, people said she were dead modern an' full of whizz-bang ideas . . . but nice with it . . . not hell bent on giving anyone who didn't agree with her their P45.'

'Anyone special in her life, do you know?' Markham asked.

'As in *romantic?*'

Noakes thought about it, rumpling his salt and pepper hair into little quills and making a porcupine of himself in the process.

'Pete Barlow mentioned some businessman . . . one of the Brylcreem tendency . . . smarmy . . . designed women's frocks or summat.'

Kevin the apprentice popped his head round the door, 'The Health and Safety guy's here, boss.'

Noakes frowned prodigiously. 'He's half an hour early . . . bleeding *typical.*'

Markham got to his feet.

'Time for me to be on my way, Noakesy,' he said. 'I'll give you a ring later. We can meet up in the Grapes and I'll bring you up to speed then . . . how about tomorrow evening?'

'*Champion.*' Noakes waved a pudgy hand at Kevin. 'Sort Mister Clipboard a cuppa while I see the inspector to his car.'

Outside, Markham patted his friend's shoulder. 'Happy New Year, Noakesy,' he said. 'Try not to worry about Natalie.' Fat chance of that. And, with a wink, 'Good luck with the artwork . . . I'll expect to see *The Fighting Temeraire* next time I come.'

'Cheers, guv,' the other said alertly, now sounding far more chipper.

There was a light in Noakes's eye which suggested he would check the historical reference in Rosemount's library before turning his attention to the far less enthralling topic of drains and plumbing. Nothing fired him up like patriotic and imperial history, particularly as he never paused to question if he was influenced by unconscious bias or colonial privilege or 'any of that bollocks'. And with the alluring prospect of the allotment murder to get his teeth into, Markham's visit was bound to have done him good.

Now for Greville Leckie and the rest of Markham's suspects . . .

* * *

Markham and Burton didn't get much out of Greville Leckie when they called at his large, white house in Old Carton. An imposing residence with generous, tall windows and large, high-ceilinged rooms, it was not unlike Rosemount though on a far smaller scale. Markham was willing to bet that the former businessman would need deep pockets to keep the place up, with signs of its having known better days in the overgrown front lawn and somewhat faded furnishings.

Leckie himself was a tall handsome man with a fine head of silver hair and patrician features including a decidedly

Roman nose. Impeccably clad in well-worn country casuals, he was courteous but steely, giving little away.

'My sister was much closer to our mother,' he said in answer to Burton's careful enquiry about rumoured family differences. 'My wife Deirdre died some years ago and we had no children, so it was really just down to us siblings when it came to organising the funeral.' His mouth tightened imperceptibly. 'I was unhappy at not being consulted . . . It seemed as if she was trying to shut me out from the arrangements.' He shrugged. 'It's a common enough story these days . . . bad feeling after a death.'

'What about the financial side?' Burton enquired delicately. 'Probate can be very stressful too.'

'She was the executor . . . I had nothing to do with it . . . only got a few hundred and some antiques but,' with a proud lift of the head, 'I didn't have expectations or anything like that . . . Besides, I'm no dog in the manger and—' with a slight curl of the lip and barely perceptible note of contempt in his voice — 'teaching in this country isn't a well-paid profession, so she's likely to need some sort of nest egg in the future.'

'Your sister was a headteacher,' Markham said quietly, finding the superciliousness distinctly unattractive. With the memory of that well-appointed shed in the allotments fresh in his mind, he added, 'I'd say she would have been well remunerated.'

The other merely raised his eyebrows. 'I defer to your greater knowledge, Inspector,' he said urbanely.

'Did you notice he never once used her name?' Burton asked indignantly once they were back in the car. 'It was "she" all the way through. When you offered condolences, he had this really strange look on his face . . . almost like he was *sneering*. And there was that weird comment about her being too trusting and impulsive . . . you'd have thought he was blaming her for being stupid enough to get herself killed.'

'Grief affects people differently,' Markham pointed out. 'But you're right, there was something very cold and clinical about his responses.'

'Had a decent enough explanation for staying in on New Year's Eve, though,' Burton conceded reluctantly. 'Sounded like he really cares about his dogs and wanted to stay in with the one that had been sick, the black lab . . . what was her name . . .'

'Meg,' the DI prompted. 'Yes, he was like a different man round his pets.'

'One of those who prefers animals to humans,' Burton agreed.

'We can check discreetly with his vet to confirm that story about colic,' Markham said. 'As things stand, it sounds credible.' He started the engine. 'Now to see about alibis for the rest of our suspects.'

'With Catherine being killed on New Year's Eve, we should be able to bump anyone "home alone" to the top spot,' Burton said happily.

St Bruno's Parish Hall was a rather soulless and utilitarian gabled red brick building, though the church next door, red sandstone in the perpendicular style with an impressive bell tower, looked like a striking example of Victorian architecture. Perhaps the money had run out when it came to the church hall, Markham thought as he took it all in.

However, there was little time to contemplate the architecture with a list of interviewees to work through.

'They're all here except for Dave Shipley, Donald Kemp and Bernadette Farrelly,' Doyle told him. 'Carruthers has arranged for you to see Shipley and Kemp tomorrow. Farrelly's coming in to the station later today.'

'Excellent,' Markham said approvingly. 'Now let's see where they all were on New Year's Eve. It's a sociable time, so hopefully no shortage of witnesses to pin down people's whereabouts.'

In the event, however, the suspects turned out to be what Carruthers witheringly called 'party poopers', virtually all of them claiming to have settled for a night in.

Peter Barlow, a barrel-chested but vigorous looking man in his seventies with a fussy manner, told them he had his sister-in-law over for a celebratory sherry to ring in the New Year. Doyle and Carruthers exchanged eloquent glances as though to say they didn't think much of *that* for a rave-up but it was consistent with the man's age and character.

Margaret Cresswell, a crop-haired large-boned woman with a booming voice and exuberant manner, waxed lyrical on the subject of allotments in general — 'places where you could get peace from the bustle of the modern world' blah blah — before getting down to brass tacks.

'I've got no time for raucousness and people getting drunk,' she said firmly. 'I'm quite happy with my own company thank you very much.' She had hunkered down with a good book and turned in around eleven o'clock. Declining to be drawn on personalities and fallings-out, she said that of course there were sometimes minor disagreements, but these generally revolved around issues to do with 'allotment etiquette': people borrowing each other's tools and not putting them back: not taking care of rubbish; forgetting to lock the gate; failing to cut back brambles or overhanging branches; forgetting to return equipment to the communal bins; leaving the main water tap running. Markham had the feeling that, as Chair of the Allotment Association, she took a tough line with offenders.

Rebecca Atherton, manager of Hope Academy's Pupil Referral Unit, was an attractive woman with curly red-gold hair to her shoulders and laughing hazel eyes that crinkled when she smiled. Not that there were all that many smiles given what had happened to her friend. 'We planned to go out on New Year's Eve,' she told them forlornly. 'But Cate cried off at the last minute, so then we decided to do something together later in January.' Asked why Catherine Leckie had cried off, she said she had no idea. 'I live on my own and it was too late to meet up with anyone else . . . In any case, I didn't fancy all the hoopla, so it was a good excuse to veg out and watch TV.'

Valerie Shipley, a hatchet-faced character with harshly dyed black hair, too much make-up and the raspy voice of a confirmed smoker, likewise claimed to have given 'all the noise and fireworks' a wide berth in favour of a night in with her husband, a scrawny doleful looking man whose resigned expression that suggested he might have preferred it if his other half *had* decided to go and whoop it up. Something implacable about her expression when Burton brought up the subject of her brother and 'issues that arose between him and Ms Leckie' confirmed the rumours that there had been some sort of incident. But all she said was, 'You'll have to ask *him* about that. It was a load of trumped-up nonsense, but these days men are sitting ducks for these #*MeToo* types with an agenda.'

Something sexual then, Markham thought as he politely thanked her. Along with what Burton had said about Catherine Leckie getting Dave Shipley chucked off the allotments for inappropriate behaviour, it amounted to a motive. In which case, Dave Shipley was looking good for the top spot.

Elsie Parker, a deputy head from Hope, was an ordinary looking middle-aged divorcée with wavy dishwater blonde hair to her shoulders and discreet make-up. Pleasant and businesslike, she commented that Catherine was a dedicated colleague and would be a great loss to Hope before moving on to say she had planned to spend the New Year with her son and daughter in Old Carton before coming down with a bad cold and being obliged to cancel.

'God,' Doyle muttered sotto voce to Carruthers. 'Apart from the old bloke, not a decent alibi between the lot of them.'

Hilary Probert was next. Thin to the point of emaciation, with wavy black hair to her waist and striking blue eyes outlined heavily in black against her gaunt, pale face, she came across as intense but sincere. 'Cate was so special,' she told them. 'Saw the good in everyone and had no time for bitching and pettiness.'

Was it Markham's imagination, or had the youth worker shot a sidelong glance at Elsie Parker and Valerie Shipley as she said this? Certainly the older women were in sharp contrast to this dungaree-wearing girl who looked like the epitome of grunge. Margaret Cresswell was eyeing her with some disapproval, as though she didn't have much time for 'free spirits'.

'I hung out with friends in the Grapes on New Year's Eve,' Hilary said. 'By about nine, I'd had enough so didn't stay till the end . . . got home around quarter to ten.'

Michael Oddie too had been in the Grapes, though he claimed to have bailed out early on account of needing to be up early the following day so he could drive to his parents in Leeds. Tall and well-built, with the body of a sportsman, he had keenly intelligent eyes behind thick, black-framed glasses and a silver-grey short back and sides. With his frank gaze and pleasant speaking voice, he looked more yuppie than allotmenteer but spoke enthusiastically about the lifestyle benefits of Beauclair Drive. 'It's kind of cut off — cut off from the world,' he said earnestly. 'Quiet and private . . . almost secret, like a hiding place.'

An interesting choice of words.

Oddie, like Hilary Probert, had clearly been fond of Catherine Leckie, though whether it had amounted to anything more than friendly admiration was difficult to determine.

Raymond Cotter, on the other hand, freely admitted pursuing her.

Markham could see why Noakes had referred to the businessman as being 'one of the Brylcreem tendency', given the man's Mediterranean good looks (Italian ancestry, Markham would have guessed) and easy charm.

'It was early days, but I was making headway,' Cotter said with what appeared to be genuine sadness. 'She was a lovely girl . . . looked on me as a bit of a Flash Harry to begin with . . . But we discovered we enjoyed the same things, and the barriers came down when we were at the allotment, like we could just be ourselves and not have to put on an act for anyone.'

'What do you mean by not having to put on an act?' Carruthers pressed.

'Well, she was a headteacher, which meant she was pretty much always on stage,' he replied. 'And my line of work — fashion and design — means cultivating a kind of persona . . . larger than life, if you know what I mean. Grubbing around at the allotments . . . dirt under the fingernails . . . it felt kind of *authentic* by comparison.'

Markham thought he understood.

'Had you arranged to see Catherine on New Year's Eve?' he asked.

'We planned to meet up on New Year's Day . . . have some food and wine down at the allotments. Cat knew I had to work late at the Artisan Centre in Old Carton because of problems with a customer's order . . . there was only me to see to it. But she understood. She was good like that.' Again a slight tremor in his voice. 'Never pushed . . . Never made me feel guilty.'

'Poor sod,' Doyle said afterwards. 'Sounded like they really had something going.'

Ninian Creech, with his small hooded eyes, thinning hair and bulbous nose, could hardly have presented a greater contrast to Catherine Leckie's boyfriend. But the ferrety caretaker appeared genuinely shaken and subdued. Apparently his wife and brother-in-law had gone out to their local to ring in the New Year, but he 'hadn't felt up to it' since he was nursing a cold.

'More like he was trying to escape the brother-in-law,' was Carruthers's verdict, and Markham was inclined to agree.

By the end of their interviews, it didn't feel that they were a great deal further forward.

'What about James Daly?' he asked.

'Coming in to the station later,' was Burton's prompt reply.

'Good.' Markham turned to the two sergeants. 'Anything from Church Avenue and Rockbourne Close?'

Doyle shook his head. 'Not so far, guv,' he answered. 'Everyone was too busy getting hammered,' he added ruefully, almost as though regretting those bachelor days when life was one long party.

'What about other allotment holders . . . the ones we haven't rounded up yet?'

'They're the ones who were away for the holidays,' Carruthers told him. 'So far that all checks out.'

'Good.' The DI realised he had been holding his breath, bracing himself for another round of interviews. 'At least we've got a manageable suspect list.'

'Even if none of 'em has a halfway decent alibi,' Doyle grumbled before subsiding at a sharp look from Burton. She noticed that Markham hadn't raised the subject of the allotment ghost with any of their interviewees and wondered if he felt as squeamish about the story as she did.

'Let's get back to the station and review what we've got,' Markham told them. 'Then it'll be time to have a crack at Bernadette Farrelly and James Daly.'

He wondered what Noakes, the one-time allotmenteer, would make of it all.

Hopefully by the time of their catch-up at the Grapes tomorrow, he would have something concrete to report.

But as things stood, the field was wide open.

CHAPTER 3

Tuesday felt like it had gone on forever, Markham thought wearily as he let himself into his apartment in the Sweepstakes that evening. Olivia was making the most of her last full day of freedom before school started and wouldn't be back from her friend Katie's till later, so there was only his own supper to worry about.

First things first, he told himself. After the day from hell, a glass (or three) of Châteauneuf-du-Pape was called for. Then he would think about food.

He took his wine into the living room and set it down on the side table next to his comfortable tartan check wing-back over by the bay window before turning his attention to the wood burner. Once that was settled to his satisfaction, he sank into his armchair with a sigh of satisfaction and savoured his drink.

When they had had this room redecorated in baroque red and gold vintage wallpaper, Olivia teased him about wanting to return to the womb, but she had come round to the rich dark colour scheme which was very comforting in winter. It worked in milder weather too, turning the room into a blaze of glory whenever the sun came out. Today, though, was increasingly sombre and windy, and he was glad to draw the heavy damask curtains against the gloom.

His thoughts travelled back to the team meeting back at the station once they had concluded their preliminary interviews . . .

'Maybe we're just looking at a maniac on the loose,' Doyle suggested. 'I mean, maybe it was some nutter who got into the allotments and there she was . . .'

'In the wrong place at the wrong time,' Carruthers finished for him.

'Mr Creech said he unlocked as usual on Sunday. So they'd have to have shinned over the gate,' Burton pointed out. 'And it's quite lethal with those pointy spikes on top.'

'Maybe they came in via Hollingrove Park or sneaked through one of the back gardens on Church Avenue or Rockbourne Close,' Doyle hazarded.

'It's possible,' Burton said consideringly. 'But that doesn't quite fit the random nutter theory . . . feels to me more like it must've been someone who knew what they were doing or came prepared.'

'A stalker?' Carruthers asked.

Burton nodded. 'Maybe. If they'd been following Catherine or knew she was going to be at the allotments that night, it was the ideal opportunity.'

'Yeah . . . and no risk of anyone catching them,' Doyle said eagerly. 'Even the oldies could've managed it,' he said eagerly. 'With a torch and stepladder, it would only take minutes.'

Carruthers pursed his lips. 'Bit risky in the dark,' he said. 'You'd need a head for heights to try breaking in that way.'

Doyle wasn't prepared to relinquish his scenario.

'There's sheds along the walls, right? So it wouldn't have been that big a drop on the other side . . . They'd just have to get onto the roof of one of those huts and let themselves down that way, then pull the ladder or whatever they used after them and hide it somewhere with all the other gardening clobber — rakes and wheelbarrows and all the rest of it.'

'I don't see anyone faffing around in the dark,' Carruthers said stubbornly. 'More likely she arranged to meet someone that night and let them in using her key.'

'*Okay.*' Doyle was thinking hard. 'But there's nothing to say it was any of the allotment crowd. Could've been some-one who had a quarrel with her from outside . . . someone unconnected to Beauclair Drive.'

'I'm with Carruthers on this,' Markham interjected, smil-ing at Doyle to take the sting out of his words. 'Catherine's murder has the feel of . . . something *intimate* . . . deeply personal.'

'Could've been a passing crackpot, guv,' Doyle reverted to his initial hypothesis. 'New Year's Eve always brings the crazies out in force.'

Something told Markham this wasn't a passing homi-cidal maniac, but he gave the young detective's theory due consideration.

'We can't rule that out, Sergeant,' he said. 'But still, with this one there's the sense of it being someone from Catherine Leckie's allotment network rather than just an individual who bore a grudge . . . The choice of her shed feels signifi-cant to me.'

DCI Sidney had precious little time for his 'hunches' or 'intuition', so they would need to come up with something concrete fairly quickly.

'Okay then . . . someone at Beauclair Drive who had got it in for her,' Carruthers pondered lugubriously. 'Someone who felt she had somehow done them down. The problem being, it's such a respectable set-up . . . boring even . . . cauliflowers and revenge crime don't really mix,' he added facetiously.

Burton frowned. 'Think of all the issues and rows that break out when people live in close proximity,' she pointed out. 'Allotments are a bit like that . . . people falling out over rules being broken . . . or just getting on each other's nerves . . . clash of personalities, that kind of thing.'

'Yeah, but it doesn't usually end in murder!' Carruthers countered.

'It can do,' she said unexpectedly. 'There was a case at Colindale Allotments a few years back where an eighty year old woman — I think she was the secretary or treasurer, something on the committee — was strangled by a fellow plot holder after a falling out.'

'What did they argue about?' Doyle wanted to know.

'It was all very sad,' Burton said reminiscently. 'The killer and the elderly woman he killed came from tough backgrounds. He ended up at the allotments via a psychotherapy group helping people who had PTSD.'

They waited expectantly.

'Anyway, to cut a long story short, it turned out there had been some sort of argument at a meeting where he shouted at the victim and she told him to shut up . . . Getting told off like that must have offended his sense of status and made him snap . . . He strangled her with the starter cord of the communal lawnmower and left her body in the shed where it was kept.'

'How did they narrow it down to him?' Carruthers asked.

'Well, his DNA was all over the shed, but there was nothing odd about that because he usually mowed the lawns. However, there were only a limited number of keys to the shed and the other keyholders had solid alibis. Plus, there was a history of bad blood between him and the victim and his account of his movements was seriously iffy. As Colindale CID saw it, there must have been another argument when he lost it and beat her in a rage. Then, after he realised this meant he was going to lose his allotment, which meant *everything* to him, he dragged her into the mower shed and killed her meaning to hide the body later. His plan backfired because her family panicked when she didn't turn up to a meeting and got the police to search the allotments . . . They were calling her mobile when they heard her ringtone coming from the mower shed. The poor woman had a fractured spine and ribs, as well as severe bruising on her face, so it was clear she'd been savagely assaulted before being strangled. '

'*Blimey,*' Doyle exhaled heavily. 'Did the bloke ever confess?'

'The jury didn't reach a verdict the first time he was tried. The second time round, he got life with a minimum of nineteen years. He insisted he was innocent and there *were* some doubts — another plot holder said he wasn't brave enough to kill anyone — but Colindale were sure they'd got their man. The creepy thing is, his plot hasn't been touched or entered since then and apparently his possessions are still there in his shed.'

'And he really lost his rag just because this old biddy told him to button it?' Carruthers demanded incredulously.

'She was apparently quite a strong-willed character . . . a bit brisk and bossy, in the mould of Margaret Cresswell . . . super-efficient, took no prisoners, made sure people paid their fees . . . The killer had been involved with the allotments for around eight years with no trouble at all . . . quite the model citizen.'

'But he had a dark side, right?' Carruthers prompted.

'Well, once the psychotherapy people cut their ties with the allotment, he got more confident . . . cockier and more competitive . . . wanted to be on the committee . . . wanted more of a role . . . needed status within the allotments . . .'

'Perhaps he just didn't like being bossed around by a woman,' Doyle speculated. 'Misogyny and all that,' he explained with a wary eye on Burton.

Burton nodded. 'It could have been a factor. He wanted another allotment holder evicted for keeping chickens and rabbits in his shed and that's when the victim told him to wind his neck in . . . He'd got it into his head that she was in a conspiracy to stop him seeing bank statements and stuff like that, so there was obviously some kind of paranoia going on. He'd had a tough life — life – been badly assaulted at one point, which left him with a wonky eye — so not surprising if he was battling demons . . . Quite a few people gave up their plots after the murder, which was hardly surprising. But Colindale's got CCTV now and they're back to full strength with a waiting list. So at least the place is still going.'

'The guy was obviously *obsessed* with the allotments,' Carruthers concluded. 'Possessive and territorial.'

'Well, that's the thing,' Burton said. 'In some quarters, having an allotment amounts to a status symbol. These associations and clubs *always* have waiting lists.'

'D'you reckon that's what was going on here?' Doyle demanded. 'Jealousy cos Catherine Leckie had that fancy pants *Grand Designs* shed . . . plus, she was a headteacher . . . pillar of the community . . . two blokes sniffing around her . . . looked like she'd got it made.'

'Jealousy is at the root of so much evil in the world,' Markham agreed. 'But we're going to have to consider the possibility of this being a random attack.'

'Dimples says she wasn't interfered with,' Burton told them, 'but that doesn't mean it wasn't sexually motivated.'

'Yeah, if they came on to her and she turned 'em down,' Doyle surmised.

'Or they got their kicks from killing because it make them feel powerful . . . like Shipman.'

Carruthers turned suddenly self-conscious as he recalled Nathan Finlayson's nickname of 'Shippers', but Burton merely said coolly, 'Of course, we can't rule out some sort of coercive sexual disorder or an associated algophilia.' Doyle's expression on hearing this suggested he was apprehensive that they were in for some kind of psychological exegesis courtesy of her beloved *Diagnostic and Statistical Manual of Mental Disorders*, but the DI shelved such discussion for the time being. 'According to Dimples, she didn't put up much of a struggle. Which suggests she was taken by surprise or at any rate never saw it coming.'

'Wouldn't there have been signs of a struggle if some nutter rocked up?' Doyle wondered. 'I mean, wouldn't she have tried to get away . . . make a run for it . . . grab her mobile or put up a fight?'

'It might have happened so fast, there was no time to react,' Markham replied gravely. 'Or possibly she just froze

. . . The SOCOs processing Catherine's flat found her laptop there but there was no sign of her mobile or handbag in the shed . . . looks like whoever killed her made sure to take those items with them.'

'Wouldn't that point to them being worried her mobile might show they'd been in contact with Catherine or arranged to meet her?' Carruthers asked.

'I think that's the most likely explanation,' Markham agreed. 'Though we can't rule out them just grabbing it on the way out . . . an impulse theft, if you like.'

Carruthers grimaced. 'Or if they were fixated and screwy, they could've just wanted something personal of hers . . . kind of like a trophy.'

'What about those flowers in her shed?' Doyle demanded. 'They could point to her having a "Secret Admirer".'

'Raymond Cotter says *he* didn't send them,' Burton interjected. 'Uniform haven't turned up anything from local florists and garden centres . . . needle in a haystack really.'

'The caretaker guy said she looked like a child asleep,' Carruthers mused. 'So it was more a case of her being posed rather than the killer just throttling her and leaving her splayed every which way . . . I mean,' he groped for the right words, 'with strangulation, it's usually ugly and untidy, but this one looks kind of *prettified* if you get me.'

'Yes, I think I do, Sergeant,' Markham helped him out. 'There was almost the sense of a *tableau*, which seemed somehow at odds with a random ambush.'

They digested this in silence for a few minutes.

'Who IDed the body?' Doyle asked suddenly.

'Her brother Greville, but the FLOs said he wasn't giving much away,' Burton replied. 'When the boss and I called round, he was well in control of himself . . . I thought he was a cold fish . . . but, like you said guv, people sometimes react weirdly.'

It was undoubtedly true, Markham thought grimly, recalling how he had heard one of the SOCOs at the scene sounding off about how Catherine Leckie was 'bloody stupid' to be hanging around the allotments by herself at that time of night. 'Just asking for trouble,' he had declared before catching sight of the DI's thunderous expression and breaking off mid-diatribe.

Needless to say, the passing homicidal maniac was DCI Sidney's preferred theory. When Markham and Burton were admitted to the inner sanctum by his dragon PA for an initial briefing before the team meeting, Sidney had been adamant about that. Anything to avoid the shadow of suspicion falling on Bromgrove's pukka citizenry.

'New Year's Eve always triggers the, er, mentally disturbed, Inspector,' he honked. 'And there she was,' in an echo of DS Doyle, 'a sitting duck.'

'With lunatics, it usually turns out to be an isolated incident, sir,' Markham conceded inscrutably. 'But if—'

Sidney's eczema, having briefly receded on Noakes's retirement, suddenly looked as angry as ever.

'No ifs and no buts, Markham,' he barked. 'We are looking at an isolated incident here. I need hardly tell you the impact on our regional statistics otherwise.'

'Sir,' Markham said stolidly. He didn't give a flying fajita for Sidney's crime data but knew he needed to ratchet his boss's blood pressure down pronto.

'We're covering all the bases,' he continued soothingly. 'DI Burton is running all the usual checks with the council and local mental health facilities.'

'Well, I suppose that's *some* reassurance,' Sidney muttered grudgingly. 'Not like you with your mania for "nuances" and "hunches", eh?'

Such was the DCI's jealous resentment of Markham, that Olivia had nicknamed him 'Judas Iscariot', her dislike only intensified by learning that Sidney sneeringly referred to her as 'Markham's lady friend' in a manner that suggested he didn't hold out much hope for their long-term prospects.

'Oh well, sir,' Markham said with charming self-deprecation, 'thanks to you, I know better than to jump in with all guns blazing.'

Pass me the sick bucket, Noakes might have said on hearing this. But Markham wanted to fend off outside interference, in the shape of Superintendent Ebury-Clarke, for as long as possible. If that meant shameless obsequiousness going forward, then so be it.

His eyes wandered to the Hall of Fame, as the photo-montage in Sidney's office was irreverently dubbed by the lower ranks.

Yep, there she was . . . Sidney's favourite royal — Sophie, formerly HRH The Countess of Wessex and soon to be Duchess of Edinburgh, newly appointed Patron of Bromgrove Horticultural Trust. Seeing Sidney's bald bonce bobbing up next to HRH, with Mrs Sidney — aka Brunhilde (for her resemblance to a Valkyrie) — making it the perfect threesome, Markham understood all too well how distasteful his boss found any prospect of blood amongst the beetroots. For once, he actually had some sympathy with Sidney's position. Whatever their mutual antipathy, it was understandable that the boss didn't want his retirement overshadowed by some kind of horrendous local scandal.

And it looked increasingly to him as if a local imbroglio might well be at the root of Catherine Leckie's murder, particularly since the house-to-house enquiries and a trawl of neighbourhood CCTV footage had failed to turn up sightings of suspicious characters lurking around the allotments on New Year's Eve. Nor had local agencies identified any 'person of interest'.

Having crossed swords with Chief Superintendent Ebury-Clarke on more than one occasion, Markham reckoned that Sidney was definitely the lesser of two evils and knew he needed to keep the DCI onside. Over time, indeed, he had come to feel if not affection, then a certain compassion for the DCI's thin-skinned sensitivity about his red brick university antecedents, social insecurity and baldness (though he did his best to look like the corporate equivalent of Pep Guardiola, having ditched the desperate millennial-style goatee and gone all out for 'bald and proud'). Sidney might have called him 'DI Heartthrob' behind his back, but the DCI nonetheless possessed a certain intrinsic decency that meant he was prepared to back him up within reason.

Within reason being the operative words.

Sidney took it quite well when Burton cunningly insinuated Noakes into the conversation by a casual allusion to their former colleague's 'familiarity with allotment culture', as though his involvement with the investigation was a *fait accompli*. Nobody could do owlish earnestness as well as Burton, Markham thought admiringly. In the DCI's book, her girl guide rectitude simply *had* to rub off on the old reprobate. Remembering Noakes's waggishness the last time he had been around Sidney — 'You can't fool me, I'm an idiot!' was just one of many side-splitting gems from that encounter — Markham wasn't so sure. As Chris Carstairs was wont to misquote mischievously, if the road to hell was paved with good inventions, then George Noakes's rehiring as an 'outside contractor' possibly came out somewhere near the top.

'Thanks, Kate,' he said afterwards when they were well out of earshot of the dragon PA. 'I think you swung it for us with Noakesy.'

'Oh, the DCI's bark is worse than his bite, guv,' she said diplomatically. 'It must be lonely at the top riding a desk. I almost got the feeling he was a bit, well, *envious* of our camaraderie . . . I mean to say, the *team's*,' she added hastily with a slight flush.

'That'll be you one day, Kate,' he smiled. 'Ensconced in lofty eminence as a DCI.'

She blinked hard. 'I'm happy with things just the way they are, boss.'

Which didn't necessarily bode well for Burton's relationship with her erstwhile fiancé . . .

Now, jerking out of his reverie, Markham padded into the kitchen and poured himself another drink before taking glass and bottle through to his study.

This was far more simply decorated than the living room, dominated by his desk that took up almost the whole of one wall and faced the picture window. As far as he was concerned, the neighbouring municipal cemetery was all he required to keep him focused on an investigation, being a reminder of numberless murdered dead who were never far away, like an invisible host imploring him to win them justice beyond the grave.

It was dark outside, but he didn't draw the curtains, content to know that this sprawling charnel lay close at hand, like a mysterious slumbering creature whose heartbeat somehow kept time with his own . . .

Markham grinned ruefully as he imagined Sidney's reaction to such flights of fancy ('maudlin', 'histrionic' and 'befuddled' were the kindest epithets the DCI bestowed on un-policemanlike philosophising), but he knew Noakes would understand. His friend liked contemplating the statues and obelisks next door, though from a relentlessly optimistic perspective. 'Death is swallowed up in victory,' he intoned with Christian certitude and the air of one fully determined to be on the winning side.

As Markham sat there feeling curiously lethargic, his thoughts turned to the final two interviews he had conducted with Burton . . .

Bernadette Farrelly, Raymond Cotter's ex-wife, was a glamorous middle-aged woman with delicate features and a sweep of ash-blonde hair that fell in a perfectly layered side-fringe bob to her shoulders. Elegantly dressed and well spoken, she presented the picture of equanimity, exhibiting no resentment or pique when Markham asked about her acrimonious divorce from Cotter.

'Neither of us behaved particularly well, Inspector,' she said levelly. 'And I did my share of shouting and throwing things.' Her mouth twisted. 'Of course I resented Catherine Leckie . . . But looking back, I can see that she wasn't the cause of our break-up. If we'd had a strong marriage, Raymond wouldn't have been tempted to play away in the first place.' A shaky breath. 'I suppose I didn't make enough effort to share his interests.'

'Like the allotments?' he prompted.

'Yes . . . It was quite funny the way he got so obsessed with all that back-to-nature stuff. But I was at a different place . . . busy with work and two teenagers . . . And one day, *phut*, that was it. I discovered our marriage had somehow gone down the drain.' For a moment she suddenly looked much older before the mask was firmly back in place. 'These days it's all very civilised and Raymond has a good relationship with the children.'

'She seems to have her head screwed on,' Burton observed afterwards. 'No crying over spilt milk or anything like that. Quite unneurotic really.' The DI looked at her notes. 'Sounds reasonable enough that she fancied a night in since her kids were at sleepovers. Yeah, her story hangs together.'

James Daly was a very different proposition.

A tall gangling youth with startlingly blue eyes, a tangle of curly black hair and features pitted with acne, he displayed a smouldering resentment towards Catherine Leckie. 'She never gave me a chance,' he mumbled. 'Just took those bitches' word for it.'

'So you're saying you *weren't* involved in bullying and sexual harassment?' Burton asked sternly.

'Look it was banter . . . and the girls were well up for it . . . they only pointed the finger at me when it looked like their grades were slipping . . . The other guys held their hands up and spouted all that feminist crap about respect and trust.' Burton's face darkened at this. 'But *I* thought Leckie wasn't being fair and said so. Plus, Mikey and Jason come from posh families headed for uni while I'm this grease monkey from the Hoxton,' he added bitterly, referring to a notoriously troubled council estate. 'Dead easy for everyone to put all the blame on me even though I wasn't the ringleader . . . and then after I got a bit mouthy with her, that was it, she didn't want to know. Until she ratted me out, I thought she was cool . . . on the level. But in the end she was just like all the rest.'

It sounded decidedly messy, but the eighteen-year-old's burning sense of injustice seemed genuine enough. Perhaps it was just that the youth reminded Markham of his dead brother Jonathan — nascent good looks marred by surliness and an attitude of 'Me Against The World' — but there was something engaging about him underneath all the truculence. It wasn't difficult to imagine either how Catherine Leckie, relatively new in the job and eager to demonstrate her credentials as a disciplinarian, might have zeroed in on Daly as the likeliest candidate for exclusion when his friends were better at covering their tracks.

The youth told them that he had spent New Year's Eve in the Duck and Olive pub before heading back to the Hoxton shortly after nine. 'I didn't have enough money to go clubbing with the others,' he mumbled. Markham concluded that he was too proud to ask for a sub.

'D'you think there was anything personal going on between him and Catherine?' Burton asked frowningly after Daly had slouched out of the interview room.

'*Sexual?*' Markham asked.

'Well, that stuff about her being cool and on the level till she "ratted him out" . . . it was a bit intense.'

'There could've been some kind of crush,' Markham conceded. 'Or it might just have been that he was hungry for her approval given his background on the Hoxton.'

'If he knew she would be at the allotments and took it into his head to confront her there . . . well, easy to see how things could have got out of hand. I mean, he's obviously got a bit of a temper, and if he'd been drinking . . .' Burton gestured expressively.

'I'll take Doyle along to Hope tomorrow morning,' Markham told her. 'See if his boyish charms will help me persuade Catherine's colleagues to open up.'

Burton laughed and rolled her eyes.

'You and Carruthers can tackle Dave Shipley and Donald Kemp,' he went on. I've arranged to meet up with Noakesy in the Grapes, so hopefully he'll have had his ear to the ground.'

Now, the rumbling of his stomach recalled Markham to his surroundings with a reminder that he needed to eat and mop up some of the alcohol.

He was in the kitchen dispiritedly surveying the contents of the fridge when Olivia arrived, flushed and glowing from the cold.

'I knew you wouldn't be up to cooking, so I got us some takeaway from the Lotus Garden,' she said happily, decanting foil trays and various paper bags from her capacious hold-all. 'I had an enormous pig-out with Katie but still fancied some of their chow mein . . . at this rate, I'm going to be the size of a house.'

There was no danger of that, Markham thought affectionately as she chatted on, amusing him with mildly scabrous gossip from her workplace spiced with the irreverent wit that was her trademark.

'So there you have it, Gil,' she concluded, tucking in to her food. 'They're all buzzing about Doc Abernathy and his toyboy . . . I mean this one's only in his twenties and Abernathy's *ancient!*'

'I always thought he was a nice chap, Liv. Good that he's found someone to share his life with. And besides, late fifties is hardly ancient.'

'It is when you're like Abernathy . . . Honestly, Gil, I really thought these days the only bloke who did it for him was John Donne.'

Markham chuckled. 'Well, being Assistant Head, I'm sure he'll ride out the storm and then you'll all move on to the next scandal.'

The vivacious features clouded over.

'Sorry, it's insensitive of me burbling on like that about Abernathy after all this business with Catherine Leckie,' she said biting her lip. 'I suppose to some extent we're distracting ourselves from what happened to the poor girl . . . it hasn't really sunk in yet.' Agitatedly twirling a strand of long red hair round her finger, she urged him. 'Tell me about *your* day. Is anyone in the frame yet?'

She listened avidly as he recounted the day's events, careful to leave Kate Burton out of it in much the same way that she avoided any mention of Mathew Sullivan.

'What was your impression of Catherine Leckie, Liv?'

'Super-efficient and not one of those dreadful micro-managers like "Call Me Tony". Trusted us to get on and do the job.'

'Fair minded?' he asked.

'She seemed so to me . . . I was so taken up with exam moderation and department schemes of work, that I never really tuned in when the bullying thing blew up with Daly and his chums. He wasn't one of mine but I quite liked him . . . had the feeling things were tough at home.'

'Any vibe between him and Catherine?'

'Not that I saw. Mind you,' she pulled a face, 'my reputation for infallibility when it comes to sniffing out workplace romance has gone for a burton with this Abernathy business.'

Workplace romance.

She shifted awkwardly as the words hung in the air between them. Was her mind on Mat Sullivan? *Again*? Markham tried to tell himself he had no right to be jealous . . . Whatever had happened with Mat was none of his business. Him and Liv had been on a break, hadn't they? And common honesty obliged him to accept that Mat hadn't been the direct cause of their break-up.

Adroitly, he turned the conversation to Noakes's revelation of Natalie's pregnancy and the baby due in summer.

His partner was dumbfounded.

But once she had taken it in, he noticed with a twinge of unease how vehemently Olivia reacted to the news that Natalie was looking into adoption.

'Surely George won't be happy if he can't be a part of the child's life,' she insisted.

'Noakesy will go along with Natalie and Muriel on this,' he said quietly. 'He'll want the best for them as well as the baby.'

Colour flared up under the pale skin, like red wine under glass.

'*Muriel!*' she spat. 'Don't tell me, Gil . . . An illegitimate grandchild isn't the right accessory? Won't strike the right note when Hyacinth Bouquet has the coven round for tea?'

'That's not fair, Liv,' he said gently, thinking of the Noakes's unusual family circumstances: how Muriel became pregnant with Natalie when she and Noakes were courting (the result of a wildly uncharacteristic indiscretion); and how Noakes married her in the belief that he was the father, only later discovering that Natalie was not in fact his biological daughter.

'You have to remember, Natalie was the result of an unplanned pregnancy,' Markham went on. 'Everything turned out all right in the end, but it's understandable if Muriel carries scars. And besides, Natalie herself isn't ready to embrace motherhood.'

Unlike Olivia, he thought anxiously. Whereas in the past his partner had rejected any suggestion that they themselves might adopt, now it appeared the tide had turned.

But he didn't want a baby used as some kind of sticking plaster in the wake of the Mathew Sullivan affair, or to set the seal on their reconciliation. Somehow that felt dishonest.

Lightly, he asked about her day with Katie and, after a moment's hesitation, she followed his lead.

In no time at all, she was delighting him with anecdotes from Katie's job as a district nurse.

'There's this family on the Hoxton, Gil,' she confided. 'Mum's just come out of hospital and there isn't much money, so Katie bought her a nice bed jacket, really pretty, with lovely fancy embroidery. But when she visited last week, guess what . . . the dog was propped up in bed wearing it. Can you imagine! She nearly died when she saw their flipping Dachshund wearing this lacy number with frilly ribbons and all the rest of it!'

'Good to know they take animal welfare seriously,' he laughed.

The earlier tension evaporated and, as he watched her dancing eyes alight with mischief, he felt the stirrings of desire.

'D'you fancy an early night,' he murmured coming up behind her a short time later as she stood tidying up at the sink.

'*You're on. Race you to the bedroom!*'

Their sexual passion was as strong as ever, he reflected later in the darkness with his arm around her, thinking that she looked more than ever like a Pre-Raphaelite heroine as she lay there with her abundant red hair spilling over the pillows. Despite the Guinevere-like ethereality of which Noakes was so enamoured, she had made love with the fervour of a maenad as though trying to exorcise something . . . or *someone*.

And yet with Olivia, despite all the misgivings and doubts about where her affections truly lay, he felt somehow complete.

For one night at least he had banished the dark secrets of Beauclair Drive.

CHAPTER 4

Wednesday morning brought DS Doyle, bright and bushy-tailed, to the Sweepstakes. Olivia, who was fond of the lanky young sergeant, insisted that he come up and have a coffee rather than 'skulking round outside'. It was a half day at Hope before the start of the term proper but she was in a cheerful frame of mind.

'There's toast as well, if you want it,' she called out before disappearing to 'do my war paint and strap on the old Kevlar vest'.

'Take no notice,' Markham said with a smile. 'She loves Hope really . . . just likes to give the impression it's right up there with *Waterloo Road*,' he added, referring to the TV series about a comprehensive school in Rochdale where riots and general mayhem were the norm.

Fancy the guvnor being up on soaps, Doyle thought admiringly. His boss was chiefly notorious for unorthodox interests — visiting mouldy old churches and tossing out obscure references that got Burton looking all misty-eyed and moonstruck — but this showed he wasn't quite such an old fogey.

The youngster's thought processes were so transparent, that Markham could read him like a book. 'Olivia keeps me

57

up to speed with all the plotlines,' he laughed. 'If it weren't for her, I'd have no street cred to speak of.'

'Is that you taking my name in vain?' Olivia bustled back in having clearly applied the 'war paint' in record time.

'Go on, sit down,' she urged the young detective as he hovered awkwardly before turning to Markham. 'Buck up and do the honours, Gil,' she instructed her partner who obediently complied, not remotely abashed at being ordered around.

Markham rarely had his subordinates back to the Sweepstakes (only Noakes was a habitué), so Doyle was decidedly self-conscious at being waited on.

Olivia Mullen was definitely a looker, he decided admiringly, shooting her shy sidelong glances. Tall, pale and willowy, though on the scrawny side, with all that red hair and the witchy grey-green eyes he could see why Noakes thought she resembled those women in the Pre-Raphaelite collection at the art gallery. She certainly didn't dress like a teacher, the Jacquard tapestry dress, tassel boots and some kind of ethnic poncho only enhancing her unconventional allure.

Things had gone wrong between her and the guvnor — he knew from canteen gossip that it had something to do with that nerdy deputy head — but you could tell from the way he looked at her and the fact they were living together that she and Markham were back on . . . The lads might sneer that Lord Snooty looked like he was dead below the waist, but it was just jealousy. Unsettlingly, Doyle had a feeling that no one knew the half of it and the DI was very hot stuff indeed . . .

Olivia's musical tones interrupted these mildly salacious musings.

'Obviously I'm going in to school separately,' she said cheerfully. 'And I'll pretend not to know the two of you should we run into each other this morning.' Then, more seriously, she added, 'There's going to be some sort of special assembly about Catherine . . . I only hope the senior leadership team don't come over all sickly and insincere.'

'Just wait till the local press gets stuck in,' Markham said coming over with Doyle's coffee and toast. 'From the *Gazette*'s obituaries, it's obvious most people think eternity consists of reading excruciatingly bad doggerel verse. Whatever your SLT comes up with, it won't be half so glutinous as *that*.'

She grinned. 'Who's getting the third degree this morning, then?'

'Elsie Parker and Rebecca Atherton,' Markham replied promptly.

'Hmm . . . I don't see you getting much out of Elsie, but Bex is all right.'

'Parker's one of the deputy heads, right?' Doyle said through a mouthful of toast. 'I just can't get my head round all these deputies and assistant heads and pastoral mentor types . . . In my day it was just the headteacher and one deputy head. Me and my mates turned out all right,' he concluded somewhat defiantly.

Markham laughed. 'Don't get Olivia started. It's her pet peeve.'

His partner tossed the long mane that fell round her shoulders like a vibrant cloak.

'I reckon all these different jobs came about after we started medicalising kids,' she said. 'When I was out for lunch with my friend Katie, who's a district nurse, she told me about this one time she was visiting a young mum about something or other . . . It turned out one of the kids' friends was off school, and when Katie asked what was wrong, this little tot sitting at the kitchen table said — without missing a beat — that her mate "had mental health" . . . I mean, for God's sake, what are we coming to when no one bats an eyelid at five-year-olds casually writing each other off as basket cases?' She sighed. 'Not that I know what the answer is, mind you,' she added, causing Markham to smile at the unwonted humility.

Privately, Doyle thought Olivia might be on to something. His partner Kelly was a teacher and fed up to the back teeth of all the carey-sharey bollocks instead of being allowed to get on with her job. By the sound of it, these days in schools the indoctrination was worse than Mao's Cultural Revolution.

'Isn't Rebecca Atherton one of the "touchy feely" brigade?' Markham continued inscrutably. 'Runs the Pupil Referral Unit or inclusion department or whatever it's called these days?'

'Yeah, but *she's* quite sane actually,' Olivia shot back. 'Not endlessly spouting PC Esperanto and navel-gazing garbage . . . Got a sense of humour too. Doesn't try to shut you down for being ideologically unsound.'

'Are we to infer that Elsie Parker is less simpatico?' Markham pressed. He hadn't probed too closely the previous night, since the whole subject of staff relations was a delicate one given Olivia's involvement with Mathew Sullivan. This morning, however, the tension seemed to have lifted.

'I suppose Elsie's not the worst,' she conceded. 'A bit stodgy and very PC. She was acting head before Catherine was appointed . . . probably figured she had the headship all sewn up, so it must've been galling to watch a youngster swan in and charm the pants off everyone. To be fair, she's a hard worker—'

'But you're not keen,' her partner observed shrewdly.

'We're chalk and cheese,' Olivia sighed. 'And she's got a habit of flagging up people's weaknesses to make herself look good . . . bit of a humble-bragger too.'

He'd met a few of those in CID, Markham reflected grimly.

'Teachers are more prone to it than most people for some reason.' Olivia grimaced. 'Including me, if I'm being honest.'

'But Elsie and Catherine worked well together?' Markham asked.

'There were rumours about the odd "personality clash", and I had an idea either Catherine or Bex — or maybe it was both of them — went to the governors with some gripe about Elsie. But it must have been smoothed over cos I never heard anything else. Wouldn't read too much into it if I were you . . . that kind of stuff happens in schools all the time.' Olivia's expression suggested that she found such jockeying for power thoroughly unattractive. 'Bex was close mates with Catherine, so Elsie probably felt squeezed out of the picture, something like that.'

'The three of them were connected through the allotments, though,' Doyle mused.

'Yes, that was a bond of sorts . . . Apparently Elsie lightened up away from Hope, though she was still quite competitive . . . She'd been an allotment holder longer than the other two, so she was able to lord it over them a bit. Look,' Olivia sounded slightly shamefaced, 'Elsie's a bit of an apparatchik, but I'm sure she's as upset as everyone else over this. And Bex will be *devastated*. Headteachers aren't supposed to play favourites, but Catherine and Bex just got on so well . . . same goofy sense of humour.' She smiled indulgently. 'They used to laugh themselves silly over some of the stuff that came out of the governors' meetings . . . not to mention loony directives from the DoE.'

Doyle's ears pricked up at this. 'Don't a couple of the governors have plots at Beauclair?'

She nodded. 'Yep, that's right. Margaret Cresswell and Peter Barlow. They're old-fashioned and a bit officious but nice with it, like Dimples Davidson. Some of the others are absolute horrors . . . can't wait to jump on every trendy initiative going, and so far up themselves you wouldn't believe it . . . Talking of which,' she grinned wickedly at the chance to take a swipe at Markham's boss, 'how's Judas Iscariot doing . . . still going for the football manager look, or is he channelling Charles Dance and Stanley Tucci these days?'

'Behave yourself, Liv,' Markham said in a tone of mild reproof. Then, to Doyle, 'Olivia's convinced the DCI fancies a career in media punditry after retirement, but I reckon he might settle for being a "Gentleman Who Lunches".'

'Not on your life,' Olivia snorted. 'Brunhilde will never let him slide into the shadows — especially not while you and George are still grabbing the headlines with your, er, "unconventional partnership"!'

'*Hmm* . . . Methinks the less said about that the better,' he retorted in a deeply sardonic tone. 'I'll be catching up with Noakesy later in the Grapes . . . very much *low profile.*'

Doyle looked sceptical about his old mentor's ability to maintain anything resembling a low profile but wisely held his peace.

After Olivia had left, the two men discussed the prospects of their learning anything useful at Hope.

'Maybe someone'll tell us more about that hoo-ha with the Daly kid,' Doyle ventured hopefully. 'Let's say Catherine had been doing something she oughtn't—'

'Like what?' Markham rapped, never comfortable with aspersions on a murder victim's character, even though his subordinate was merely voicing concerns he himself had raised with Olivia the previous night.

'Like leading him on, guv . . . making him think she had feelings for him or he was somehow special . . . then when he got nasty or threatened to tell, that stuff about bullying and being a sex pest gave her the perfect excuse to chuck him out. If he ever accused her of anything, no one would believe him because he was just this badass who was trying to get back at her.'

Aware that his boss didn't particularly care for Americanisms, Doyle amended, 'A no-gooder, guv, that's what I meant.'

'Relax, Doyle, I'm with you.'

Markham was pleased that he had thought to invite the young sergeant to meet him at the flat as a mark of confidence. There was a risk of him being overshadowed by the more cerebral Carruthers, so it was important to demonstrate his professional regard.

Right,' he got up from the table, 'we should be on our way.'

* * *

It was decidedly awkward that Mathew Sullivan was now acting head, Markham thought as they sat opposite Olivia's one-time lover in Catherine Leckie's office at Hope Academy.

However, Sullivan, a charismatic drama teacher whom he and Noakes had always regarded as 'one of the good guys', showed a lightness of touch that Markham admired, enquiring after the former sergeant with an affection that was evidently genuine.

'I've missed some five-a-side fixtures, Gil. Got myself knocked out so often, I should've been awarded the Sputum Cup of the Year Award.'

Somehow this broke the ice, and in no time at all the two men were chuckling over their un-politically correct friend in a manner which totally perplexed Doyle.

Wasn't Sullivan meant to be the bloke Markham's missus went and had a fling with?

So how come they were laughing away like old buddies?

The DS felt like he would never in a million years understand Markham. But somehow him and Sullivan were managing to put a good face on things, so it was a case of going with the flow.

Not that Sullivan gave them anything particularly helpful about James Daly other than readily agreeing to hand over all internal school documentation to the police. It seemed like the school had nothing to hide on that front, but of course these days you could never be sure.

Elsie Parker turned out to be just as dreary and humourless as Olivia had indicated.

'Made me think of Theresa May,' Doyle told Markham afterwards as they sat in his car by the school gates mulling things over. 'You know, when they nicknamed her the Maybot cos she was like some kind of android.'

'Ms Parker gave us one interesting nugget, though.'

'Oh yeah.' Doyle was keen to show that he hadn't missed it. 'That about the leftie youth worker having a thing for Leckie.'

'Yes,' Markham said thoughtfully. 'She rather made a point of getting that in.'

'Seemed to me . . .' Doyle hesitated.

'Go on, Sergeant.'

'Well, it sounded almost like she was hinting Leckie an' Probert could've been lezzers . . . er, lesbians,' he amended, belatedly remembering Markham's pronounced dislike of canteen speak.

'A "king size crush" was how she summed up Ms Probert's feelings,' Markham responded austerely. 'But for all her PC credentials, she struck me as being deep down the kind of ultra-conventional woman who would be quick to disparage a relationship that didn't fit the mould or one she didn't understand.'

Doyle turned his thoughts to their suspects' movements. 'Leckie and Raymond Cotter couldn't party on New Year's Eve cos of that fashion order or whatever it was he had to get sorted . . .'

'Correct. So Catherine arranged to go out with Ms Atherton but then texted her around eight o'clock to cancel because something had come up . . . Possibly she planned to see someone at the allotments. Or it could just be she felt tired and fancied some time to herself.'

'Yeah, if she planned to spend New Year's Day swinging from the chandeliers with Cotter, then she could've wanted to get some beauty sleep 'stead of clubbing,' Doyle pronounced with a mature, man-of-the-world air that made Markham smile inwardly. 'These days, me and Kell don't have time for going out and getting hammered just cos you feel you have to.' Was it Markham's imagination, or did the youngster sound ever so slightly wistful as he endorsed the millennial puritanism? 'Not very classy, Kell says,' it being clear that 'Kell' was the oracle in such matters. 'We just had a nice meal and watched telly.' Markham duly made approving noises.

'Leckie had to be something special,' Doyle continued. 'There's Cotter and the Oddie bloke sniffing about . . . looks like she had Atherton and Probert dangling on a string too.'

'I think she was one of those generous, open-spirited women to whom people were naturally drawn,' Markham replied slowly. 'Both men and women.'

'Parker implied she was dramatic and OTT . . . the type who liked to get down with the kids,' Doyle mused. 'But Atherton said she was really quite shy.'

'The two aren't irreconcilable,' the DI commented. 'According to Olivia, you have to be a bit of a thespian . . . almost play the clown to win kids over—'

'Yeah,' Doyle interjected eagerly. 'I remember my form tutor Mr Hart from Medway High. He was *brilliant*. Didn't bat an eyelid when I said Socrates was a sweeper from Brazil.'

'Indeed,' Markham said, hiding his amusement. 'Well, it sounds as if Catherine Leckie was very much of that ilk, despite being more of an introvert in her private life.'

'Atherton's a bit of a joker too,' Doyle reflected. 'Parker didn't like it when she said the school motto should be 'Hit Him Again' rather than that Latin quote on Hope's badge.'

'They're coming at school discipline from different angles, Doyle,' the DI commented. 'And don't forget the generation gap . . . Catherine and Rebecca did their teacher training a couple of decades after Ms Parker, so it's understandable they're poles apart.'

'Anyroad, I *liked* Atherton,' Doyle said decisively, 'and when we were walking around, you could tell the kids rated her. It was cringe when Parker boasted about knowing all the students personally and then she called that big lad Darren when his name was David . . . What a bleeding *pseud*!'

'You're sounding more like Noakesy with every passing day,' the DI sighed. 'And no, I wouldn't necessarily take that as a compliment.'

As they drove out of the car park, Doyle observed, 'The buildings at Medway are crummy, but Hopeless is much worse, guv . . . reminds me of a bunker . . . an FBI facility or something like that.'

It was true. Markham thought. No wonder Catherine Leckie had craved grass and apple trees and the great outdoors. It would be pure bliss after that three-storey brutalist cement building, its submarine-like corridors aggressively plastered with Day-Glo laminated posters like something out of an Orwellian nightmare. *Big Brother Is Watching You.*

He glanced at the manila folder on his knee. 'I have a feeling there's nothing particularly illuminating about James Daly in this lot.'

'Yeah,' Doyle agreed. 'HR were happy to hand it over, which means we'll get sweet FA,' he added cynically.

'Maybe the other two are having better luck with Dave Shipley and Donald Kemp,' Markham said as they picked up speed, Doyle curbing his boy-racer tendencies despite an inviting stretch of open road.

'Shipley . . . he's the bloke who got chucked off the allotments for perving, right?' Doyle rather begrudged his colleagues bagging that one. It sounded a whole lot spicier than their session with the two schoolmarms.

'Well, we don't know what was at the bottom of it, but it's a fair inference given the venomous way his sister quoted #MeToo at us when we did the initial interviews.'

'He sounds more promising than Kemp, guv . . . I mean, it's hard to imagine a councillor's son strangling the local headteacher.'

'Let's not make any assumptions, Sergeant,' the DI replied heavily. 'It was obvious Ninian Creech didn't care for Donald Kemp one bit.'

'Probably afraid Kemp will set the council on him for something,' Doyle concluded sagely. 'Creech looks the type to be up to all sorts. Wouldn't be surprised if it turned out *he* got off on peering through shed windows and that sort of thing.'

'Well, he'd have been disappointed if he was spying on Ms Leckie the night she died,' Markham observed drily. 'She wasn't dressed for a romantic encounter . . . if you recall the crime scene pictures, it was jeggings and a sweater.'

Doyle repressed a shudder. Leckie wasn't much older than his Kelly, but the bastard murderer had turned her into some sort of gargoyle with bulging eyes . . . *horrible*.

With a pang of compunction, it occurred to him that the guvnor never referred to victims by their surnames, being scrupulous about according them full respect in death. He didn't reprimand his subordinates for doing so, however, as though he understood their need to detach themselves from the despair and ugliness.

Hastily, Doyle turned their conversation away from the subject of crime scene photographs.

'Sullivan didn't seem to know anything about a bust-up where the governors got involved.'

'Well, Olivia didn't attach much significance to it.' Markham laughed. 'I don't think Dimples would appreciate Mat saying that most of them were "nice old buffers" . . . reckon he thinks he's got a bit more going for him than the likes of Margaret Cresswell and Peter Barlow.'

Doyle sniggered appreciatively, having been on the receiving end of an occasional withering put-down by the pathologist.

'No,' Markham said reflectively, 'it didn't sound as though there was anything to that . . . Ms Atherton looked blank when I mentioned it, so maybe it was just Catherine who had a personal issue with Elsie Parker . . . and in the end, it didn't cause any ripples.' With a mischievous gleam in his eyes, the DI added, 'I'll leave it to you to review the minutes of the governors' meetings just in case.'

'Cheers, boss.' Glumly, Doyle concentrated on the road.

* * *

While Markham and Doyle visited Hope Academy, Burton and Carruthers were tackling Dave Shipley and Donald Kemp.

It turned out that Shipley, a driving instructor employed by BSM, was living in a one bedroom flat above a chip shop a short distance from Hollingrove Park. Which presumably accounted for the pervading smell of grease, Burton thought as she perched gingerly on a shabby armchair in the poky living room. Despite his surroundings, however, the man wasn't entirely unprepossessing, being well muscled with a boxer's build, a head of wavy brown hair and lop-smiled smile (he was clearly self-conscious about a chipped tooth which presumably awaited the dentist's attention). Like his sister Valerie, he had the voice of a smoker, but little of her raddled venom. There was even a curious dignity in the way he insisted that Catherine Leckie had got the wrong end of the stick.

'Sure I liked her,' he told them. 'I went round to her shed now and again for a chat. She even made me a cuppa if she was brewing up. But there wasn't anything else to it. I knew she had a fella . . . and anyway,' his voice was regretful, 'it would've been punching above my weight. She was way out of my league.'

'Why did you get chucked off the allotments then?' Carruthers asked unsympathetically, taking the lead as previously agreed with Burton.

'Catherine got it into her head that I'd been spying on her . . . peering through windows, leaving notes by the door of the shed, that kind of thing.'

Carruthers looked up alertly. *This* sounded promising.

'What kind of notes?' he asked.

'I never knew. Must've been poison pen or something like that. Anyway, apparently Margaret Cresswell,' he gritted his teeth, 'told her to flush them down the loo and forget about it.'

'*And?*' Carruthers prompted.

'Well, the notes petered out, but then there was all this about someone watching her.' He hesitated. 'I wondered if she wasn't doing it to get Raymond Cotter to pay her more attention . . . y'know, pull the damsel in distress number so he'd feel he had to dance attendance.'

'Rather strange that Mrs Cresswell didn't tell us about these notes and the stalking or whatever it was,' Carruthers commented suspiciously.

'She's a great one for *respectability* and *appearances*,' the other said bitterly. 'Plus, deep down I'm not sure she totally believed Catherine's histrionics . . . Of course it wouldn't do to say so, and there I was — this divorced bloke who'd been hanging around her . . .'

'You weren't the only one. What about Michael Oddie?' Burton interjected.

'*Get real!*' Shipley said contemptuously. 'The respectable accountant from a nice home counties background! As if *he* was ever in the frame! No, *I* was the best bet for a stitch-up. Besides, Cresswell and my sister don't get on. Val wasn't mates with Catherine either, so it was one way to stick it to her . . . keep her down.'

God, the guy sounded like he was developing a full-blown persecution complex, Carruthers thought wearily.

'Doesn't the committee have to hold a meeting or a hearing or something before they chuck folk out?' he asked.

'I knew it was a foregone conclusion. There are eight of them on the committee, but basically they do whatever Cresswell says. So I jumped before I was pushed.' With a note of satisfaction, he said, 'Plonked my resignation on the table before Cresswell had a chance to open her beak. It was almost worth all the aggro to see the look on her face.'

'Do you reckon he was perving, ma'am?' Carruthers asked after the interview as they made their way back to Burton's car.

'He looked a bit of a saddo,' was the reply. 'But he was convincing enough when he talked about the injustice of it all . . . seemed genuinely indignant and upset.' The DI sighed. 'We'll have to check up on this "lady friend" he says he spent the night with on New Year's Eve.'

'If it was a case of them drowning their sorrows,' Carruthers's lips curled, 'he could've sneaked out to the allotments once the girlfriend was three sheets to the wind . . . she wouldn't have noticed him disappearing for a bit. The allotments are only minutes away, and he's easily fit enough to scale the wall.'

'Shipley and his sister aren't particularly pleasant characters,' Burton said thoughtfully. 'But that doesn't mean they aren't telling the truth.'

'Valerie Shipley was a school secretary at Hollingrove Primary back in the day,' Carruthers mused. 'Probably didn't like teachers queening it over her. Margaret Cresswell's a retired head . . . St Gregory's in Calder Vale. That might be why she took Catherine's side—'

Burton frowned. 'You mean because she thought teachers should stick together?'

'Yeah, closing ranks or something like that . . . It's hard to see how the Shipleys managed to wangle their way into Beauclair Drive in the first place, seeing as they stick out like sore thumbs.'

'Presumably they were on the waiting list . . . that's down to the council, so Mrs Cresswell and her well-heeled chums don't have it all their own way.'

Carruthers rolled his eyes. 'There's something downright *incestuous* about the whole set-up, if you ask me. Like a dysfunctional family, the lot of them.'

'Come on, let's see if we fare any better with Mr Kemp.'

Donald Kemp could hardly have presented a greater contrast to Dave Shipley, being a tall, fair-haired young man with what might be called classical good looks, were it not for a prominent, slightly hooked nose and an expression of petulance about the mouth. His minimalist flat in the centre of town spoke of an affluent lifestyle and, as Carruthers pointed out irritably afterwards, he made sure they didn't miss the fact that his father was *Councillor* Kemp.

'His alibi seems airtight,' Burton mused.

'Yep, you can't really argue with "supper chez the parentals",' Carruthers said in a mock Hooray Henry accent. 'Though, seeing as this is *murder*, his parents aren't likely to mention it if boyo happened to slope off early.'

'Doesn't come across as the kind of allotment holder with a passion for nature and the great outdoors,' the DI went on thoughtfully. 'And Mr Creech said his plot's an absolute tip.'

'Probably just a gimmick,' Carruthers retorted. 'Some kind of Marie Antoinette shtick . . . playing at farmers and all that . . . eyeing up the talent while he's at it.'

'Maybe . . . but I don't see him as Catherine Leckie's stalker . . . too conceited to waste time on someone unless he got encouragement.'

'Yeah, he looks more the type to chat up the ladies in town . . . then back to his place for a quick leg-over.'

Burton winced at the vulgarity, but she had to admit it fitted her impression of the man.

'What's his game, I wonder,' she murmured.

'Drugs? Underage girls?' Carruthers suggested helpfully. 'And maybe Leckie got wind somehow and threatened to dob him in the same as she did with Shipley. If her and Cresswell were on some kind of moral crusade — rooting out undesirables and pervs — it could've meant she was cramping Kemp's style.'

'Or someone else's.' Burton knuckled her eyes. 'God, it feels like we're going round in circles. We should get back to the station and check if the boss has done any better at Hope. While we're at it, we can have a word with Chris Carstairs and see if anyone from the allotments is on his radar.'

'Kemp was pretty shifty about what he does for a living. I mean "entrepreneur" covers a multitude,' Carruthers grunted as he looked back at the mansion block. The guy probably had daddy's solicitor on speed dial. If that was their man, he'd be a tough nut to crack.

* * *

Noakes was decidedly intrigued to hear Markham's account of the day when the two friends met up that evening at the Grapes.

Their favoured hostelry was a delightfully quirky establishment which, despite its recent renovation by fearsomely bee-hived proprietor Denise, retained an old-world charm that held little appeal for Bromgrove's chattering classes. Markham found the pub a very cosy place to unwind, its multiple nooks and crannies, nautical curios (Denise had seafarers in her family tree) and creaky, sloping floorboards in the back parlour like something out of *Hornblower* or *The Onedin Line*.

The menu was good too, and they tucked into their toad-in-the-hole (Noakes) and chicken schnitzel (Markham) with gusto. 'I remember being in Sainsbury's a while back when this kid pointed to an avocado an' asked what it was,' Noakes commented, eyeing the vibrant salads that accompanied their mains. 'His mum said "Them's what posh people eat". An' now bleeding avocados are *everywhere!*'

Markham grinned. 'An interesting barometer of progress,' he said, reflecting that Muriel doubtless wouldn't like it to be thought that an avocado was anything out of the ordinary at *her* table.

'So you got fobbed off at Hopeless then,' Noakes pronounced with the gloomy satisfaction of one who could have predicted such an outcome. With unusual circumspection, he refrained from mentioning Mathew Sullivan but looked pleased when Markham said that Sullivan sent his regards. 'He ain't the worst. You c'n have a laugh with him. I loved that story about the time he found that note on his desk from the kid in detention: "Sir, I have wrote one hundred times, *I have gone home*, and then I have went home." Priceless, even if he *did* make it up.'

'I wouldn't be too sure about that, Noakesy. I've heard real howlers from Olivia.'

'How's your girl doing then?' Noakes enquired affectionately. 'Putting some manners on 'em, I hope.'

'When she's allowed to,' he grimaced. 'Apparently, it's all woke snowflakery these days, so she feels increasingly like a square peg in a round hole.'

'Mebbe she should have a shot at being head,' Noakes suggested with his head on one side. 'Then *she'd* get to make the rules.'

'All the politics and jealousy and petty backstabbing would drive her mad,' Markham rejoined decisively. 'Not to mention the SLTs.' Despite himself, he smiled on recollecting that his partner invariably called them STDs.

'D'you reckon that poor lass snuffed it cos of some school quarrel?'

'I honestly don't know what to think . . . I've got Kate checking the digital media angle to see if there was any online harassment or trolling going on, but nothing's come up as yet.'

'I bumped into Peter Barlow the other day.' Accidentally on purpose, if Noakes's past form was anything to go by. 'He were proper discombobulated by it all . . . According to Pete, Leckie an' another teacher had the odd whinge about the Parker woman . . . said she was always talking herself up at their expense.'

'Olivia tells me it's a bitchy profession. That's what gets her down sometimes — colleagues preaching to the pupils about kindness while going for the jugular!'

Noakes scratched his head. '*My* lot were all pretty decent.'

'Yes, I had a good experience too, though of course a fair number wore dog collars, so kindness was part of the job description . . . And Doyle seems to have happy memories.'

'P'raps the bitchiness is cos there's more women than men,' Noakes said warily, knowing that Markham disliked anything that smacked of misogyny.

But the DI merely nodded. 'Men can be as bad, though,' he said ruefully, thinking of Sidney and some of the top brass. 'And I suppose these days schools are like pressure cookers — all that competition to get the best results—'

'Or be most liked by the kids,' Noakes put in sarcastically.

'There's probably a fair amount of dark humour in the mix too, with folk being contentious or un-PC to let off steam.'

His friend looked somewhat self-conscious at this. 'Could be it's jus' the playground rubbing off,' he muttered.

'Well, even if there *are* undercurrents and cliques at Hope, so far we haven't made a connection with what happened to Catherine.'

'What about the Daly lad? I've heard he's not the worst on the Hoxton. Ackshually—'

Whatever he had been going to say was interrupted by Markham's mobile.

'I'd better take this, Noakesy. Kate may have turned up something in the background checks.'

The other finished off his lager, watching closely as a range of expressions chased each other across Markham's face.

Apprehension. Concern. And finally, horror.

'Not good news then?' he said at the conclusion of the call.

'The worst.' Markham's voice was suddenly hoarse, as if the thing he dreaded had suddenly grappled him by the throat.

'Raymond Cotter is dead. It happened a short time ago at the allotments.'

'Heart attack . . . on account of the grief?' But Noakes knew even as he asked the question that this was clutching at straws.

'Kate seems to think he took something . . . says she'll be with us in five.'

Noakes lumbered to his feet, much gratified at Markham's use of the first person plural.

So Catherine Leckie wasn't a one-off.

Their shadowy killer had struck again.

CHAPTER 5

Beauclair Drive was already a hive of activity when Markham and Noakes arrived, illuminated by powerful search lights with a tent screening the latest victim.

'Forensics for Catherine Leckie were finished by Tuesday evening, sir,' Burton pointed out. 'There was no justification for keeping the place closed . . . but to be honest, it didn't seem likely that anyone would want to hang about her, so we advised people to stay away for now.'

'Who found him?'

'Mr Creech doing his rounds,' she said without needing to add, *Again.*

'Mr Cotter must have believed that he was quite safe,' Markham said wearily.

'Knew how to handle himself,' Noakes observed. 'No danger of anyone taking him by surprise . . . not like that poor lass.'

The tent flap lifted to disclose Dimples Davidson.

'Your victim didn't think to check his tea,' the pathologist said, beckoning them in, having completed his preliminary examination.

Raymond Cotter was sitting hunched over at a garden table clad in cords and a dark sweater. His arms were resting on the table with his forehead bowed down on them so that they couldn't see his face.

'Looks as if he's sleeping in that position, but supple enough for me to manipulate,', Dimples told them gesturing to the recumbent corpse. Then he drew their attention to a flask next to the body. 'Somehow he ended up having a swig from that. Possibly a shot of something along with Rohypnol to lower his defences, followed by a more potent ingredient which kicked in once he was oblivious.'

'Any chance this could have been suicide?' Markham enquired. 'A guilty conscience because he murdered Catherine?'

'Very unlikely in the circumstances,' the other said decisively. 'That sawhorse posture and the claw-hand point to strychnine. There are other indicators too — frothing, lockjaw and so forth . . . I've seen it before. *Nasty* . . . guaranteed to achieve a painful exit. Not something most people would opt for. But we'll know more after the tox screen.'

'So, Mr Cotter met someone here and they doctored his drink,' Markham said.

'It had to be someone he trusted,' Burton said. 'I mean, after Catherine's murder, he wouldn't have sat down for a chat with just anyone.'

'There are no signs of a struggle — no defensive injuries — so I'm inclined to agree with you, Inspector,' Dimples told Burton. 'I'd say he was taken unawares.'

'It looks almost peaceful,' she replied. 'Like something out of *Hamlet* . . .'

The pathologist regarded her quizzically.

'Sorry, doc . . . Hamlet's wicked uncle gets poison poured down his ear when he's sleeping in the garden.'

'I'm with you now, m'dear . . . *Things rank and gross in nature possess it merely*,' he recited softly.

Noakes harrumphed noisily. In his experience, it was always a bad sign when folk started quoting the Bard.

Dimples looked from the two men to Kate Burton and back again. Markham knew it was a chivalrous quirk of Davidson's that he wanted to spare their female colleague the dismal and humiliating realities of violent death, despite Burton's own resolutely phlegmatic composure in confronting everything head on.

'Everything will be clear after the PM,' he said. 'I'll just get finished up with him.'

With that, he disappeared back inside the tent.

Markham had the feeling that Dimples needed to unwind, but would feel constrained by Burton's continued presence. A shamefully anti-feminist reaction, no doubt, but the DI understood such old-fashioned reticence. Dimples was in his sixties but might be said to have been "born old". Certainly his shire antecedents made the pathologist something of a throwback.

'I need you to get back to HQ and brief the others, Kate,' he said easily. 'Dimples could be a while and you're better deployed back at base.'

Once upon a time, she would have been agitating to attend the PM, but these days she generally trusted Doyle or Carruthers to do the honours.

'Righto, sir,' she said briskly. 'I'll get on with checking alibis for this one.'

Good luck with that. Noakes was surprised to find he actually felt positively benign towards the guvnor's peaky-looking number two. Whatever was amiss with her and Shippers had hit her hard, he thought compassionately. Just so long as it didn't send her ricocheting back towards Markham . . .

Once she was gone, it wasn't long before Dimples re-emerged, summoning waiting paramedics to organise the removal. Instinctively, the SOCOs, uniforms and assorted personnel bowed their heads respectfully as Raymond Cotter's body left the allotments.

After the remains had been carried away, Dimples sank down wearily on one side of a neighbouring potting table, apparently not ill disposed for talk. Observing furrows and grooves in the pathologist's face that seemed almost to have sprung up overnight, Markham sat across from him. After a moment's hesitation, Noakes joined them, sliding in next to Markham though with a grunt that suggested it was a tight fit. Despite being mid-evening, it wasn't particularly cold and there was plenty of illumination from the police arc lights.

'Why is it folk are so keen on allotments?' the medic wondered before answering his own question. 'Must be that whole Beatrix Potter thing. Country is good, town is bad.'

'At a level, I guess there's some sort of moral subtext,' Markham observed mildly. 'Particularly now so many people are obsessed with caring for the land and sustainability . . . And then, with towns and cities so densely populated, we shouldn't be surprised if there's this hunger for fields and wildlife and nature. Maybe evolution plays a part too . . . moving from hunter-gatherer mode to settling down and digging one's own patch. Or perhaps it's just some deep-seated primeval urge to be outside.'

'My uncle Jim got evacuated to Wales during the war,' Noakes put in. 'Thought he'd died and gone to heaven . . . seeing animals an' climbing trees . . . no more dog shit an' traffic an' smog . . . His asthma,' Noakes pronounced it 'assm-mar' like Piggy in *Lord of the Flies*, 'cleared up over-night.' He shuffled, trying to get comfortable. 'An' it were all organic food an' sugar rations, so he didn't need the dentist neither.'

Markham smiled. 'When she first started teaching at Hope, Olivia was shocked that some of the more deprived youngsters she taught had never seen cows or sheep . . . I think she wouldn't mind having her own garden. When she first moved in with me, I was forever falling over pots of ferns and trays of seedlings.'

With the easy chat, Dimples visibly relaxed, some of the strain leaving his face.

Watching the medic's expression, Markham reflected that the job no doubt got to him at times as he weighed and measured and sluiced in Bromgrove General's mortuary along with his team of grim-faced technicians. No doubt the same thought had occurred to Noakes, since he too appeared content just to sit there and chew the cud.

'The missus wants us to get a pergola,' he confided. 'One of them fancy trellis jobbies with roses climbing all over.'

Markham tried not to imagine Olivia's likely reaction when she heard about Muriel's latest step towards turning the Noakeses' pleasant three-bedroom Tudorbethan detached home into one big country cliché or pastiche of The Simple Life. He knew Noakes hankered after an Old English sheepdog, but while roses round trellises might be indispensable to Muriel's comfort, a shaggy dog certainly was not.

'Nice idea,' the pathologist said politely before asking, 'Didn't you have an allotment here at one time?'

'Yeah, thass right . . . before the fun went out of it . . . But I get to do some digging an' stuff at Rosemount, an' the missus is planning a kitchen garden.' No surprises there, given Muriel's fixation with Merrie England lifestyles as depicted in the pages of *Country Life*.

'I thought community gardeners were meant to be a friendly lot . . . you almost imagine funny handshakes and passwords . . .' Dimples gazed round at the SOCOs busy about their various tasks and gestured helplessly. 'But now *this* . . . Beauclair's always seemed pretty middle-class to me, so you don't expect bodies turning up.'

'I think allotments were originally designed for the labouring poor, and some places still have strong welfare credentials,' Markham replied, recalling Burton's words of wisdom on the subject and her account of the site at Colindale. 'But I imagine you're right about most of the plots here belonging to people who are relatively well off.'

'Didn't they took off in the war when grub was short?' Noakes asked. '"Dig for Victory" an' all that.'

'Yes, but it's rapidly becoming a middle-class fad,' Markham told him . 'These days it's all *From Soil to Fork* . . . River Cottage . . . *Make Do And Mend*—'

'Fearnley-Wotsit an' Kirstie Allsopp an' all them poshos doing the nostalgia bit an' pretending to be in touch with the ancestors,' Noakes finished dourly. 'Load of hippies if you ask me.'

Dimples chuckled, suddenly looking ten years younger. He had always enjoyed the banter with Noakes, thought Markham.

Now the pathologist mused, 'It's understandable people want to be at one with things growing and flowering, when you remember that the Good Book says we started out in a garden—'

'An' got chucked out for bad behaviour.' Noakes made short work of Adam and Eve.

'At any rate, allotmenteers in *this* neck of the woods aren't hippies or dropouts,' Dimples continued. 'There's the old school brigade . . . Rumour has it that Peter Barlow regularly turns up wearing a tie.'

'Nice to know *some* folk have standards,' the other sniffed.

They lingered on in companionable silence, Dimples being clearly in no hurry to get back to the 'slicing and dicing'. Markham was well aware he himself needed to return to base — could almost hear Sidney honking, 'Less talk, more action' — but he knew Burton would already have set wheels in motion and it somehow felt important to allow Beauclair to *speak* to him. Even though it was just a typically dullish January day, he had the sense of spring being not just a calendar promise but something that was imminent, with bulbs and buds poised to burst out all over the place . . . an earthly transformation that Catherine Leckie and Raymond Cotter would never see. So what could have impelled someone to desecrate this paradisiacal sanctuary? What was its significance for the killer?

Or maybe Beauclair was just a convenient dump site and the connection lay elsewhere . . .

Markham's thoughts returned to the first victim's workplace.

'Did you ever get the sense that something was wrong at Hope, Doug?' he asked the pathologist.

'What kind of wrong?'

'Professional rivalries . . . school politics. This all started with Catherine Leckie, so I'm wondering who might've had it in for her. I mean, that appointment can't have been universally popular . . . With you being a governor, I just wondered if you were aware of problems.' He reflected that even if there had been problems in the work environment, it must have been something pretty radical for the teacher to end up murdered.

'She *did* drop hints that she was finding it difficult to win over the old guard . . . you know, the likes of Elsie Parker.' Dimples scratched his chin. 'Even though she was young and progressive, Catherine didn't have a whole lot of time for what she called "woke nonsense",' he air quoted ironically, 'whereas Elsie was always on some kind of soapbox . . . micro-aggressions, unconscious bias and something called white resentment . . . To be honest, me and a few others like Peter Barlow didn't understand the half of it, but I remember Margaret Cresswell was quite keen.' He snorted. 'Talked about Hope needing to be more inclusive and less archaic.'

'I don' get it,' Noakes cut in. 'You'd think the older ones would be all for tradition an' history . . . y'know, the status quo . . . keeping things the way they've always been, not the other way round.'

'It's not always age-related,' Davidson retorted.' Just look at King Charles — too woke for words . . . always sniping at the Tories and meddling in politics.' Muriel wouldn't like to hear such criticism, Markham thought.

'I'm not so sure Elsie didn't hitch her wagon to those "identitarian" liberal causes partly to make mischief,' the medic continued.

'What sort of mischief?' Markham asked.

'Well, Elsie taking the opposite stance to Catherine and being all holier than thou was one way of undermining her . . . getting her own back because she was passed over for the job . . . She was quite clever about getting the teaching assistants and support staff on her side.'

'Sounds like summat out of the middle ages,' Noakes knew his history. 'Folk setting up rival courts an' trying to do each other down.'

'Not a bad analogy,' Dimples agreed. 'You see, there's a lot of jealousy in schools. The previous head didn't take a tough enough line.'

'Thass cos he was a slimeball.' Noakes scowled, recalling Tony Brighouse's reign of terror as relayed by Olivia in lurid detail.

Dimples affected not to hear. 'I reckon another reason women like Elsie and Margaret are so keen on all the victim-hood and class warfare stuff is, that it keeps the lower orders in their place.'

'That's a bit cynical even for you, Doug,' Markham laughed.

'Well, it's the wife's theory actually, but I think she may be on to something . . . You *could* say all that bottom-of-the-pile narrative about disadvantage and kids being oppressed is one way of keeping them down — a kind of inverted snob-bery cos it's so negative and doesn't challenge them to break the cycle . . . Catherine's line was all about having 'em climb out of the failure pit, but you got the feeling the other lot were quite happy to keep them there.'

'Manipulative then?' the DI asked bluntly.

'Yes, something like that . . . It gives power-mad types the whip hand, plus all the virtue signalling and parroting the latest fad du jour makes them feel superior.'

Dimples shrugged. 'Sorry, guess I'm out of my depth when it comes to all of that.'

'No, it's an interesting slant on the reality of school poli-tics,' Markham replied, reflecting that it was a debate capable of arousing strong passions. He grinned. 'Olivia would cer-tainly agree with you about all the posing and virtue signal-ling being a way of getting one over on Ms Leckie.'

'What about the Daly lad?' Noakes demanded suddenly. 'Did Parker an' the bleeding heart lot make trouble when Leckie chucked him out.'

Markham's lips twitched at the obvious partisanship. Dimples, being well used to Noakes's approach and (as Markham suspected) inclining to his side of the debate, replied easily, 'Yes, there was a tussle over that. Even Rebecca Atherton sided with Elsie on that one — and let's just say those two weren't natural soulmates . . . But I reckon Catherine didn't really have a choice, given all the complaints from parents, and in the end the governors backed her. If anything, me and Barlow and some of the others thought she hadn't been tough enough with Daly when he first went off the rails, but at least she didn't let it turn into a crisis. Sure there was lots of criticism and muttering, but Catherine made sure Daly wasn't just cut adrift . . . got her youth worker mate from the allotments to keep tabs on the lad and check that he was okay.'

There was silence as Markham and Noakes digested what was clearly a complicated picture.

'Look, I wouldn't want you to think Elsie's just some troublemaker,' Dimples protested, clearly alarmed lest he had been lulled into major indiscretion. 'When it comes to all that progressive stuff, the likes of Mat Sullivan and Doc Abernathy are singing from the same hymn sheet, but I think with her it's a case of mixed motives . . . like Margaret Cresswell.'

'*Oh?*' Markham was keen for a new light on the Chair of the Allotment Association.

'Between you and me, Margaret felt a bit threatened. She's a former headteacher herself, you see . . . used to being queen bee and everyone deferring. But Catherine wasn't a forelock-tugger . . . very confident and authoritative. I'm not sure Margaret was entirely comfortable with that. She was used to having things her own way as a governor and down at the allotments — had her own little clique — and didn't care for competition. Oh, don't get me wrong,' he added, seeing that Markham was deeply intrigued by this take on Dimples's fellow governor, 'she's a thoroughly good woman — salt of the earth — but not as secure as she appears on the surface.'

'I understand Mrs Cresswell actually took Ms Leckie's side when it came to getting an allotment holder expelled for inappropriate behaviour,' Markham pointed out. Though, from what Burton had said after her interview with Dave Shipley, the man had resigned before any formal hearing.

'I heard there'd been some kind of trouble,' Dimples replied. 'Margaret wouldn't want the allotments associated with any kind of seediness. She was a stickler for keeping up appearances.'

This tallied with what Dave Shipley told Burton and Carruthers. Interestingly, it appeared that Shipley too had detected Margaret Cresswell's suppressed hostility towards the young headteacher and suspicion of her 'histrionics'. Of course, Val Shipley was no fan of Catherine Leckie and this was bound to have coloured her brother's account.

'Did you know anything about stalking, Doug?' Markham asked.

The medic was startled. 'What, as in someone pestering *Catherine* . . . here at the allotments?' Slowly, he shook his head. 'No, but I can easily imagine the committee trying to keep it under wraps.' Emphatically, he added, 'That kind of thing wouldn't do their image any good at all.'

'Sir.' A young SOCO had materialised at Markham's elbow. 'There's something you should see.'

The DI got up, followed by the pathologist and Noakes.

The forensics officer led them to a gnarled deciduous tree on the far right of the allotments.

Noakes was bewildered.

''S jus' a big old tree,' he said. 'So what's the big deal?'

'There's a knot-hole, Sarge,' the other replied respectfully (like many of Noakes's former colleagues unable to drop the honorific). 'Quite deep, but if you look inside . . . well, go on,' he urged, 'see for yourself.'

Noakes duly peered in and then made way for the other two.

'Chiffon scarf . . . print hairband . . . a couple of hair clips . . . and a perfume bottle,' Dimples said slowly. 'I'm pretty sure the hairband is Catherine's . . . almost certain I saw her wearing it at some shindig or other.'

'Why would her things end up in a tree?' Noakes asked blankly.

Then he recalled the stalking.

'Chuffing Nora . . . That weirdo she thought were spying on her must've pinched them as keepsakes . . . like the pervs who nick ladies' undies from clotheslines.' This being a mindset with which Noakes was all too familiar from his long police career. 'But why stash 'em here? Why not take the stuff home so they could drool over 'em all nice and private?' The words conjured up a disturbing image.

'What drew your attention to this tree, officer?' Markham enquired.

'My brother's a tree surgeon,' was the unexpected reply. 'He does wood carving on the side . . . I noticed this tree cos it looked kind of interesting . . . as though it had hobbit holes . . . like in *Lord of the Rings*.. Just fancied taking a quick look . . .'

He trailed off, uncomfortably aware that Noakes was unlikely to be an aficionado of Bilbo Baggins and fairy folk.

'Lucky for us that you have a curious mind,' Markham said kindly. 'Good work. We'll leave you to get these items bagged up.'

'Sir.' The lad saluted smartly and whipped out a plastic evidence sack as the three men moved away, conferring in low voices.

'I don' get why chummy squirrelled the lass's bits an' pieces inside a bleeding *tree*.' It was clearly beyond Noakes.

'I'm a bit baffled myself,' Markham admitted. 'There must be some particular meaning behind it . . . an associated memory or ritual.' He thought for a moment. 'It's almost like *To Kill A Mockingbird* where Boo Radley puts objects inside the hollow of a tree.'

Noakes had read the book on Olivia's recommendation, finding it surprisingly enjoyable. 'Yeah, but *he* leaves little gifts for the kids to find cos he's a mentalist an' too shy to say hello face-to-face . . . kinda sweet . . . whereas *this* is plain freaky.'

Dimples thought about it. 'If your murderer has a kink — and it looks that way — then they could be caught up in some kind of romantic fantasy,' he suggested. 'I'd get your criminal profiling guru on it pronto, Markham.'

'Will do.'

Despite watching just about every true crime documentary going, Noakes was deeply sceptical of forensic psychologists. 'Them Cracker types always dress it up, when we're probl'y looking at some sicko who jus' wants to get his end away playing with women's things.'

'Very evocative, Noakes,' was the pathologist's dry retort before adding, 'Of course, there's always the possibility the stalking and thefts aren't related to these murders.'

Markham groaned. 'Give us a break, Doug. What are the odds on there being *two* deviants targeting Beauclair?'

'Vanishingly small,' the other grinned. 'Just keeping you on your toes.'

As the medic departed with a cheery wave, Noakes groused, 'Why's that one so chipper all of a sudden? He had a face like a smacked arse before.'

'I got the impression he was down in the dumps, Noakesy. Needed some time out before the next PM.'

'Oh aye,' His friend felt he could afford to be magnanimous. 'If we're talking hobbits an' *Lord of the Rings*, then poor ole Dimples is worse than Gollum, being stuck in that creepy basement all day.'

'Well, I reckon we've galvanised him with a vengeance. And there was certainly food for thought in what he said about Elsie Parker and Margaret Cresswell weaponizing ideologies for their own ends.'

'But, as Dimples pointed out, school politics can be murky, so perhaps we shouldn't read too much into problems at the chalkface.'

'What next, guv?'

'A late-night brainstorm for me and the others back at base followed by the usual humdinger with Sidney.' Noakes's expression was one of profound commiseration.

'Why don' we have a workout at Doggie's tomorrow, boss?' This was a reference to Bromgrove Police Boxing Club in Marsh Lane, a frequent resort of Markham's in times of stress or difficulties with the DCI (the two being virtually synonymous). 'You'll need it after going ten rounds with Sidney.'

'Right, you're on . . . Let's say we meet there four-ish and I'll give you the lowdown.'

The allotments were haloed in an eerie nimbus as the two men walked towards the gates, the forensic teams still flitting about their tasks like giant moths.

False paradise, Markham thought with one backward glance. But how had evil infiltrated Eden?

Here they had found no tree of life, only death and desolation.

And somewhere out there was a killer who, just like the ominous serpent, slithered unseen with a camouflage that had everyone fooled.

We have to penetrate that disguise, Markham thought desperately.

Before another death.

CHAPTER 6

Despite the late hour, with news of a second murder, the team was waiting in his office when Markham returned from Beauclair Drive shortly before 11 p.m. It was obvious that adrenalin levels were high, with Doyle and Carruthers visibly excited at the prospect of the allotments enquiry moving up a gear while simultaneously trying not to be too obvious about it in case they appeared callous. *Déjà vu*, the DI thought wryly.

'FLOs are with Bernadette Farrelly and the kids,' Burton told him, having wanted to provide support even though she and Cotter were divorced. 'Sounds like the family's holding up okay.'

'I'll be round there tomorrow, Kate, but interviews can wait until they're ready.'

'Bernadette was out with Bromgrove Harriers for an evening run then went for a cool-down by herself.' Compassion for the bereaved never clouded Burton's investigative focus. 'The kids were over at a friend's, but they'd been dropped home by the time she got back just after nine . . . they're sensible youngsters, used to getting their own tea.'

'No clear alibi then,' Doyle said.

'Not from about eight o'clock . . . that's when she peeled off from the other runners to do her own thing.'

Which might or might not have included poisoning her ex-husband.

'What about alibis for the rest of our suspects?' Markham wanted to know.

'Initially, we've just focused on people who were around when Catherine Leckie was killed, guv, as opposed to all the Beauclair membership.' Her voice held a question.

'Quite right, Kate,' Markham confirmed. 'There's no doubt in my mind that these two murders are connected. We should run routine checks on all allotmenteers, obviously, but I want to focus on suspects who were in Bromgrove over the New Year.'

Burton turned her attention to Hope Academy. 'The spring term kicks off tomorrow Thursday the fifth,' his colleague said punctiliously. 'According to Rebecca Atherton and Elsie Parker, they were at home getting stuff ready.'

'Very virtuous,' Markham replied tartly. 'Anyone able to vouch for them?'

'Unfortunately not . . . hard at it all evening apparently.' She grinned. 'Perfect martyrs to duty.'

Now it was Doyle's turn. 'Hilary Probert was WFH too . . . social work notes and conference calls.'

'Was this video or audio?' Markham asked.

'She had a listen-only PIN for her mobile. That's the usual routine for non-essential stuff or where it's not your particular team . . . "housekeeping" was what she called it. It's not unusual for them to log in for remote catch-ups in the evenings.'

Again, nothing to say these administrative chores had prevented her from slipping out to meet Raymond Cotter.

Next up was Carruthers. 'The Shipleys were over at Valerie's. It was her husband's darts night, so Brother Dearest came round for some home cooking.' His tone was sardonic. 'The Alibi Siblings.'

Doyle sniggered. 'Makes 'em sound like an indie band.'

There was a distinct hint of frost in Burton's tone as she took over. 'Michael Oddie had a colleague over for a meal. Apparently, they made a night of it.'

Great, it looked like they were going nowhere fast, Markham thought in exasperation.

Aloud, all he said was, 'Any joy with Donald Kemp?'

Burton sighed. 'Home alone . . . Mind you,' she perked up slightly, 'Chris Carstairs says there's been rumours about him and underage girls.'

Markham's eyes narrowed. 'Ever had his collar felt?'

'Not so far . . . Carstairs reckons the councillor made any trouble go away.'

Something about this stank to high heaven, but the DI knew they couldn't charge in all guns blazing. Sidney would never wear it . . .

Burton could see the way his mind was working. 'Up till now, Kemp's always been two steps ahead, but with these murders the rules have changed — whoever's had his back at this nick won't be so keen to cover for him in future . . . *way* too risky.'

'D'you think he might have been using the allotments for, er—' Doyle groped for a suitably decorous word — '*dates* . . . ply them with drink and then . . . into his manky shed for a bit of how's your father . . .'

'Knock it off, mate,' Carruthers exclaimed scornfully. 'They may be teenagers out for some fun . . . but it'd take more than a couple of Bacardi Breezers in a shed to get them in the mood.'

Burton wasn't so sure. 'Kemp's a sophisticated older guy. If they're vulnerable, they might think it was romantic.'

'And the secrecy would be a turn-on,' Doyle suggested with some hauteur, clearly nettled by Carruthers's response. *Like you would know,* he thought indignantly.

'If Catherine Leckie knew what was going on with Kemp and threatened to make trouble, that might give him a motive for murder,' Burton concluded.

'He wouldn't just roll over,' Carruthers insisted, ignoring Doyle's smirk at the *double entendre*. 'Not unless she could prove it.'

'Bandying accusations like that around would put her in the council's bad books,' Burton mused, 'and it's the local authority that holds the purse strings. Peter Barlow said she was always having to go cap in hand to them.'

'What about Mr Barlow's movements, Kate?' Markham enquired, though without much hope.

'A district nurse from Marsh Lane Surgery did a late-afternoon house call because he was poorly with a chest infection . . . dropped off his antibiotics and told him to go straight to bed. He was supposed to be playing bridge at Margaret Cresswell's later but didn't feel up to it.'

'Did Mrs Cresswell's bridge evening go ahead?'

Burton shook her head. 'It turned out she was sick as well. Sounded like the two of them had the same bug.' Burton consulted her notes. 'They were both pretty groggy when I rang . . . Cresswell's niece is taking her to the surgery drop-in clinic first thing tomorrow. To be honest, if this is the same norovirus infection everyone seemed to go down with just before Christmas, I can't see either of them managing a late-night rendezvous at the allotments.'

'It would've taken a cool head to lull Mr Cotter into thinking he was safe so they could slip the poison into his drink,' Markham agreed. 'Difficult to imagine anyone with the lurgy being up to it.'

'Greville Leckie claimed to be down with the same thing,' Burton went on, frowning.

'I feel a "but" coming,' Markham said heavily.

'It's just that he didn't *sound* particularly sick, not like the others. And he was so, well, *incurious* somehow . . . didn't even want to know why I was asking about his movements.'

'We have to remember he's been bereaved too,' Markham said. Then, in case she took this as a reproof, 'I didn't care for his manner at our first meeting.' A mixture of captain of industry and Coldstream Guards, as per his CV. 'But we don't have anything to indicate he had a connection to Mr Cotter or any reason to bear the man a grudge.'

'Perhaps the killer went after Cotter because they wanted revenge on him and Leckie for something they did in the past,' Carruthers surmised.

'Like what?' Doyle demanded.

'Dunno,' the other threw up his hands. 'Could be some sort of sex triangle for all we know.'

'Or maybe Cotter knew something about the killer,' Doyle countered. 'Something compromising . . .'

'Talking of compromising material,' Markham said quietly, 'the SOCOs found certain items hidden in a tree hollow at Beauclair Drive.'

He had their attention now, three pairs of eyes riveted on his face.

Succinctly, he outlined the discovery at the allotments.

'Stalking and trophies,' Carruthers breathed, enraptured by the unfolding possibilities. 'So it's *gotta* be a sex crime.'

'Not necessarily,' Markham demurred.

'Sidney'll *love* it,' Doyle insisted. 'He always goes for those nutter-on-the-loose scenarios if it gets nicey-nicey types off the hook. Veg growers and outdoorsy folk don't fit the profile . . . way too wholesome . . . I mean, Beauclair Drive's practically wall to wall teachers and respectable types . . . downright boring really.'

'What about Donald Kemp and Dave Shipley?' Carruthers challenged.

'Okay, those two and the caretaker are a bit iffy,' Doyle admitted. 'But I still can't see them creeping round stuffing women's gear into tree holes . . . that's *properly* mental.'

'There's always James Daly,' Carruthers pointed out. 'Wasn't he in trouble for harassing girls at Hope?'

'True.' Burton checked her aide-memoire once more. 'His mum swore blind he'd been at home all evening.'

'So that's another one without a decent alibi,' was Carruthers's ironic verdict.

'And we've got Ninian Creech bringing up the rear,' Burton sighed. 'Apparently Mrs Creech got in from visiting a friend at around ten and the brother-in-law was off doing his own thing, so Ninian was by himself for the first part of the evening before going out to "check on the allotments".'

After some further lively speculation, Markham dismissed his team, grateful that at least he had a few reasonable "lines of enquiry" ready for Sidney. He suspected that Doyle was right about his boss favouring the notion of a deranged sex maniac. But to his way of thinking, it just didn't fit the peculiar precision with which those objects had been hidden at the allotments nor the cool deliberation of Raymond Cotter's poisoning.

His eyes were gritty with fatigue. Time to get home to Olivia.

* * *

Thursday got off to a bad start with Sidney breathing fire about a headline in the online edition of the *Gazette* which proclaimed, "Hoxton link to murdered teacher."

The byline indicated that the scoop came courtesy of Gavin Conors, the paper's lead gossip columnist (or 'sleazeball in chief', as Noakes had dubbed him).

'How the *hell* did this happen, Inspector?' Sidney hissed. 'Conors all but accuses some schoolboy of murder, not to mention insinuating that there's this hotspot for violent crime smack on our doorstep. As you can well imagine, the Chief Constable is *furious.*'

Markham quickly scanned the article. None better than Conors at the subtle art of insinuendo, he thought ruefully.

'*Well, Inspector?*' Sidney's eczema, always a reliable indicator of his mood, was more florid than a pepperoni pizza topping.

'It's Conors's usual shtick, sir . . . guesswork tinged with salaciousness . . . stops short of naming names or anything defamatory,' he said with grudging admiration. 'As for the stuff about Catherine Leckie's zero tolerance for sexual harassment and "tough love" approach, it's no more nor less than what you can read in the tabloids about headteachers any day of the week.'

'Community leaders are *bound* to make mischief . . . just when we'd got the Hoxton on an even keel,' the DCI lamented.

'We can organise a caring counterstrike, sir.' Markham felt decidedly cynical as he made this suggestion but knew it was the kind of language Sidney understood. 'I believe a social worker's been dealing with the family in question,' he continued smoothly, omitting to mention that Hilary Probert also happened to be a suspect, 'so it's just a question of fielding someone from children's services to say they offer a range of support to all students who've been excluded and to the best of their knowledge there's no overlap with any police investigation blah blah . . . give the impression that Conors's piece is just a stab in the dark and he doesn't have a clue.'

The pulsing vein on Sidney's right temple gradually slowed. Clearly the prospect of making Gavin Conors, the perennial thorn in his side, look like a clown held considerable appeal.

'I suppose that *might* work.'

Markham forged ahead. 'At least the *Gazette* hasn't said anything about Raymond Cotter's murder . . . once Conors hears about that and latches onto Mr Cotter's relationship with Catherine Leckie, he'll forget all about schoolboys on the Hoxton estate.'

'We'll need a press bulletin about Cotter. Something to take the heat off CID.'

'*Naturally*, sir,' Markham said with his best bedside manner. 'We give it the usual spiel . . . early stages of the investigation, no stone unturned . . . need to avoid unhelpful speculation and respect the privacy of the families etcetera.' He paused to let the bland phrases sink in before continuing. 'Mr Cotter's parents are dead, and his ex-wife won't be talking to the press, so no leaks from their side.'

'Someone tipped Gavin Conors off . . . sent him sniffing round the Hoxton for dirt on that lad who was excluded,' Sidney said sourly. It sounded almost as though he suspected one of Markham's team.

'Anyone with a grudge against the boy could have done it,' the DI replied with a steely glint in his eye. The tip-off could have come from their murderer for that matter, he thought grimly. 'But I don't see Conors giving up his sources.'

The DCI grunted acknowledgement.

'Right sir, if there's nothing else you need from me . . .' Which translated as: *Let me do my blank blank job.*

At least Dimples had some news for him, confirming that Raymond Cotter had died from a massive overdose of strychnine 'with a morphine and cyclobenzaprine chaser to seal the deal.' The pathologist sounded as though he was back to his usual brisk, bluff self. 'I'll send over a breakdown of quantitative determinants for your earnest sidekick to computate,' he added with affectionate condescension. 'And before you ask, Markham, I estimate time of death somewhere between seven and nine since rigor in the face muscles was fairly well advanced by the time we got to him.'

'So he suffered.'

Somehow it felt important to remember that.

'Undoubtedly.'

'And you can confirm there were no defensive injuries?'

'None.'

There was no need to spell it out. As with Catherine Leckie, it seemed to him as if there was a strong probability that the victim knew their killer and had no reason to be fearful.

'Cheers, Doug,' he said, making an effort to sound upbeat.

But there was no fooling the other.

'Very bad with the DCI, was it?' the medic enquired sympathetically.

'Let's just say Gavin Conors sent his blood pressure through the roof.'

'*Ah.*' There was a pause before Dimples went on, 'I heard a rumour at the golf club the other day that the Sidneys may be having some marriage problems.'

'*Seriously?*' It was the last thing Markham would have expected to hear.

'Well, she lost all that weight last year — empty nest syndrome, most probably — and seems to have hit the social scene with a vengeance . . . Your boss is having a hard time keeping up with her by all accounts. Plus, my other half reckons she's impatient with him for not being ambitious enough . . . not reinventing himself as a celebrity policeman, John Stalker Mark Two or whatever.'

'Olivia's always been under the impression it was *Sidney* who hankered after a slot on CBS Reality . . . you know the kind of thing — *Scotland Yard Files*, *Descent of a Serial Killer.*'

There was a chuckle on the other end of the 'phone.

'I know your good lady isn't a fan.' Apart from Noakes, Dimples was the only man he knew who used such old-fashioned expressions, Markham reflected with a wry smile.

'Too right,' he retorted. 'Well, I'll make sure to cut the DCI some slack then . . . This is a bit of a turn-up for the books seeing as he'd taken to condoling with me on my,' assuming an ironic basso profundo, '*disastrous* love life.' He didn't expand on how the DCI came to know all about his break-up with Olivia, being sure that Dimples had already heard all the gossip about that.

'You're back on track now, though, so the boot's on the other foot,' the pathologist said cheerily. 'Tough on your boss if all he really wants after retirement is pipe and slippers while *she's* ready for Botox and the bright lights.' Markham heard an echo of Mrs Davidson in this waspish pronouncement.

'I think there *was* a time when Sidney fancied some celebrity exposure,' Markham said slowly.

'Understandable seeing as his handsome hot-shot DI invariably got all the attention,' Davidson observed slyly.

'Being a bean counter and playing CID politics seems to have taken it out of him somehow,' the DI went on as if the other hadn't spoken. 'Though he's as keen on royalty as ever, so maybe there's the chance of a gong.'

'Good luck to him! Though now his missus has got the bit between her teeth, she might be after something more glamorous.'

'God, Doug, you make it sound like she's ready to ditch Sidney for a toyboy or something!'

'You heard it here first!'

* * *

Noakes was vastly tickled by Davidson's intel.

'*Well, I never!*' he said as they sat after work in the euphemistically entitled VIP Locker Room at Doggie Dickerson's gym in Marsh Lane. 'Mrs S must be having a midlife crisis or summat . . . Poor old Sidders.'

The proprietor of Bromgrove Police Boxing Club caught the tail end of their conversation as he shuffled in to greet his 'fav'rite 'spector' and Noakes.

'My Evie's brother is having one of them midlife thingies,' he said lugubriously. 'Sixty odd but thinks he's a youngster . . . busy making a fool of himself over some PA dolly bird down at the council.'

'Sorry to hear that, Dogs,' Markham said politely. 'Family break-ups are always painful.'

'Well, Bill's not married, but Evie worries about him getting hurt in the end cos of the age gap. Plus, he's spending money like water . . . trying to buy the woman. It just ain't dignified.'

Doggie (best not to enquire into the provenance of that nickname) was not exactly the epitome of dignity himself, resembling a villainous extra from *Pirates of the Caribbean* with his yellow tombstone teeth, eyepatch and lopsided horsehair wig the mere sight of which unnerved even local villains and ne'er-do-wells. Today he was wearing one of his funereal frockcoats over flapping striped trousers and trailing whisky fumes that contended for supremacy with the locker room's smell of cheap disinfectant (Johnnie Walker narrowly winning the day).

Sidney and Bromgrove CID high command utterly disapproved of Doggie's grimy and insalubrious outfit, but it had proved a surprising hit with detectives and the criminal fraternity alike, these time-honoured foes going at each other in the ring with no questions asked and no quarter given before resuming their usual cat and mouse once outside the confines of the gym.

Markham had always enjoyed Doggie, consoling him though a litany of romantic vicissitudes that ended when he became engaged to Evelyn ('Evie') who had never yet graced the premises with her presence but clearly knew how to keep the old reprobate in order. As for Doggie, he appreciated the inspector's grave courtesy and gratifying assumption that they were somehow brothers under the skin.

Noakes too was well liked by the rheumy-eyed proprietor, not least as the former sergeant's world view was, if anything, even more reactionary and un-PC then his own. The fact that both men were ex-army (though Doggie's military record, like his moniker, doubtless didn't bear close inspection) made another bond, likewise the blithe disregard for anything approaching sartorial appropriateness.

Doggie sighed wheezily in acknowledgement of human degeneracy before recalling the obligations of hospitality.

'Mr Carstairs was in earlier. Said you've got your hands full with these gardening murders.'

Oddly enough, nobody in CID ever worried about Doggie blabbing to anyone outside the gym, a strange brand of ethics ensuring that the Fagin lookalike never betrayed any of his 'gentlemen'. His motto was ever, *What's Said Here, Stays Here.*

'It's weird all right,' Noakes gloomed before recounting their travails to date, right down to the tree-hole finds.

'Sounds a bit screwy,' Doggie said doubtfully at the conclusion of the recital. 'Maybe they've got a thing for fairy trees.'

'There's these crackpot folk who go in for *tree marriage*,' Noakes informed him. 'Insist trees are like humans . . . go round stroking 'em an' all sorts.'

'Thass *gotta* be the midlife thingy,' Doggie cackled disbelievingly.

'Nah, they're mostly kids — eco-warrior types,' Noakes sniffed disdainfully. 'Make your Evie's brother look positively normal.'

'I never knew anyone who had a tree kink,' Doggie said almost wistfully, as though it was his life's ambition to plumb the depths of human depravity.

'Oh aye . . . There'll be a name for it an' all.' Noakes winked at Markham. 'One of them paraphilia wotsits Burton's always droning on about.'

'*Nasty*,' Doggie observed with a pleasurable shudder. 'Like they can't go courting same as normal folk.'

After he had disappeared back to his back office (and the bottle wedged in the top drawer of his rickety filing cabinet), the two men quickly got changed.

'Right, Noakesy, let's head out there for some cathartic pummelling,' the DI said, trying not to laugh at the other's porky physique in billowing Artex shorts and off-colour T-shirt.

'Reckon I c'n give you a decent workout, guv . . . Young Kevin's got me on to these special milkshakes an' they're not half bad.'

'Excellent. And then you can come and sit in on my session with this criminal profiler Kate's lined up.'

'Ain't Shippers on it?' his friend frowned.

'Apparently he's double-booked, but this one comes highly recommended.'

'Okay, boss . . . It's Kev's shift at Rosemount but,' Noakes puffed his chest out, 'he knows to call me if there's owt he can't handle.' Markham nodded gravely, amused by his friend's executive tone. 'How about we swing by Greggs an' pick up some grub on the way,' the other suggested. 'We c'n bat ideas around while we're at it,' he added craftily. And undo all that hard work in the ring.

But Markham smiled agreement. 'Lead on, Macduff,' he urged. 'Time for you to deliver!'

He had the uneasy feeling that he had missed something during the last twenty minutes or so of easy chat in the locker room. *Something important.* But looking back, he couldn't for the life of him think what it was.

Allotments and midlife crises and fairy trees . . . all swirling round and round in his head.

And a killer still on the loose . . .

CHAPTER 7

Dr Eleanor Shaughnessy, the psychologist Burton had brought in from the university, was a striking woman who put Markham in mind of a Norse goddess. Tall and statuesque with long blonde hair loosely secured back from her face, piercing blue eyes and a strong jaw, she possessed an aura of assurance and serenity that he found immediately appealing. Her voice too fell agreeably on the ear, being melodious and gentle with just a hint of Irish brogue. Markham was able to judge of her effect on Noakes by the way the other self-consciously checked his flies and straightened his tie on being introduced, blithely unaware that the unmistakeable spicy aroma of that BBQ meal deal from Greggs wasn't entirely compatible with an impression of corporate efficiency. Burton's long-suffering expression certainly suggested she didn't care for it at all.

The visitor listened attentively as Markham brought her up to date on the case, paying particular attention to the strange discovery of Catherine Leckie's possessions in the tree hole at the allotments.

'Secreting trophies like that points to your killer's need to keep the victim close,' the psychologist told them. 'The trophies are also symbolic in that they serve both as a reminder of the perceived relationship the killer had with the victim and an expression of power over her.'

'Like Ian Brady an' his freaking photo album,' Noakes pronounced.

She looked at him enquiringly.

'Well, Brady never told the police where he buried that poor lad who were never found . . . the one whose mum went out on the moors in all weathers looking for him.'

'Keith Bennett?'

'Thass the one. Brady were always creating about getting his photo album back from the police an' later on they figured he wanted his snaps of the moors cos it gave him some creepy power over the lad . . . his pervy little secret . . . like him an' Keith still had this connection in spite of him being locked up in prison, an' every time he looked at the pics it meant *he* were the one in control . . . It's how he got his jollies.'

'That's an interesting analogy, Mr Noakes,' she said, causing him to blush with pleasure. 'Yes, I would say possessiveness and control are crucial to your killer. Even though Brady's mementoes were all about giving him power over dead victims whereas Catherine Leckie's things were presumably stolen while she was still alive, the principle is the same . . . It's all about reliving the connection and experiencing feelings of power and omnipotence.' She let that sink in before continuing. 'I believe there would also have been a sexual kick or some form of excitement from knowing that they had been able to steal items belonging to Catherine without her being aware of it.'

'Does that mean you think her attacker was male?' Markham asked.

She shook her head. 'No . . . If anything, the way her body was found — positioned almost *decorously* as though sleeping — suggests a fastidious distaste for mess, though of course it's a trait found in men too.'

Definitely not in George Noakes, Burton's expression seemed to say.

'An' don' forget how Cotter died . . . poison's a woman's weapon,' Noakes pointed out.

'True,' the profiler acknowledged. 'There aren't obvious gender markers in these murders, and female criminals are also motivated to keep trophies.'

'Why hide Catherine's things in a tree, though?' Burton asked impatiently. 'Wouldn't it make more sense to take them home . . . then the killer could pore over her belongings in private with no risk of being disturbed. I mean, stashing stuff at the allotments doesn't really make sense.' Clearly it offended Burton's sense of logic.

'Risk can be a component in sexual excitement, remember,' the psychologist pointed out. 'But it's more likely the killer derived intense satisfaction from using the allotments as their hiding place.'

'But *why*?' Burton still wasn't satisfied.

'Perhaps because Beauclair Drive was the scene of previous encounters with Catherine Leckie and her boyfriend — possibly involving some humiliation at their hands — and the place had thereby assumed some outsize significance in the killer's mind . . . That might also explain why they chose to dispatch both victims at the allotments.'

'A way of rewriting the script so that this time *they* were in control,' Markham suggested.

'Exactly, Inspector.'

The psychologist regarded them calmly, content to let them digest the implications in silence. Markham found that he liked her self-effacing style. Not that Nathan Finlayson was by any means strident or pushy . . . it was more that this woman had a uniquely *restful* quality about her even as she discussed sociopathic variables.

'So you think that Ms Leckie and Mr Cotter might *both* have antagonised the killer?' he asked, recalling Carruthers's hypothesis that this was a revenge attack against them as a couple.

'I would say it's a strong possibility, Inspector. Actually, I would go further and say that the allotments have an almost mystical value for your killer — an overwhelming representational significance that holds the key to it all.'

Hearing her say this, Markham thought of a recurrent dream he had of the semi-detached house he and his dead brother shared with their mother in the idyllic days before the arrival of an abusive stepfather changed their lives forever. So strong was its magnetic pull, that he could not pass the property on Bromgrove Rise without experiencing a mad impulse to stop and ask the householders for permission to revisit his old home and the magical mint-scented garden. Only the thought of Sidney's likely reaction ('You really need to control your *poetical impulses*, Markham, etcetera') prevented him from succumbing to this homesickness. Of course, as Noakes was wont to point out mordantly, 'Nostalgia ain't what it used to be,' but the DI had the feeling of being permanently haunted by the ghosts of that vanished paradise. *His* ghosts felt like benevolent entities, but it sounded as though their killer's recollections had a more tormenting character.

'Don' take this the wrong way, doc.'

Oh God, this kind of preamble generally meant Noakes was gearing up for some monumental piece of offensiveness.

But his friend merely observed, 'It's *obvious* chummy's got a squirrelly hang-up about gardens an' all that.'

'Well, to you and me maybe, Mr Noakes,' the psychologist said courteously. 'But then, we've a long acquaintance with criminal dysfunctionality.'

Oh, you're *good* at this, Markham thought admiringly, as his former wingman preened complacently.

Noakes was on the front foot now.

'Watcha reckon to the weirdy teenager that got expelled?' he demanded.

'I've a lot of sympathy for young men like that, Mr Noakes,' was the gentle reply. 'Despite the positives in terms of social progress, some feel there's been this massive cultural shift against them and that the *#MeToo* and *Everyone's Invited* movements seem to cast virtually every teenaged lad as some kind of predator or sexual deviant.'

Noakes, all pursed lips and furrowed brow, looked as though the popular perception corresponded precisely with his own assessment of the anathematised social group in question.

'It's entirely possible that the youngster in question developed an unhealthy preoccupation with Catherine Leckie and her partner,' the psychologist continued evenly, 'in which case there's likely to be some kind of social media trail.'

'We're working on it,' Burton said. 'But so far, nothing's shown up.' She regarded Shaughnessy hopefully. 'Can you give us any pointers as to the killer's age, doc?'

'It's rare, though not unheard of, for seniors to commit serious violent homicide,' she replied. 'Usually in such cases, it's a question of financial gain, though issues of power and dominance are also relevant to that demographic. The problem being, that there's nothing to indicate your well-heeled older suspects had any impetus for murder — no obvious social insecurity or vulnerability vis a vis the victims . . . As for the absence of any social media indicators, that doesn't necessarily mean you can rule out a perpetrator in the higher age brackets.'

'Lemme get this straight,' Noakes said heavily. 'You reckon we're looking for someone with a thing for gardens who had some sort of run-in with Leckie an' her boyfriend . . . mebbe felt inferior to them or got the idea they looked down their noses . . . so killing 'em evened things up an' made everything square again.'

Dr Shaughnessy smiled at her portly interrogator. 'I'd say that's a fair summary, Mr Noakes.'

She's like Freya or another of those ancient Scandinavian deities, Markham thought, observing with amusement how Noakes blinked as though dazzled.

There was a knock at his door.

'Sorry for interrupting, sir.' Markham recognised a pimply member of the civilian staff and tensed, aware that only a major development would justify the interruption.

What have you got for us?' he enquired crisply.

'Reported fire at Beauclair Drive, sir.'

Burton was already out of her seat.

'We'll be there in ten,' she said, looking across to Markham for his approval. On receiving the nod, Burton turned to Dr Shaughnessy. 'Would you mind taking a look, doc?' she asked. 'See if anything jumps out at you?'

'Happy to help,' the other replied.

Seeing that his former sergeant clearly had no intention of being left behind, Markham said, 'Right, you're with me, Noakesy. Kate can take Dr Shaughnessy.'

Out in the car park, it had turned cold, though with a sharp clean tang that was bracingly welcome after the stuffy office.

'Jus' gets better an' better,' Noakes said sarcastically. 'A bunch of alibis leaking like sieves an' now there's arson in the mix . . . *Bleeding perfect!*

The DI's countenance was taut. 'Apparently Superintendent Bretherton has described my elite unit's approach to homicide as "Four Cops Talking",' he said bleakly. 'So maybe he'll be happier now it's a case of Action Stations.'

'Bretherton don' know his arse from his elbow,' was Noakes's withering verdict. '*Ackshually,*' he added, 'I reckon that trick cyclist of Burton's said some interesting stuff.' As well as being easier on the eye than Finlayson, Markham thought wryly.

When they got to the allotments, an apologetic uniform approached Markham. 'Two hourly mobile patrols as per the updated instructions, but no sign of anyone hanging around.'

'What happened?' Markham asked tersely.

'A small blaze behind one of the sheds, sir. Didn't take hold though, so the fire service sorted it quickly.'

'Who raised the alarm?'

'Dog walker in Hollingrove Park spotted smoke and called 999.'

'Where's the caretaker?' Noakes demanded.

'Off sick with the flu,' the uniform replied.

'More like he's afraid he might be next.' Noakes clearly didn't see Ninian Creech as the courageous type.

It came as no surprise that the shed behind which the fire had started was Catherine Leckie's.

'They used an accelerant,' Simon McLeish of Bromgrove's Fire Investigation Unit informed them in his strong Northern Irish accent. 'Petrol by the look of it.'

Markham introduced the sandy-haired FIO to Dr Shaughnessy.

'Any thoughts, doc?' McLeish asked amiably.

'I would say this was an almost primal reaction to painful memories connected with that shed,' she said thoughtfully. 'Though the fact that they started the fire *behind* it suggests they couldn't bear to damage the structure directly for some reason. Clearly, whatever pain or hatred is eating your killer hasn't subsided with Mr Cotter's murder, so they've felt compelled to strike out again.' She frowned. 'In which case, it's a very short cooling-off period.'

'Do you see this escalating?' Burton asked anxiously. 'As in more murders?'

The psychologist took her time before answering. 'If there's a complete break with reality, then they might attack others based on a distorted perception of those individuals' relationship to the victims.'

Burton whistled in dismay. 'Are we talking some kind of psychotic break then?'

'I would say more like PTSD or emergent schizoaffective disorder,' was the calm reply.

The FIO took in their discombobulated reactions.

'At least nobody was killed this time,' he said in a feeble attempt at reassurance. 'And you're not up to three.'

Yet.

'I'll get Doyle and Carruthers on to mental health checks,' Burton said desperately. 'There's got to be red flags in *someone's* background.'

'Not necessarily,' the psychologist said. 'This could have taken a long time to come to the boil, so it's only *now* that hostile cognition is taking over.' Her tone apologetic, she added, 'Sorry, I know that's *not* what you want to hear.'

'We appreciate your frankness, Doctor,' Markham said, despite his plunging morale. Without any knowledge of their killer's internal triggers, how could they predict which of the allotment holders was potentially at risk from this derangement?

The uniform who had initially greeted them suddenly reappeared, eyeing the disconsolate group warily.

'There's a woman from Church Avenue at the gate, sir,' he told Markham. 'Says she may have seen something.'

'*Here we go!*' Noakes groaned. 'Another know-all who's OD'd on *Silent Witness* an' wants to give us their two penn'worth.'

'I'll be over in a minute, Constable,' replied Markham, ignoring Noakes.

The sun had finally come out and it showed every sign of turning into a glorious day, the branches of the site's majestic trees silhouetted like delicate fretwork against clear blue skies. Markham's gaze travelled over the allotments, where the peaty smell of compost and fertiliser mingled with the scents of grass and budding vegetation, before returning to the trees with their silvery-green trunks and sun-dappled canopies.

'There's something implacable — almost cruel — about all that beauty, isn't there,' said Eleanor Shaughnessy softly, following his glance. 'Nature still going strong while humans turn to dust . . . under a headstone, oblivious of everything.' A shaky laugh. 'All done in!'

It was so close to his own thoughts that Markham started, taken aback. Her face was sad, and in that moment he wondered about her personal history.

There was a brief silence broken by McLeish.

'Better leave you to it,' he said. 'I'll email you later, Markham.' With a polite nod to the others, he returned to his team.

'I should be heading back to the university,' Dr Shaughnessy declared at the same moment as Burton, unsettled by that moment of communion between the guvnor and the tall blonde, announced her intention to give the psychologist a lift.

Noakes too had noticed the chemistry between Markham and Eleanor Shaughnessy. His boss had an eye for female allure, and it sounded like this one was another fan of 'Big Words', but in his book the Irish colleen couldn't hold a candle to Olivia.

'Thought she were going to break into poetry,' he grunted once the psychologist was out of earshot. 'Though I'd sooner listen to your Liv any day of the week.'

Subtle as a hang-gliding flasher, Markham thought, divided between exasperation and laughter.

'Let's see what this public-spirited citizen has for us,' he said briskly, heading for the gate at speed.

The mild-mannered elderly woman, resident of a block of flats with an excellent view of Beauclair Drive, was the antithesis of an attention-seeker. She informed them that she had noticed a young woman hanging around outside the allotments earlier that morning but didn't think anything of it until she saw the fire engines come roaring up.

The description she gave — 'scrawny and looked like one of those Goths' — matched Hilary Probert.

'Let's pay Ms Probert a visit, Noakesy,' Markham suggested once they had sent the civic-minded OAP on her way. 'I recall her saying she's based at St Bruno's Youth Centre Thursdays and Fridays, so she should be there now.'

Noakes being nothing loath to accompany the guvnor, they duly returned to Markham's car.

The DI had expected Noakes to raise the subject of Olivia once more, but was surprised when the conversation took an unexpected direction.

'Your Liv said you an' her might be in the market for a baby,' his friend confided after much harrumphing and clearing of his throat.

'*In the market?*' Markham temporised, taken aback.

'Looking to adopt . . . mebbe start by fostering an' then go the whole hog an' make it official.'

'Are we talking about *Natalie's* baby by any chance?' the DI asked, his brows contracting at the revelation that Olivia had actually gone so far as to broach this with Noakes without telling him. It felt like she had crossed a line behaving like this behind his back. And yet, he was keenly aware of the trauma from that botched abortion — understood how it might have skewed his partner's normal sensitivities.

Now Noakes was shuffling his feet like a child who needed the loo, uncomfortably aware that the guvnor's mood had suddenly turned Siberian.

'*Relax*, Noakesy. I'm just surprised, that's all . . . I had no idea Olivia was thinking along those lines.' Which wasn't strictly true, he thought, uneasily recalling his partner's passionate interest in Natalie's pregnancy and insistence that Noakes's grandchild shouldn't be lost to him.

Dammit, she shouldn't have put his friend in this position, Markham thought irritably. It was unfair, not least as there was no way on God's earth that Muriel would countenance such an arrangement. Not just on account of her personal ambivalence towards Olivia, but because it would drastically change the dynamic were they to assume parental responsibility for Natalie's child, making them and the Noakeses practically in-laws. Oh there was no doubt he would be able to swing it — had all the contacts — but he knew it would not be right. The very idea was ludicrous and he couldn't see Natalie coming on board in a month of Sundays.

'I guess it's your Liv's maternal side coming out,' Noakes said awkwardly. 'Stands to reason she'd be thinking about adoption if . . . that's the only way, like.'

His friend knew nothing about the procedure that had left Olivia unable to have children and, out of loyalty, Markham was happy to give the impression there were fertility issues. Let Noakesy think *he* was "firing blanks" if necessary!

In the wake of Olivia's affair, or whatever it was, with Mathew Sullivan, she probably believed that becoming parents might bring them closer together and patch up the cracks in their relationship. No doubt Noakes, being an incurable romantic where Olivia was concerned, thought so too. But Markham instinctively felt that such a scheme would somehow be *false*. And, truth be told, deep down his own childhood experiences made him doubt his suitability for such a role.

He felt that he had many lives in him, but not that of a father.

Selfish maybe, cowardly undoubtedly, but that's how it was.

He and Noakes never explicitly acknowledged the childhood nightmares that had crippled Markham's youth despite his old ally having intuited it early in their friendship. Now, all the other said with gruff embarrassment was, 'Nat's only just found out about the baby, so she's got plenty of time to make plans. You gotta do what's right for *you*, boss. Being a parent ain't for everyone . . . half the time it's a thumping great pain in the neck. Your Liv'll come round, never fear.' The clumsy attempt to give comfort was as touching as what had preceded it was bizarre. Signalling that the subject was closed for the time being, Noakes grunted, 'Right, let's see what Little Miss Goth has to say for herself.'

St Bruno's Youth Centre was, from an architectural point of view, as lacklustre and uninspiring as the Parish Centre, being constructed in the same liverish red brick and possessing all the charm of a municipal library.

Hilary Probert, far from being unsettled by their arrival, appeared perfectly cool and collected, though her eyes were red-rimmed and swollen.

'I went there to lay some flowers for Cate,' she said composedly as they chatted in her tiny cubicle of an office. 'But then at the last minute, I just couldn't face going into the allotments.'

'What did you do with the flowers?' Noakes demanded.

'Brought them back here,' she said, pointing to what looked like a sad little bouquet of Michaelmas daisies and nasturtiums in a jam jar on her desk. 'I felt it was overdoing it somehow and Cate would prefer me to put them in here for the kids to enjoy.'

Noakes looked highly sceptical at the idea of any such botanical therapy but held his tongue.

'We know you and Ms Leckie were good friends,' Markham said gently before asking, 'Did you have much to do with her boyfriend Mr Cotter?'

The youth worker was very still at this, only the hunched shoulders suggesting a rigid self-control that she was determined to maintain at all costs.

'I didn't really know him,' she answered. 'He didn't strike me as really being at all Cate's type . . . way too brash and controlling. But he paid her lots of attention and she seemed dazzled by him.'

Once they were outside, Noakes cut straight to the chase.

'*Hell hath no fury* an' all that, guv . . . Whatcha reckon to *her* being Leckie's stalker? She looks jus' the type to go a bundle on fairy trees an' superstition an' nicking dead folks' clobber.'

'I'm not sure the mere fact of her wearing those denim overalls or boiler suit automatically justifies our assuming that she's a two-time killer, Noakesy,' was Markham's dry response. 'It seemed to me that she had herself well in hand.'

'Yeah, but if we're looking at an emergent psycho wotsit like Blondie said back there, then Probert wouldn't be giving us the screaming abdabs cos it's only early stages, right?'

'If by "Blondie" you mean Dr Shaughnessy, then yes, her theory would seem to point to some kind of dormant personality disorder with no overt signifiers.'

'Probert looked like she'd been up all night crying a river,' Noakes said beadily. 'What if *she* wanted to, er, get it on with Leckie an' couldn't cope when she got the brush-off . . . so then she flipped her lid an' went on the rampage.'

'Sergeant Doyle is very much of your opinion, Noakesy,' Markham said tersely, recalling the youngster's view that this might be a sapphic imbroglio.

Noakes was the picture of gratification.

'There you go then, boss,' he said, patting his paunch as he was wont to do in moments of high glee. 'If Leckie turned Probert down, then she'd want to stick it to her an' Cotter. *Crime Passionel.*' Noakes's accent was so execrable, that he made it sound like a dodgy continental dessert.

'You seem to forget, Ms Probert has an alibi for both murders. Noakesy. Granted they're not the strongest,' he said, forestalling his friend's objections, 'but my gut just doesn't like her for these killings.'

Noakes's countenance suggested that he felt his guvnor's radar could be way off beam.

'*Right*,' Markham said crisply. 'You need to get back to Rosemount.' Seeing that his friend looked mulish, he said firmly, '*Yes you do, Noakesy.*' And craftily: 'Kevin needs you at the helm, and I don't want mutiny on the quarterdeck.' The nautical allusion was nicely calculated to recall Noakes to a sense of where his priorities ought to lie (not that they necessarily did).

'Right-oh, guv.' A pregnant pause. 'How about you an' Liv come to ours for your dinner on Sunday? We c'n check out the service at St Bruno's first,' he added craftily, 'seeing as that's where all your gardening folk go.'

Oh no, Olivia would kill him. But Markham felt there was no hope for it.

'Delightful, Noakesy,' he said faintly. Please God let Natalie not be of the party. 'Tell your lady wife not to put herself out on our account.' Fat chance. Muriel would go into *MasterChef* overdrive the moment she heard about it. On the other hand, maybe it wasn't such a bad idea if it meant he could put the kibosh on any notion of adopting Natalie's baby . . . He would need to get a strong grip on his resentment of the way she had behaved before he saw Olivia. Ideally, he wanted to have it out with her — clear the air somehow. But maybe that should wait till after Sunday lunch once he had gauged the lie of the land . . .

In the meantime, the interview with Hilary Probert had got them precisely nowhere. He knew from Burton's background reports that Probert's supervisors spoke warmly of the social worker's trustworthiness and integrity, and he found her explanation of the visit to Beauclair Drive convincing.

Which left them back at square one.

Everywhere he looked, tensions were mounting. And resolution was nowhere in sight.

CHAPTER 8

Friday and Saturday brought no new developments in the case, a carefully drafted press bulletin taking the heat out of the storm over James Daly and the Hoxton while pacifying Sidney and the brass.

Olivia's reaction to the news of Noakes's invitation to lunch was predictable.

'*Oh no*, Gil,' she groaned on Saturday morning. 'Muriel will come on like a piranha, making digs about our break-up and implying that I don't deserve you. I can hear it now — non-stop drivel about "the love of a good man" till I want to *puke*.'

'No, Liv. She'll be too busy sweeping Natalie's little difficulty under the Axminster to worry about you.'

Another heartfelt groan. 'You don't think the poison dwarf will be there, do you? One's bad enough, but *two* . . .'

He didn't blame her for not relishing the prospect of a mother and daughter tag team but merely murmured reassurance. 'It'll be fine, Liv. As someone once said, if you can fake sincerity, you've got it made. Besides, you know it'd mean a lot to Noakesy.'

Her affection for his former bagman was always the trump card.

Saturday proved uneventful. They enjoyed an invigorating walk through Hollingrove Park and a lazy wander through Bromgrove Market before repairing to their flat for an evening binge-watching *The Bridge*, though Markham's thoughts occasionally reverted to his stalled investigation and the increasing pressure to come up with a tangible lead. By mutual consent, they avoided any further discussion of Natalie's pregnancy, though Markham sensed his partner's mind, like his own, was travelling down byways unconnected to the Scandi Noir drama.

It was with difficulty that he clamped down on his urge to confront her over what she had said to Noakes, but he stuck to his resolution to wait until the weekend was over.

Sunday was a still, overcast day with sunshine struggling to pierce the clouds.

They had agreed to meet Noakes at St Bruno's at half past ten, allowing time for an inspection of the allotmenteers' local church before the eleven o'clock service.

The exterior was nothing special, being largely constructed of sober dark brick. A campanile bell tower with quaint little overlapping louvres and blue copper dome at one end looked distinctly incongruous, as though the architect had sought to relieve the overall drabness by throwing in a minaret.

Inside was a distinct improvement, however, being warm and glowing and mysterious with the scents of incense resin, candles, flowers and invisible generations of faithful.

The trio wandered up to the front for a closer look at the sanctuary's decorated wood panels, floor of green and black honeycomb slating, raised copper-gilt tabernacle and pale rose marble altar behind a finely carved communion rail. Above the altar, a stained-glass window showed a white-robed monk in the countryside, absorbed in prayer before a crucifix. 'St Bruno,' Markham told them. 'The Chair of the allotments gave me and Kate a run-down on the church's history,' he added by way of explanation.

'Seems like there's lots of chained demons,' Noakes observed, somewhat disconcerted by the multiplicity of strange little gargoyles engraved on the reredos and oak lectern. 'An' the skinny bloke lying stretched out like that across all them skulls an' bones is downright depressing.'

'Not completely, Noakesy,' Markham reasoned. 'Your dead man's head is lifted up towards the Almighty . . . as if he's hoping for a merciful judgement.'

'Dunno why they always make God look like a weirdy beardy,' Noakes muttered balefully. 'He's the dead spit of that PCC . . . the one who's always sounding off to the *Gazette* about hate crime an' irrelevant lefty bollocks nobody gives a stuff about.'

Now that his friend mentioned it. Markham *did* detect a certain resemblance between the Deity and Bromgrove's local crime commissioner . . . along with a petulant disgruntlement that suggested God the Father was decidedly weary of humanity's grievances.

As they wandered along the far-right aisle with its richly coloured stained-glass tableaux and quaint statues, Noakes's thoughts turned from the subject of human dignity *in extremis*. 'It's always like *The Da Vinci Code* or summat in places like this with all the little symbols an' whatnot to show how the saints an' holy folk snuffed it . . . dragons an' dark caves an' towers an' forceps—'

'*Forceps?*' That pulled Olivia up short.

'Oh aye, there's a Saint Apollonia . . . had all her teeth pulled out an' — get this — *no anaesthetic.*'

'You're a marvel, George,' she laughed. 'Like a walking compendium of religious knowledge . . . Butler's *Lives of the Saints* or something!'

Noakes endeavoured to look suitably modest and failed miserably. 'Reckon it's down to the guvnor dragging me round all them mouldy old churches.'

Dragons were certainly a recurring motif in his career, Markham reflected, along with dark caves. As things stood, he had no idea how to keep the dragon in this particular investigation leashed and helpless.

Noakes peered closely at the statue of a burly figure with a large-good-humoured face who held a copy of the Gospels.

'St Thomas Aquinas it says on the little plaque thingy.'

'He was a great scholar, Noakesy,' Markham said.

'Don' look like he sat up all night studying,' his friend grunted. 'Bit of a fatty really.'

The DI chuckled. 'My old religious studies teacher told us he had to have a semicircle cut out of the table in the friars' refectory so that he could get within touching distance of his plate.'

'Nice to know at least *one* of 'em enjoyed his grub,' Noakes rejoined. 'Not like this lass here.' He squinted warily at the neighbouring small miniature of an anaemic looking young woman who had a palm in one hand and what looked like a spray of flowers in the other. 'Chuffing Nora,' he took a step back. 'That's not primroses or geraniums she's holding . . . they're eyes on stalks!'

'That's St Lucy,' Markham informed him.

'Oh aye.' Noakes could just imagine Burton and the boss lapping up all that the allotments Chair had to relate of the church's history, unlike Doyle and Carruthers who would have given Mrs Doo-Dah a wide berth.

'St Lucy gouged out her own eyes rather than succumb to a persistent suitor.' Mischievously, Markham continued, 'That's after she survived a range of other tortures, including burning, having her teeth pulled out and her breasts cut off.'

Olivia examined the leaflet she had collected on their way in. 'Apparently, she's the patron saint of the blind . . . St Bruno was famous for standing as a light of Christ against the darkness of the devil and Lucy's name means light, so there's a connection. It says here the picture was gifted to the church by a grateful parishioner in 1864.'

Noakes looked as though he didn't think much of said parishioner's taste.

'Proper ghoulish, if you ask me.' He halted in front of another gilt-framed miniature. 'Thass more like it,' he said approvingly as he took in the romantic image of a tall woman with abundant blonde hair standing in front of a medieval

tower. 'More calm an' peaceful like you expect with saints
. . . nice little castle too.'

'Saint Barbara.' Olivia's voice held merriment. 'She's
another one who had it tough. Her father locked her up in a
tower so he could control access to her.'

Noakes was intrigued. 'Bit of a control freak, then?' he
said, thinking that he'd sometimes wished he could do the same
with Natalie. 'Didn't want her falling in with the wrong type?'

'Well, it started out with him wanting to protect her from
the lures of the outside world. But he took it to extremes,
George, seeing as he eventually betrayed her to the authorities
for being a Christian and then beheaded her.' She smiled at his
rapt attention. 'But God struck Daddy-O down with lighten-
ing, so it all came right in the end.'

She could tell Noakes wasn't sure this really counted as a
happy ending, not least with divine retribution being visited
on the saint's *father*. 'Come on,' she urged, to distract him,
'Let's have a shufti over the other side.'

At the top of the left-hand aisle were three confes-
sional boxes and next to them an impressive statue of Saint
Michael the Archangel routing a hideous creature of serpen-
tine deformity. A little further along was another devotional
painting which depicted a pale young girl with long dark
hair reclining in some sort of bower, with what looked like a
helmeted guardian angel peering in at her.

'St Cecilia asleep at her organ,' Olivia recited.
'Reproduction of a Victorian painting by Frederick Appleyard.
Donated by Beauclair Drive Allotment Association.'

'Weren't Cecilia beheaded?' Noakes asked.

'Yes . . . but looks like this painter fancied something more
on the lines of the Lady of Shalott,' Olivia retorted. 'Sans gore.'

The sleeping figure reminded Markham of Catherine
Leckie curled modestly on her side, features half concealed
by her flowing chestnut hair. It made him uneasy, though
he couldn't for the life of him say why. Perhaps it was the
inclusion of that shadowy angel whose pose struck him as
leering and voyeuristic rather than protective.

In fact, something about the interior of this church troubled him, as though it was trying to communicate a warning, only he couldn't decipher the message.

Olivia too appeared vaguely unsettled.

'It's meant to be romantic and dreamy,' she said thoughtfully. 'But somehow that angel looks threatening . . . almost as if he's creeping up on St Cecilia, sort of coming up behind her.' Brows contracted, she went on. 'Like those strange paintings by Walter Sickert which made some people think he must have been Jack the Ripper, because he had a thing for stalkers and peeping Toms.'

'*Oh yeah.*' Now Noakes was hooked. 'I saw a documentary about him. Some crime fiction writer were positive old Walt were Jack . . . traced it back,' a furtive glance around the church to check no one was within earshot, 'to him having problems *with his wedding tackle.*'

'That's right,' Olivia said. 'That was Patricia Cornwell. She turned up horrific details about possible hermaphroditism and genital surgery . . . maybe even some sort of castration.'

Noakes gulped as though he didn't care to embark on such topics before his Sunday 'meat and two veg'.

'Any road,' he said hastily, 'Walt painted prostitutes an' criminals an' dodgy types . . . not *saints* . . . So that angel's *gotta* be a stand-up guy . . . like Gabriel or Michael or one of them warrior types.'

Markham suppressed a smile. Clearly his friend was having no truck with any unsavoury comparisons of the seraphim with Jack the Ripper. And yet he could not rid himself of a chill sensation of dread, as of an omen borne unseen on the air.

Now Noakes and Olivia were gazing up at the stained-glass windows.

'Mary out in the garden an' Gabriel come to say hello,' Noakes said approvingly. 'Very nice. Lots of fruit trees an' flowerbeds an' birds . . . You c'n see why the gardening crowd would like it.'

'With Adam and Eve being thrown out of Eden in the windows on the other side,' Olivia said thoughtfully, looking across the nave with its black and white chequerboard tiles. 'Damnation on one side and redemption on the other.'

'Yeah,' Noakes nodded sagely. 'Kind of cancelling each other out.' He spoke as if the Almighty was a celestial accountant engaged in balancing the books, Olivia thought, doing her best not to laugh.

'It's a beautiful church,' she said as they returned to the back of the church and the glassed-in alcove that appeared to be some kind of piety shop. Then, suddenly, she recoiled.

Markham followed her gaze.

'Reproduction of *The Three Ages of Man and Death*,' she murmured, leaning in to a small framed painting next to the recessed stall. 'Only,' she wrinkled her nose, 'it's not man but *women.*'

They looked at the picture whose medieval original was apparently enshrined in the Prado.

It depicted three figures: firstly, a pert young woman; secondly, a withered hag with sagging breasts; and in third place, a desiccated skeleton with scant, tufty hair holding an hourglass. In the foreground, a sinister owl and dead infant offered their own silent commentary on human folly, while in the background a lifeless moss-covered tree and ruined buildings seemed to shriek: *To This All Must Come.*

Olivia shuddered silently. Shooting a sideways glance at his partner's pinched features, Markham remembered the legend of the dead baby that was supposed to haunt the Beauclair allotments and was glad he hadn't shared that story with her. Given her current sensitivity on the subject of chil-dren, it was best to steer clear of tales of ghostly infants. He hadn't mentioned it to Noakes either, in light of Natalie's circumstances.

'What a strange little painting,' Olivia said finally. 'It almost seems to be saying that women are sneaky and deceit-ful and don't want to accept their mortality.'

'Fits with those windows,' Markham said, gesturing back towards the stained glass of right-hand aisle, 'and the idea that the expulsion from paradise was all down to Eve . . .

The Victorians were obsessed with fallen women, so it's hardly surprising that they went in for misogynistic memento mori.'

'I think it's *horrible*,' she said with unusual vehemence.

An awkward silence followed these words before a trickle of arrivals in the church porch put an end to their sightseeing.

The Sunday service for the Baptism of the Lord was unexceptionable, meaning that Markham's attention drifted as the etiolated elderly celebrant droned on. It struck him, however, that the liturgical references to opening the eyes of the blind and being a light for the nations dovetailed neatly with the histories of Saints Bruno and Lucy. The officiating clergyman duly flogged their stories to death, including some neatly turned metaphors about life's candle being snuffed out in the twinkling of an eye amidst the trappings of vanity.

All the way through the service (and disconcertingly happy-clappy hymns churned out by the venerable organ as if it was some kind of hurdy-gurdy), Markham had the nagging feeling that this church held a vital clue within its precincts . . . something lurking at the periphery of his vision that he just couldn't pin down. The harder he tried to catch the will-o'-the-wisp impression, the more persistently it eluded him.

Margaret Cresswell and Peter Barlow made a point of coming over at the conclusion of proceedings, though Markham detected a certain stateliness in their manner that might be construed as disapproval of CID's handling of the investigation. They looked to be over the worst of the lurgy, though still raspy-voiced and somewhat wheezy. Being of the 'stiff upper lip' generation, clearly only double pneumonia would prevent their attendance at the Sunday service.

From a forensic point of view, coming to St Bruno's had been a total waste of time, he thought dispiritedly. But Noakes and Olivia appeared to have enjoyed it, vying with each other in their aspersions on the hapless priest who shuffled off at the end like a benevolent tortoise.

'We shouldn't laugh, George,' his partner said with some compunction as the church emptied. 'He oozed kindness . . . the poor man can't help it if he had a charisma by-pass.'

'Imagine going to confession with *him*.' Noakes was by no means finished with the deficiencies of St Bruno's parish priest. '*Ackshually*,' he turned confidential, 'one of Muriel's mates from the Women's Guild — ever so holy — said she went into one of them tardises at St Mary's,' such being Noakes's term for the confessionals in Bromgrove Cathedral, 'an' launched into this big fat recital of sins — the whole nine yards, right. Well, the padres are all pretty much old an' deaf,' he continued irreverently, 'so she practically screamed the shopping list. Nada, just silence, so she did it all again slower an' louder . . . She were going to give it another whirl when she heard someone clanking around with a bucket an' mop. Then this woman in overalls popped her head out of the tardis on the other side an' said, "There's no one here, luv." *Can you imagine!*

Olivia's bell-like laugh rang out, attracting disapproving looks from the remaining worshipers.

'I bet her response was forceful enough to add one more to her list of sins,' she gurgled.

'Yeah, she were dead embarrassed . . . didn't know where to look. Put her off big style.'

'You're as bad as each other,' Markham said indulgently. 'Which is why I made an especially generous donation when the plate came round.' That had been a tricky moment due to his conviction that Noakes was quite capable of demanding change!

His friend, looking sheepish, adroitly changed the subject. 'Any road, reckon we've earned Muriel's roasties,' he said. '*Plus* apple crumble for afters.'

* * *

Olivia hadn't expected to feel compassion for Muriel Noakes (or 'Mrs Fratefully Naice' as she thought of her) but, as she watched their hostess patting the stiffly lacquered blonde bouffant and cranking her voice up one degree of poshness, she couldn't help having sympathy for the woman's gallant efforts to put a good face on what she undoubtedly considered to be a family crisis of the first magnitude. Wearing a navy-blue dress more suitable for a cocktail party than Sunday lunch, heavily made up and trailing Chanel No 5, it was evident that Mrs Noakes had devoted her entire morning to burnishing her image for Markham's benefit. Olivia had long since come to terms with the knowledge that Muriel found her partner divinely attractive while having little enthusiasm for herself (flighty, bohemian, too clever by half yada yada yada). The snide insinuations that she had trapped Markham by sexual wiles were a constant provocation, but she knew how much Noakes meant to her and Markham and simply gritted her teeth.

Yes, there was no doubting that Muriel was maddeningly adept at getting under her skin, the arch gaiety, fake concern about her and Markham's 'little rocky patch' and mini lectures on the 'responsibilities of being a policeman's wife' calculated to make Olivia feel like necking a whole bottle of the Bordeaux that accompanied their Sunday roast.

But beneath it all, she sensed high-octane anxiety and embarrassment about the prodigal daughter's latest bombshell and guessed that this had revived painful memories about Muriel's own youthful seduction and the unplanned pregnancy that had resulted in Natalie. Notwithstanding her marriage to (and, in a sense, rescue by) Noakes, the resulting insecurity had left its mark, heightening her obsession with social standing and bourgeois respectability.

Of course, she had no idea that Markham and Olivia had guessed the truth of Natalie's parentage (this having emerged during the notorious Bluebell investigation). It had never even been explicitly broached between the DI and Noakes, the most personal topics lying buried in the substratum of their unique relationship, but was at the heart of the old-world courtesy with characterised Markham's manner towards Muriel. He knew Noakes was immensely proud of his wife and regarded her in the light of an oracle on everything from royalty (an abiding passion) to Renovation (most notably of the Mock Tudor cum Country Cottage variety). Even her propensity for what Olivia termed 'crushettes' on distinguished older men (particularly medics and clergymen) failed to dent Noakes's devotedness and, never much concerned with his own dignity, he was watchfully protective of his wife's.

Olivia knew the union was rock solid, even if Noakes's partiality for herself nettled Muriel. With honours more or less even, they managed to conceal their mutual dislike, to the point where Noakes actually fancied they were well on the way to becoming bosom buddies. It was less easy to deceive himself where his daughter was concerned, however. Equally as susceptible to the personal charms of 'DI Dreamboat', Natalie disliked Olivia even more than her mother, convinced that the willowy teacher with her smart alec talk and sharp repartee was privately laughing at them. This feeling had subsided somewhat since she had started her studies at the university (since it put them more on the same level), but she remained prickly on the subject of Markham's partner.

Markham too was alert to the various undercurrents. All in all, it was just as well that Natalie had decided not to grace Sunday lunch with her presence, he thought with a marked sensation of relief. He had a feeling that the one-time leading light of what he euphemistically termed Bromgrove's club scene was unlikely to look favourably on any desperate scheme Olivia might nurture for adopting her baby.

Over the meal — pure Mary Berry all the way, from the onion gravy to the crème anglaise that accompanied their apple crumble — Muriel assiduously papered over the cracks in her family's facade.

'Of course, Natalie and Rick look forward to starting a family *eventually*,' she gushed. 'They both *dote* on children . . . But they want to wait till a few years down the line, seeing as things are just starting to *take off* for them. As young *entrepreneurs*, they have to think about the *timing* and *pace themselves*.' A falsetto laugh. 'Accidents will happen and there's no question of anything *hole-in-the-corner*.' In other words Rick Jordan wasn't going to be strongarmed into a shotgun wedding, Olivia thought grimly. 'They're both terribly *well-adjusted* and *sensible* and *grown-up* about everything,' Muriel continued, her italics proclaiming, Move Along, Nothing to See Here.

She's probably praying the Bolshie One will have a miscarriage, Olivia thought sourly. That would get everyone off the hook nicely. Suddenly, she felt appalled at her own callousness, not least as she knew what it felt to lose a child.

As Muriel chuntered on about '*arrangements*' and '*doing the right thing*', sounding more than ever like a character out of *Downton* or some other period drama, Olivia felt her half-formed dream splinter into a thousand pieces. Her hopes needed to go back to where they had come from, she told herself dejectedly.

Nothing could be more obvious than that Muriel wanted things to return to normal as soon as possible, with this inconvenient contretemps consigned to oblivion. Her rapt attentiveness to Markham demonstrated a cast-iron determination to maintain the status quo with no alteration in their respective relations to each other, still less any possibility that she and Noakes might become grandparents-in-law (was there even such a thing?) of a child adopted by Olivia and Markham.

Pregnant pauses, she thought savagely as Muriel disappeared to prepare coffee (she always called it the 'perculator' for some reason) while her guests exchanged polite commonplaces and Richard Clayderman tinkled away in the background. Noakes fiddled awkwardly with his serviette (despite all Muriel's strictures on "U and non-U", he was always letting her down by forgetting to call them napkins), before abandoning his origami and padding off to help his wife.

In the end, Olivia supposed she had to hand it to Muriel who had passed the whole thing off almost as if Natalie's news wasn't (in her eyes) a social faux pas to end all others. The woman deserved her moment of victory, she grudgingly admitted to herself, as the other bustled back in with her hostess trolley, the Spode china and amaretti biscuits doubtless intended to show Olivia — who favoured chipped mugs and hobnobs — the importance of 'not letting things slide'.

Sipping the excellent coffee, Olivia longed for them to be able to make their excuses and leave. But courtesy demanded that they stay a while longer.

Muriel, having spent much of the meal on damage limitation, was now graciously disposed to take an interest in Markham's current investigation.

'We *did* love having an allotment. So *beneficial* from a health point of view. But really, there's quite enough to keep us busy here.' She gestured complacently towards a back garden that was manicured and weeded to within an inch of its life, privet hedges, shrubs and well-behaved narcissi presenting an attractive aspect in a burst of late-afternoon sunlight. 'And we've plans for some *landscaping*, so it would be *greedy* to want more . . . After all, those without access to outdoor space have the greater need,' she intoned piously.

'An' there's always Rosemount for some extra digging,' Noakes put in.

Seeing Muriel frown at the image of her husband as a horny-handed son of toil, Markham interposed suavely, 'Do you know anyone from Beauclair Drive, Muriel?'

'Well, Margaret Cresswell and Peter Barlow are stalwarts of Bromgrove in Bloom . . . real committee people,' this with an air of faint disparagement, 'but of course being on their own leaves them plenty of time . . . I know most of the others by sight, but Woodsorrel in Old Carton would probably be my preferred choice.' She nodded significantly. 'Very particular about their membership.'

In other words, they had a caretaker who didn't look like Ninian Creech and not too many social worker types, Markham thought wryly. Plus, the proximity to Old Carton Hall was bound to appeal, given Muriel's decidedly soft spot for the aristocracy.

'Are you making progress with the case, Gilbert?' His hostess paused as though in genteel reluctance to broach distasteful subjects. 'I gather there may be some kind of *sexual obsession* with the victims . . .' She let her voice tail off with just the right inflection of horrified reticence, but Olivia noticed that the small black eyes were alight with prurient curiosity.

'It certainly looks like one possibility,' Markham replied. 'Right now, the profiler's looking into dissocial personality traits and psychological maladjustment,' he added, knowing that Muriel liked to feel she was in his confidence. 'Various lines of enquiry have sprung up but you know how it is,' with a charming smile and a shrug that she could interpret whichever way she wanted.

'Of course.' An arch twinkle that made Olivia feel distinctly nauseous. '*Mum's the word!*'

She fought down a wave of hysterical mirth at the realisation that Mum definitely *wasn't* the word in *her* case, with any prospect of motherhood disappearing rapidly over the horizon. It had been utterly stupid to entertain fantasies about scooping up Natalie's baby like some kind of demented fairy godmother. Middle-aged hormones had swollen the longing for a child to flood tide, she told herself, but now it was time to face reality. Hers and Markham's.

Markham was anxiously aware of his partner's rigid posture. Damn Natalie's pregnancy and the whole baby nightmare, he thought irritably, more than ever glad that he had never breathed a word to her of the infant found buried at Beauclair Drive. Thank heaven there were no secret offspring to worry about in their current enquiry . . . or at least, he reflected gloomily, none that had so far come to light.

He started as his mobile trilled loudly, interrupting the brittle postprandial chat. Instinctively, he knew this wasn't good news.

Kate Burton cut straight to the chase.

'There's been another one.'

CHAPTER 9

The body had been found by walkers along Old Carton Reserve Path, which was essentially a nature trail that wound around the perimeter of the sleepy hamlet on the outskirts of Bromgrove. The only other local attractions — Carton Hall and the neighbouring Artisan Centre — weren't due to reopen to the public until the end of January, but the woods and wildlife offered an invigorating prospect for weekend visitors and ramblers.

Rebecca Atherton lay in a little clearing some distance from the main footpath. It was almost a grassy meadow and dotted with evergreens.

The bobble-hatted middle-aged couple who found her explained that they had veered off the main route and somehow got lost.

'We knew straightaway that it wasn't an accident,' the woman told them, her plain weather-beaten features furrowed with distress. 'Because of how she was left . . . all exposed and indecent.'

Indecent was the word, Markham thought grimly, contemplating the obscenely splayed legs with jeans pulled down to just above the knees, along with jumper and bra yanked up to expose the victim's breasts and what looked like a scarf stuffed into her mouth.

'We figured it had to be a sex attack.' The husband resembled a ruddy-faced Pop Larkin, but his Adam's apple was bobbing up and down convulsively in time with the left leg that jackhammered into the rutted earth. 'So we called 999 right away.'

Burton, gently reassuring, guided the pair away towards a group of hovering uniforms as Markham and Noakes (who had his coat on, ready to accompany the guvnor, the very second the news came in) contemplated the tableau. Around them, crime tape was going up and SOCOs gathering. A forensics officer proffered paper overalls and latex gloves and, their eyes never leaving the dead woman, the two men duly gowned up.

Dimples Davidson appeared alongside them similarly attired and lost no time getting down to business as Markham quietly filled Noakes in on the background.

Markham was surprised to see the pathologist suddenly rock back on his haunches as he removed the trailing scarf from Rebecca Atherton's mouth, looking unusually upset as he uncovered the ugly bruises on her neck.

Instinctively, the DI moved a step forward, remembering that the pathologist was a governor at Hope and knew the victim.

'You're all right, Markham.' Dimples's voice was gruff. 'It was just the braces that threw me . . . reminded me how young she was.'

'Braces?' Noakes echoed in puzzlement.

'She wore aligners,' Markham said quietly. 'I remember thinking they made her look like a teenager.'

They moved closer.

The woman's mouth was wide open, wire braces shockingly contradictory against the backdrop of such malevolence. Her eyes were filmed over with florid petechiae at the corners, and the red-gold hair was crusted with blood.

Markham was acutely aware of the loamy smell of earth and moss and wildflowers.

A robin redbreast, oblivious of the drama, hopped jauntily along the sward, fluffing himself out with cheery bonhomie.

'It's a sign she's still somewhere about,' Noakes whispered hoarsely. 'My old nan always said that's what it means when you a see a robin . . . when someone dies, their spirit hangs around to watch for a while . . . before moving on to the next plane.'

The clumsy words were oddly comforting to the DI, feeling as he did that there was always something very spiritual for him at any murder scene, in those moments when he somehow made peace with the victim and envisioned the gates of death opening to disclose a new landscape beyond . . . a vista not unlike this tranquil country setting with its rich promise of springtime after a long cold winter . . .

He grimaced, imagining how Sidney would react to such speculation about the realm that lay beyond the physical and his hope that it marked a new beginning. *Fey claptrap*, the DCI would snap. And he would have a point. For whatever Markham's ideas of Rebecca Atherton's future destiny in the hereafter, it was her *past* that now confronted him fixed in letters of blood. His job was to work back from the endpoint and uncover whatever had led to this lonely death out in the woods.

Burton returned. Her manner was calm and clinical, because she knew it was required and any messy emotions had to be boxed up somewhere safe in her brain. Only later would she allow herself to dwell on Rebecca Atherton's final moments, when the young teacher saw death staring her in the face.

'Are you thinking it's the same person who did the other two?' she asked Markham.

'Has to be,' the DI replied softly, as if the dead woman was merely sleeping and he feared to wake her.

'Different M.O., though,' Noakes pointed out. 'Like the woolly jumper pair said, this one looks like a sex attack . . . The others were left neat an' tidy. I mean to say, no underwear or *bits* showing.'

'The killer could just be aiming to send us on a wild goose chase — going after rapists and sex pests,' Burton pointed out. 'Alternatively,' her face tightened ominously, 'this could be the kind of escalation Dr Shaughnessy mentioned . . . some sort of slow-burn sexual kink which makes them want to degrade and humiliate their victim.'

Noakes looked baffled.

'I get the idea of them wanting to stick it to Leckie an' Cotter cos of some obsession with the two of 'em . . . a crush on Leckie that went nowhere on account of her being shacked up with lover boy . . . mebbe hating them for summat they'd done. But why strangle *this* poor lass? What's *she* ever done?'

'She was very friendly with Catherine Leckie,' Burton said slowly. 'So maybe it's all tied up with the idea of punishing Catherine by wiping out those who were dear to her . . . Or it could be that Bex was somehow involved in whatever happened at the allotments—'

'Something that took over the killer's mind,' Markham finished.

Burton's eyes narrowed in thought. '*Exactly*, boss. Some kind of distorted mythology which meant that Catherine, Raymond Cotter and Rebecca Atherton had to die, because it was the only way the killer was able to keep their sense of self intact.'

Noakes blinked. He didn't like the sound of this one little bit.

'What if a whole crowd were in on it . . . this thing or whatever it was happened at the allotments?' he asked. 'Are you saying chummy's going to pick 'em off one by one?'

'Raymond and Bex were the boyfriend and close friend,' Burton reasoned. 'So my best guess is, that it's tied up with Catherine's *intimate* life as opposed to some wider vendetta or revenge scenario.'

'Mebbe Bex were having an affair with her at the same time as Cotter,' Noakes suggested with attempted nonchalance, as though to signal he was entirely au fait with the notion of sexual musical chairs. 'An' *that's* why the killer offed them both . . . cos he saw them as rivals.'

Dimples cleared his throat in a reproachful manner, as though he detected a certain want of respect in such debate while Rebecca Atherton was barely cold.

'Time of death, doc?' Burton enquired, embarrassed at her own want of propriety. Noakes, needless to say, appeared totally unrepentant.

'She's still semi-supple . . . Judging by that and the bruises, I'd say sometime early this morning.' The pathologist looked round the clearing swarming with SOCOs. 'Your lot will be able to say if she was killed out here . . . It's fairly overgrown, so plenty of cover once they got her off the main path.'

'What about dog walkers?' Noakes objected. 'Bit of a risk if Lassie came sniffing around.'

'They don't allow dogs on this trail, Noakes,' Dimples informed him briskly, 'though the local animal lovers are petitioning to get the rules changed. Your man, or woman, knew there was an infinitesimal risk of discovery . . . Joggers stick to the main track and there'd be no reason for anyone to come out here.'

Anyone but a murderer.

'She was a decent woman,' Dimples said sadly. 'Schools can be strange places . . . all the spying and gossiping and knives-in-the-back carry on. It's why I didn't want any of my kids to go in for teaching. But Rebecca and Catherine Leckie were the right sort . . . really cared about the kids, as opposed to the type who'd sell their own grandmother for promotion.' Clearly, like Olivia, Dimples had no very high opinion of headteachers in general or Hope's senior leadership team.

Markham was glad to hear this tribute to the murdered teacher, as though it had somehow released her from the threat of futility and pointlessness. In his mind's eye, he saw her surrounded by all the youngsters she had taught and nurtured, like some kind of mysterious affirmation of her legacy.

'I need to move her now, Inspector,' Dimples said as two paramedics with a folding stretcher and body bag came towards them.

The paraphernalia of removal seemed a hideous anomaly in such a peaceful setting, Markham thought as they watched the little cortege vanish through the trees.

For a time, no one spoke. Then Burton said softly, 'It's beautiful here . . . When I first saw her lying there, it made me think of the movie *Snow White* . . . that part where she falls asleep after eating the poisoned apple and all the animals come to care for her. But then . . . seeing how she'd been posed—'

'You realised it ain't Disney after all,' Noakes said with his customary bluntness. Looking round, he said, 'What's the betting all the cranks an' nutters will make a beeline for this place . . . probl'y put it on TikTok.' Markham suppressed a smile at this, reflecting that Noakes's young apprentice Kevin appeared to be expanding his friend's social media horizons.

'All they'll find is an ordinary English field and trees that you could see anywhere,' he said firmly.

'For all we know, the killer could still be round here somewhere,' Noakes said ghoulishly. 'Looking forward to her being found . . . mebbe getting off on it.'

Markham felt a chill crawl down his spine, as if the other had conjured up the spectre of a shadowy figure watching from the trees . . . *enjoying* what they had done.

'Everywhere's cordoned off,' Burton said crisply, well and truly jolted out of her earlier meditative mood. 'Nobody's going to get anywhere near this place, least of all Gavin Conors or anyone from the *Gazette*.'

'Good.' Markham said approvingly. 'We'll need to check out any CCTV footage for this area,' he mused.

'The only CCTV is up at the Hall, sir,' she told him.

'Bleeding typical,' Noakes snorted. 'Make sure the toffs are covered while the rest of us have to slum it.'

'Take that chip off your shoulder, Noakesy,' Markham admonished. 'Bridleways are bound to be low priority and this isn't exactly a crime hotspot.'

Burton was looking round thoughtfully. 'I wonder if the killer arranged to meet her here . . . or if they were following her.'

'You mean stalking her the same way they did with Leckie?' Noakes asked. 'If she were jogging or power walking or whatever, then they'd have to be fit to keep up—'

'Not to mention clever at keeping out of sight,' Markham interjected. 'I'm more inclined to think they came here by arrangement . . . an outdoorsy type like Ms Atherton probably didn't think there was anything to fear from a Sunday stroll in the countryside.'

'She could have trusted the killer,' Burton observed.

'Indeed,' Markham agreed, 'and probably never suspected them for a minute.'

'What line did they spin her?' Noakes wanted to know. 'They must've needed some sort of pretext to get her down here for a heart to heart.'

'Something like, they had suspicions about who'd done the murders,' Burton suggested. 'Or they'd found something out but didn't know what to do about it, wondered if they should go to the police blah blah . . . Her head was probably all over the place after Catherine was killed, so she didn't think to be cautious.'

'I want the PM results asap, Kate,' Markham instructed. 'We need to rule out any sexual interference for a start.'

'I'll get Doyle to observe,' she said whipping out a notebook.

There had been a time when Burton never passed up the opportunity to attend a post-mortem, but now she followed Markham's advice to conserve her energies for command and control. Her fellow DI was willing to bet she was also itching to consult one of her specialist manuals on psychosexual criminal drivers. *Crime and Human Nature* or *Sexual Homicide: Patterns and Motives* by Ressler and Douglas, her all-time favourite FBI profilers.

As they walked back to the start of the nature trail, she said, 'Don't you think this case is a bit like the Carton Hall investigation?'

'In what way, Kate?'

'It's that thing about villages and little local communities being the ideal camouflage for murder because they've got a veneer of respectability and ordinariness . . . easy for a killer to blend in and no one have any idea what's going on beneath

134

the surface.' She gave a little shudder. 'Living their sedate life in middle-class suburbia and nobody any the wiser.'

'*Some* of 'em stand out, though,' Noakes challenged. 'There's the bloke who got chucked off the allotments for being a peeping Tom.'

'Hmmm.' Burton looked straight ahead, her forehead creased as if she was trying out different scenarios. 'Dave Shipley . . . We need to go over people's alibis with a fine-tooth comb, and after what went on between him and Catherine Leckie, he's top of the list.'

They walked on for a time in silence, undisturbed save for the odd squirrel whisking across the path and wood pigeons cooing softly overhead.

'What about Rebecca Atherton's next-of-kin, Kate?' Markham asked as they finally reached the reserve's car park. Sometimes in murder investigations, he felt like he had started reading an unputdownable thriller and couldn't wait to see what the next chapter would bring. However, he never forgot the real people who had been sentenced to a lifetime of grief and, unusually, never dodged the dreaded bereavement visits.

'Her mum and dad live in Medway, guv. There's a brother based in Birmingham.'

'Text me the address for the parents, Kate. I'll get over there and see them right away.' He was back in his professional bubble, deliberately forcing down his feelings about what he had seen back there in the woods — all that promise and potential erased in an instant. 'I'll drop you off on the way,' he told Noakes. 'You and Muriel need to salvage what's left of your Sunday. And don't worry, we'll be sure to keep you in the loop.'

'There's a memorial service for Catherine Leckie at Hope on Tuesday morning, guv,' Burton informed him. 'The funeral's at St Bruno's on Friday at three. Apparently, Greville Leckie has friends in high places.' Judging by the intent look on Noakes's face, it was clear that he meant to be there. 'Count me in,' he said as the two DIs exchanged resigned smiles.

Markham noticed that Burton was looking tired. 'You should get off home too, Kate,' he urged gently. Guiltily, he added, 'I forgot to ask if you've had a good weekend.'

'Not bad thanks, boss,' she replied, perking up at the enquiry. 'I went to a talk at the university yesterday. One of Nathan's mates was giving a paper on Richard III. With that film *The Lost King* coming out, suddenly he's flavour of the month.'

'Oh yeah, the one with Steve Coogan . . . great story, what with Quasimodo being found under that car park, but can't get my head round Coogan being in it,' Noakes grunted. 'Keep expecting him to shout "Aha!" like Alan Partridge.'

Burton winced slightly but persevered. 'All that about Richard being hunchbacked was probably wide of the mark, Sarge. It's more likely he had scoliosis which meant his right shoulder may have been higher than the left.' She paused. 'It didn't stop him being a great fighter . . . incredibly brave on the battlefield.' That was well calculated to appeal to Noakes as an ex-serviceman, Markham thought with amusement.

'Some people from the Bromgrove Ricardian Society were there,' she went on.

Noakes frowned. 'Come again?'

'It's an offshoot of the Richard III Society . . . Kind of an amateur history society, quite sweet really . . . Margaret Cresswell and Peter Barlow and a couple of teachers from Hope belong to it.'

'Might've known them two would have a finger in the pie,' Noakes grunted.

'Michael Oddie and Greville Leckie were there . . . It was all very civilised and nobody said a word about murder.'

'What about the Princes in the Tower?' Noakes demanded beadily. 'Don' tell me Tricky Dicky being a dab hand at infanticide didn't come up.'

'I meant no one said anything the *allotment* murders, Sarge.' As if he didn't know it. 'Obviously the other stuff came up, but Dr Ashworth set it in *context*.'

'Oh aye.' Normally Noakes would have told her to bore off, but part of him was intrigued.

'He explained the dynastic and political *drivers*,' Burton loved that word. 'It was interesting how he showed Richard had a conscience about it all but in the end was left with no choice.'

'There's *always* a choice,' Noakes muttered, clearly unsympathetic to the socio-political milieu of medieval England.

'I was afraid the lecture might be a bit dry,' she continued brightly, 'but there was some interesting stuff about Richard having incestuous feelings for his niece,' Burton added.

Noakes's head came up. *That sounded more like it!*

'Remind me to give you the lowdown, Sarge.'

Having whetted his appetite, with a cheery wave, she was gone, and shortly afterwards, the two men also pulled away.

When Markham got back to the Sweepstakes, Olivia was unusually quiet and subdued. Announcing her intention to have a long soak in the bath and an early night, she made no further allusion to the Noakeses' domestic affairs or the possibility of adopting Natalie's child. Selfishly, he was glad that she appeared to have given up on the scheme which he did not see as a route to breathing life back into their relationship. Despite his previous resolution to have it out with her concerning the underhand way she had approached Noakes, he decided it would do no good to tackle her about the deceit. And, selfishly, he was relieved to be able to shelve the entire subject of parenthood.

Living his cases in the way that he did was bound to take its toll, he thought as he took coffee into his study. He knew that he used his job as a protective shield, in much the same way as he had been building walls around himself since adolescence, some crucial part having sealed off when he witnessed his brother's dead body twitching and dangling in the disgusting squat where he had committed suicide. In a sense, he felt his stellar police career was a way of making it up to Jonathan for the fact that he had somehow survived their messy, traumatic upbringing while his sibling had not. He knew this was irrational and illogical — their stepfather was the abuser and his alone the responsibility — but when he looked down at Jon's body, ravaged by drink and drugs, it was almost as though he was looking down at a sacrificial victim whose death was the price for his own success. Along with those childhood experiences and their mother's complicity (though he had long since forgiven her), it made him doubt his ability to be a good parent. He had considered resorting to therapy in an attempt to prod his feelings loose but had never been able to take the final step.

His professional habits were all he knew.

Work and more work was the only cure for the hollowness at his centre.

Suddenly, he remembered what Burton had said about the killer's desperate attempt to keep their personality intact and cover up the cracks.

That defence mechanism was proving insufficient, he reflected grimly.

Bizarrely, he experienced a reluctant pity for their quarry — the superficially unremarkable allotmenteer (and he felt increasingly sure that it *was* an allotment holder) whose bland, apparently well-controlled exterior hid boundless contempt and rage.

Feeling tired to his bones, Markham decided to turn in. The meeting with Rebecca Atherton's devastated parents had been draining. In their seventies, they struggled to take in the news of their daughter's death, her mother poignantly asking 'if he was sure it was really her' and 'could the police have made a mistake'.

Tomorrow morning meant a trawl through the alibis, though the murder having occurred on a Sunday morning made it unlikely they would come up with anything useful.

They also needed another press statement to head off the possibility of the *Gazette* coming up with even more lurid headlines. The last thing he could afford at this stage was for Gavin Conors to stir up another hornets' nest on the Hoxton . . .

The to-dos swirled round and round in his head until as he prepared for bed.

Perhaps tomorrow would bring the breakthrough they so desperately needed.

* * *

In the event, it was Valerie Shipley who stored up a hornet's nest mid-morning the following day, arriving at the station like an avenging angel.

'She's screaming about police harassment, sir,' Doyle informed the DI as the latter sat in his office submerged in paperwork. Looking at the latest memos with what to him seemed like pidgin PC nonsense about 'correct pronouns' and 'gender neutral inclusivity', he felt like topping himself. Just as well Noakes had retired, he told himself. Otherwise his friend would have been in and out of 'Aitch-arrr' on pretty much a revolving door basis.

'How come?' Markham's tone was wintry, since he did not care to be taken by surprise and the Hoxton debacle was continuing to prove an almighty headache.

'Well, alibi-wise, it's like you thought, guv . . . Everyone was having a lie-in or at home Sunday morning, 'cept for Hilary Probert who went for a jog in Hollingrove Park and Michael Oddie who had training with the Bromgrove Territorials . . . oh, and Greville Leckie took the dogs out to Calder Vale but that wasn't till the afternoon. Looks like none of them are off the hook . . .'

Dimples had put death at somewhere between seven and nine o'clock in the morning, which meant all the runners and riders were still in contention, Markham thought with mounting frustration.

'What's Mrs Shipley's beef with us then?' he enquired acidly.

'One the teachers from the allotments — Elsie Parker — said Shipley had made a bit of a pest of himself with Rebecca Atherton—'

The DI was taken aback. 'You mean in addition to bothering Ms Leckie?' he asked.

'Yeah, a regular Casanova of the cucumbers . . . Mind you, Carruthers thinks Parker's being wise after the event . . . fancies herself a bit of an armchair sleuth and doesn't like the Shipleys . . .'

'Out to make trouble in other words?'

'Well, it didn't sound like she had all that much to go on — just saw Atherton giving Shipley the brush-off or blanking him . . . pretty vague, if you ask me.'

The DI leaned back in his chair, tapered fingers steepled together as he considered this.

'Ms Atherton never said anything about Shipley bothering her. And after what happened to Catherine, surely she wouldn't have held something like that back.'

'Like I say, boss, Carruthers thinks Parker's making something out of nothing . . . maybe wants to boost her own importance . . . attention-seeking.'

'Does anyone else back her up?'

'She said Peter Barlow had noticed it too but the old gent was dead embarrassed when we asked him about it — almost like we were talking dirty about his favourite niece or something. Mumbled stuff about it being down to the allotment Chair.'

Markham thought he understood. Peter Barlow had the kind of old-fashioned chivalry that meant he would feel it was casting aspersions on the dead woman to speculate about unwanted sexual attentions.

'We didn't get much change out of Cresswell either,' Doyle continued. 'She looked at us like we were toerags from the *Gazette* and came over all hoity-toity.'

Markham could well imagine it. 'So Mrs Parker's out on a limb with this,' he sighed.

'Well, Hilary Probert said Shipley gave her the creeps . . . but that's a long way from saying he came on to Atherton.'

'Quite.' Markham felt almost sorry for Shipley who sounded like Beauclair's resident scapegoat.

'Donald Kemp said it wouldn't surprise him if Shipley hadn't tried it on.' Doyle pulled an expressive face. 'Takes one to know one.'

'What about Messrs Oddie and Creech?'

'Oddie looked completely blank . . . Creech just leered and winked like we'd made his day.' Doyle shuddered. 'If anyone's creepy, it's *him* . . . Shipley comes off like a choirboy by comparison.'

The DI's thoughts returned to alibis.

'There's definitely no one to vouch for Dave Shipley's whereabouts on Sunday morning?'

'Nope, he was nursing a hangover . . . banging headache and all the rest of it. Definitely looked rough.' But Markham remembered the boxer's physique and wondered.

'I suppose it's too much to hope that James Daly has a strong alibi for Ms Atherton's murder?' he enquired resignedly.

Doyle grinned apologetically. 'Just his dear old mum, guv . . . She's got some mouth on her,' he said ruefully, 'even worse than Valerie Shipley.'

Markham was fast losing the will to live.

'What about Bernadette Farrelly?'

'Lazy morning with the papers. Her parents had the kids, so—'

'Home alone.'

''Fraid so, sir.' The lanky youngster suddenly brightened. 'The Shipley woman dished some dirt about her.'

'Oh?'

'She said things got so bad between Cotter and Farrelly, he threatened to get an injunction against her for harassing Catherine Leckie.'

'Where did she hear that?'

'Greville Leckie was spitting mad about his family name being dragged through the mud . . . Apparently his cleaner overheard him telling someone about it on the phone. Turns out she cleans for Valerie Shipley.'

Markham's mouth twisted with distaste.

He got to his feet, 'I suppose I had better pour oil on troubled waters before Mrs Shipley starts shouting from the rooftops about police harassment.'

'We're not bringing Shipley in then, guv?' Doyle sounded disappointed.

'As things stand, we don't have enough to go on. But I'd be interested to hear if Mrs Shipley has any more little drops of poison to bestow. There's a memorial service for Catherine Leckie tomorrow at Hope, so any gossip might prove useful.' Bernadette Farrelly had kept secrets from the police, he thought. It was more than likely others had done likewise.

Ten days in and counting.

Something had to give.

CHAPTER 10

The memorial service for Catherine Leckie at Hope Academy on the morning of Tuesday 10 January proceeded as such occasions generally did.

There was a crossover with the allotments' investigation in that Elsie Parker, Margaret Cresswell and Peter Barlow appeared on stage at the school assembly, the latter pair looking somewhat frail and papery whereas the deputy head radiated an almost defiant purposefulness. As she read a Victorian poem about allotment holders being shot through with golden sunset-shine, Markham was acutely aware of Noakes shuffling mutinously next to him.

'What the chuff's she on about?' his friend muttered. 'Leckie were a teacher, not some presenter on *Countryfile*.'

Olivia and Mathew Sullivan stood at opposite ends of the school stage, looking impenetrably grave, though Markham could well imagine they shared Noakes's discomfiture.

As Hope's choir burst into a rendition of 'All Things Bright and Beautiful', Markham reflected that it was hardly surprising the school authorities wanted to sanitise Catherine Leckie's demise, not least as news would now be filtering through about the death of a second teacher. The DI could scarcely believe CID's good fortune in managing to keep a

143

lid on the latest developments, but his department's truce with the *Gazette* was unlikely to last the day and he dreaded to imagine the spin that Gavin Conors would put on Rebecca Atherton's murder. 'Teacher in love triangle killing' would sandwich Leckie, Cotter and Atherton in a titillating three-some, with no way of countering the salacious narrative . . . short of producing a cast-iron suspect.

Suddenly he became aware of a disturbance at the back of the hall.

Gesturing discreetly to Mat Sullivan — *I'm On It* — he left his seat, followed by the team and Noakes.

He wasn't surprised to find that the source of the com-motion was James Daly.

'Why won't they let me come in? I've as much right as anyone else.' The youngster was wild-eyed and dishevelled.

With a combination of arm and elbow, Markham manoeuvred him out into Hope's foyer.

'Now isn't the right time, James,' he said quietly, pri-vately appalled by the boy's distraught appearance.

'You're not a student here anymore,' Burton added.

'Decent of you to come along.' Noakes's voice was full of compassion. 'But they're all bawling hymns at the top of their voices back there . . . like *Songs of Praise*. Reckon you should wait till the funeral on Friday when it's all about her *private* mates . . . the ones who ain't part of the herd.'

Cheers Noakesy, Markham thought. Talk about putting off the evil hour!

But he had to admire his friend's understanding of human nature, as he saw James Daly's vision suddenly clear.

'I'm sorry,' Daly mumbled. 'Just wanted to show I rated her . . . in spite of everything.'

'Good on you,' Noakes said kindly, slapping him heartily on the back so that the youngster staggered. 'See you Friday.'

With that, the former sixth-former and his supporters melted away.

'Nice one, Noakesy,' Markham said. 'Reckon we dodged a bullet there.'

'He's jus' a poor lad in a bit of a mess,' Noakes said. 'Happen once the funeral's over, he'll straighten hisself out.'

On returning to the assembly, they didn't appear to have missed a beat, 'O Praise Ye the Lord' being followed in quick succession by 'Morning Has Broken' and various other conservationist style hymns.

'Sod this for a bunch of soldiers,' Noakes announced at the conclusion of proceedings. 'I better be getting back to Bri and the wrinklies. *Ackshually*,' Markham braced himself, 'we're looking at a painting of Christopher Columbus for the residents' lounge.'

'Isn't he beyond the pale these days, Sarge?' Doyle ventured. 'What with slaving and bullying the indigenous lot and all the rest of it?'

'They're called the Taino,' Noakes responded with dignity. 'An' I reckon the folk who criticise have got it all wrong. Columbus were a diamond geezer . . . even if he never made it to Japan.'

After seeing his friend off, Markham suddenly couldn't bear the thought of returning to CID.

Dispatching Doyle and Carruthers with instructions to review all suspects and alibis, he turned to Kate Burton.

'Let's you and me head back to Old Carton, Kate,' he said. 'There's an eatery in the Artisan Centre that beats our canteen hands down!'

* * *

'This is a nice tearoom, guv,' Burton said, looking round shyly at the café with its old-fashioned vintage decor, local pottery displayed on antique dressers and charming prints of Carton Hall adorning the duck egg blue wall panelling.

Markham smiled at her. 'Well, I figured long enough had passed since the Old Carton investigation, that you wouldn't run screaming from the place.'

'Oh, I've been back to Old Carton since then,' she confided. 'It's still a great day out despite everything that happened.'

Placing an order with the befrilled waitress, Markham surreptitiously contemplated his number two, thinking that the vivacity in her face was somehow dimmed down to about three-quarter strength when normally at this point in an investigation her energy levels would have been sky high.

He knew that with Burton, you had to approach personal stuff crabwise. Equally as proud and private as himself, she would never just come out with it and say what was wrong. Somehow he had to try and winkle it out of her over tea and chat.

'You haven't made good on that promise to Noakesy, you know, Kate,' he said casually. 'Those cliffhangers about Richard Crookback had him practically salivating.'

He thought he detected relief in her face, as though she was grateful he didn't propose to come over all pastoral and grill her about where things stood with her personal life.

'I think it might not be as juicy as Sarge imagined,' she said. 'Nathan's friend Dr Ashdown pretty much debunked all the myths about Richard being a villain. Actually, it turns out he was quite a devoted husband, though he *did* have a couple of illegitimate kids before getting married,' she added primly. 'It was after his wife Anne died of TB that there were all these rumours about him having a thing for his niece Elizabeth and being desperate to marry her . . . People even said he poisoned Anne when she didn't die quickly enough.'

'What was your speaker's take on it all?' thinking that scandal-wise it put Prince Harry and the Windsors in the shade.

'He thought it was most probably malicious slander, though he *did* say maybe there was a kernel of truth in there somewhere, what with Richard losing his baby son and then being told by the doctors to stay away from Anne because she was contagious . . . Maybe after all the unhappiness he just fancied the idea of starting over . . . having a second chance with this beautiful young girl. But it caused a massive outcry, and he didn't exactly help matters by making a big fuss of Elizabeth while Anne was still alive and kitting her out as if she were queen. She was Anne's lady in waiting, which just fanned the flames.'

Burton's eyes must have been tired (too much late-night delving in FBI manuals perhaps) because she was wearing her second-best specs which had a habit of sliding halfway down her nose whenever she became especially earnest. With a hair clip keeping the bob out of her eyes, she looked endearingly youthful, Markham thought.

'Noakesy's imagination went into overdrive at the mere whiff of incest and scandal,' he said wryly, thinking that it had at least distracted them from a murder investigation that seemed to be going nowhere.

She grinned. 'Yeah, looked like he was going all *Time Team* on us,' she said, alluding to one of Noakes's favourite TV shows.

'What did Richard III's son die of?' Markham asked, his thoughts returning to the Plantagenet king.

'TB, the same as Anne . . . I suppose him eying up his niece was all about proving his virility or something. Dr Ashdown said he was totally obsessed with making sure that his great rival Henry Tudor couldn't have her. Of course she ended up with Henry in the end, which makes it all the more pathetic.'

The waitress arrived with tea and scones.

'What *is* it with these medieval widowers?' Markham asked quizzically, buttering a scone. 'Presumably in Richard's case, it wasn't just lust,' he added in an ironic tone, 'seeing as dynastic considerations trumped pretty much everything else back then.'

'I reckon underneath it all, they weren't so very different from us, guv. Richard's wife was sick, so who's to say he didn't just fancy a change . . . On the other hand, apparently he was quite religious and puritanical. When his brother Edward died, he made Edward's mistress do public penance for being a harlot . . . And he was mad keen on St Anthony who lived in the wilderness and had this pet boar which warded off demons and sexual temptation; that's why he designed a boar badge for his servants to wear.'

'Sounds a very curious mixture, Kate.'

'Well, he might have had this secret passion, but at the same time he took a hard line on sexual immorality. Elizabeth's mother was generally reckoned to be a bad influence and eventually ended up being confined to a nunnery. So maybe he was just ultra-protective of Elizabeth cos he was being a decent uncle and worried about her being corrupted.'

She slathered strawberry jam onto a scone. 'Dr Ashdown thinks Elizabeth might not have been as innocent as all that, because she apparently wrote to some nobleman about wanting to marry the king and being fed up that Anne was taking so long to die. Then there was another letter saying she belonged to Richard in body and soul . . . though there's lots of debate about the evidence, so no one can be sure what was going on.'

Markham smiled. 'So Richard wasn't a villainous lecher then, and the niece might have been looking for a sugar daddy?'

'Well, there's plenty of people who think she might've been quite manipulative . . . worked out that Richard *did* have feelings for her and played on it.'

'Still, he never went ahead and married her.'

'True. His advisers weren't keen and public opinion was against it because the uncle-niece thing made some folk queasy.'

'To say nothing of the rumours that Richard killed her little brothers,' Markham suggested, recalling what Noakes had said about the Princes in the Tower.

'What was the age difference?' he asked.

'Richard was thirty-two, fourteen years older than her . . . not bad looking, despite the scoliosis, and desperate for an heir . . . but whatever he felt about her privately, he wasn't your average debauched nobleman, so something held him back.'

'A split personality, would you say?' He knew his colleague was always fascinated by such warring impulses.

'Yeah, I reckon he must've been a pretty tormented character . . . difficult to get a handle on him cos he seems this blurred figure, dark . . . Shakespeare and the history books make him out to be some kind of psychotic tyrant, but he was terrifically pious . . . took his prayer book with him into battle . . . they found it in his war tent after the Battle of Bosworth.'

Markham chuckled. 'Well, Noakesy is bound to approve of *that*, at any rate.'

'Won't be so keen on the goaty side, though,' she said doubtfully.

'Oh, he'll be thoroughly intrigued.' He smiled at her. 'As am I.'

After a companiable pause, he asked, 'What did the allotment Ricardians make of all this?'

'Oh, they couldn't get enough of it, guv. In the Q&A session, Margaret Cresswell talked about how Richard was ever so devout and arranged chantry chapels so Masses could be celebrated for the souls of his enemies. Peter Barlow came out with stuff about him being a lawgiver — people glazed over cos he went on a bit too long — and then some priest from St Bruno's did a spiel comparing Richard's castles to the true heavenly home.' Biting her lip, she admitted, 'I drifted off a bit during that part, guv. The lecture theatre was quite warm and, well, you know how it is.'

'Don't I just.'

'Michael Oddie said something about brass rubbings,' she continued.

'I didn't have him down as that type,' Markham remarked.

'Nor me, boss. But apparently there's medieval inscriptions and whatnot in St Bruno's graveyard . . . Him and Greville Leckie were quite enthusiastic about it. Elsie Parker and a couple of teachers chipped in as well . . . something about a creative project on medieval kingship. To do with the Battle of Bosworth, maybe.'

'Bosworth would be great for a school project.' Markham smiled.

Sitting there, he felt, as always, that something in him was tranquilised — *unsnarled* — by Burton's company. Like Olivia and Noakes, she had an omnivorous interest in all things historical, together with a relish for legends and tales of the uncanny. But where Olivia was frequently spiky and Noakes downright bellicose, there was a tranquillity about his fellow DI.

As they sat enjoying their scones and jam, he had the feeling that he had missed something vitally important in their conversation, only he could not bring it to the surface.

Never mind, he told himself. Perhaps if he let his mind drift, it would come to him.

'I dreamed about those woods on the nature reserve that night after we found Rebecca Atherton,' Burton said unexpectedly. 'Storybook woods where you'd imagine little ones playing hide and seek . . . Only in my dream, the trees had eyes and saw Bex being murdered . . . and they were going to tell me the killer's name.' She took a long gulp of tea. 'At least she didn't end up lying in the open for the animals to get at her . . . I'll never forget that case where the poor mum kept talking about finding her kid's bones so she could put him back together again in the coffin. That was just *awful*.'

'Mrs Atherton tried to convince herself we must have got the wrong girl,' he said grimly. 'She and her husband couldn't seem to take it in, but the FLOs will drip-feed them the details.' And then their daughter's death would be in constant, cruel replay in their minds.

'It takes around three and a half minutes to strangle someone to death,' Burton observed. 'Catherine and Bex must have been so scared realising they were going to die.'

The young waitress who had come to replenish their tea looked startled at this, but was reassured by Markham's calm, steady smile.

After she had moved away, Burton went on. 'If Catherine, Raymond and Bex knew their killer, then odds-on we've met them too.' Her voice sank to a whisper. 'But so far they're just some ghost-face.'

'Very evocative,' Markham said lightly, thinking that it was unlike his prosaic deputy to be so melodramatic.

She flushed and laughed shakily.

'Sorry, guv. This whole case has got to me . . . the murders and that baby they dug up at the allotments . . . somehow all jumbled up in my head along with Richard III's dead wife and his poor little boy . . . like a riddle that I'm too stupid to decipher.'

Markham regarded her thoughtfully.

'Having a ringside seat at trauma is a trauma in itself . . . affects our personal lives,' he said carefully. 'Heaven knows I've struggled with it.'

Some of the tension left her face, but he still wasn't sure what was going on behind her eyes.

'Nathan thinks once we get married and have a family, things will get better,' she confided. 'And maybe he's right but I feel mixed up somehow . . . can't take the plunge, like I'm subconsciously afraid and pushing back on the whole idea.'

Ah, so *that* explained the preoccupation with dead infants and intense interest in a medieval monarch riven by conflicting impulses. Markham felt an uncomfortable pang of guilt as he wondered if the affinity with his colleague was an additional obstacle to her finding Happy Ever After with Nathan Finlayson.

It sounded very much as though Finlayson, like Olivia, was clutching at children as a way to cut the Gordian knot, while Kate baulked at putting sticking plaster on a problem that ran much deeper.

What a bloody mess, he told himself in dismay, wondering for the umpteenth time if he shouldn't get Burton transferred from his team.

The problem being, he was too damn selfish — needed her too badly. And besides, not only would she be upset at such interference, there was no guarantee it would resolve the personal dilemma.

'*Sir?*'

Burton was clearly anxious that she had overstepped the mark. It was up to him to reassure her.

'You're a first-class detective, Kate,' he said warmly. 'It's an occupational hazard that we get tunnel eyes and sometimes struggle to connect with the world. So don't be too hard on yourself. If you ever need time out for anything, just say the word.'

Aware that she had taken the minimum compassionate leave after her father died, he suspected that delayed grief might also have thrown her personal life off track. Sometimes it seemed to him as if her happiness switch had been flicked off, though the tea and free ranging chat had brought colour and animation flooding back. Whatever the perils of their relationship — hero-worship on her side and an answering tenderness on his — they would find a way through.

Pretending not to see as she blinked away tears, he poured himself some more tea.

Being Burton, she composed herself in record time.

'Thanks sir, but there's a case to solve first.' She cleared her throat. 'We've got a meeting with the DCI first thing tomorrow followed by a press conference.'

'Should be fun.'

'And then there's two community leaders from the Hoxton due in.'

'No doubt today's shenanigans will be on the agenda,' he grimaced before adding, 'We need to check the arrangements for Catherine's funeral at St Bruno's on Friday, because I don't want a repeat of this morning's performance.'

All business now, Burton folded her napkin carefully and brushed stray crumbs from her immaculate trouser suit. 'Maybe the press conference will shake something loose,' she said with more confidence than she felt.

That or another murder.

But he didn't say it.

It takes around three and a half minutes to strangle someone to death.

Burton's words hammered in his brain likes strokes on an anvil.

Three and a half minutes.
Three victims.
Three days to Catherine Leckie's funeral.
Three days to catch a killer.

CHAPTER 11

'So what you mean to say, Inspector, is that we are no further forward in this investigation?'

DCI Sidney, along with Chief Superintendent Ebury-Clarke and Superintendent 'Blithering' Bretherton, regarded Markham dourly as they sat in his office the following morning.

Ebury-Clarke, aka Toad Face (qua Noakes), looked more than usually dyspeptic. Bretherton of the beaky nose and bald dome sat stodgily alongside the other two as though his role in life depended on rubber stamping whatever they decreed.

'It's been just over a week, sir,' Markham said, privately cursing Sidney and his cohorts.

Kate Burton spoke up.

'The geographical coefficients mean we can pretty much discount everyone outside Beauclair Drive, sir . . . Triangulation points to an allotment holder being implicated.'

Triangulation! Not for the first time, Markham blessed his fellow DI for her mastery of the scientific jargon. Sounded like she had been overdosing on David Canter *et al.*

'The murders have the hallmarks of a personal vendetta rather than being random attacks by a mentally disturbed individual fixated on the allotments,' she continued, 'though of course we're liaising with mental health services.'

Both inspectors were well aware that Sidney invariably preferred 'lone wolf' scenarios to anything that cast suspicion on upstanding pillars of the community.

'Councillor Kemp has complained about oppressive questioning of his son,' Ebury-Clarke barked.

If Noakes had been in attendance, he would doubtless have said something provocatively un-PC about Donald Kemp being a 'big girl's blouse'. But Burton knew better.

'Oh, that must have been a misunderstanding, sir,' she said politely. 'Obviously we're checking people's movements for Sunday morning, but there's no question of Mr Kemp being singled out.' She beamed winsomely. 'I'll have a word with the team, but you know how it is . . . the troops desperate to do you proud and get a result, especially with these murders striking at the heart of the community.'

In other words, a better class of victim, Markham thought cynically.

But Ebury-Clarke cracked what passed for a smile and the atmosphere thawed a couple of degrees. Somehow, Burton in girl guide mode was always irresistible to the top brass, which was why Markham invariably brought her along.

Bretherton roused himself to ask, 'Are you of the view that the murders are somehow sexually motivated, Markham?'

'Dr Shaughnessy believes so,' he replied, casting his mind back to the Skype session with the psychologist earlier that morning . . .

Even in a virtual conference, the profiler had been impressively 'together' and authoritative, leading him to hope that there would be further opportunities to work with her, given the way they somehow clicked.

Having examined the crime scene photographs, she advised that the suggestive positioning of Rebecca Atherton's body wasn't a red herring intended to send them in the wrong direction but an eruption of intense anger.

'It's possible the killer's warped thinking led them to envisage some kind of good witch, bad witch scenario, with

Catherine Leckie cast as the innocent led astray by her friend . . . and by Raymond Cotter too, if it came to that.'

'So they had to be punished,' he pressed.

'Yes,' she agreed, 'and I would say it's likely the killer derived gratification from exhibiting Ms Atherton's body in that way . . . a paraphilic sadism that undoubtedly had its roots in sexual frustration or inadequacy.' She had declined to be drawn on the perpetrator's gender, but was positive there would be some kind of trail leading back to Catherine Leckie.

Catherine Leckie, who was the start of it all . . .

Now, avoiding all mention of paraphilic dysfunction (even though this was pretty much psychology graduate Burton's 'specialist subject'), he simply told his superiors the team would be conducting intensive background checks based on Dr Shaughnessy's conviction that they were looking for someone with a personality disorder.

'What about the press?' Ebury-Clarke wanted to know. 'Now that the *Gazette*'s got wind of that hoo-ha at Hope with the lad who was expelled, they aren't going to let it go.'

'We're seeing two representatives from Hoxton Together this morning, sir,' Burton interjected brightly, 'along with Mr Daly's social worker.'

'Hoxton Together?' Markham hid a smile at Ebury-Clarke's dubious tone, which made the local housing collective sound like some kind of disreputable reggae band.

'That's right, sir, from the Hoxton housing estate.' Burton's tone of determined optimism never wavered. 'We're confident we can reassure them that Mr Daly has nothing to fear and no prejudice attaches to his exclusion or disciplinary issues at the school.'

'Dr Shaughnessy is of the opinion that Mr Daly's behaviour falls within the range of normal adolescent attention-seeking and "acting out", whereas the pathology behind our three murders indicates a more complex incubation of violent thoughts and fantasies.' Markham was glad he could be positive on at least one point.

'You're saying Daly can be ruled out?' Sidney honked eagerly.

'It appears so, though obviously we can't be explicit at this stage of the investigation.'

Exonerating Daly was a stretch, but Markham badly wanted to escape the inquisition and get back to his investigation. One reason he could never imagine himself riding a desk at HQ was the interminable amount of time and energy expended in this kind of political arse-covering which not only bored him rigid but drained his intellectual reserves. The trio facing him were hardly the greatest advertisement for climbing the greasy pole, he reflected wryly, looking from his own DCI to the other two. He supposed if it came to it, Sidney was the least worst option, given that they had developed a grudging respect for each other over the years. Moreover, he felt a sneaking sympathy with Sidney over his rumoured marital difficulties, knowing all too well the toll the job had taken on his own relationship with Olivia.

As Burton continued talking energetically about 'lines of enquiry going forward,' he was amused to note that she had somehow managed to trick Ebury-Clarke and Bretherton into a more benign state of mind. Never servile, she managed to convey the impression of respectful deference to their rank and experience while fighting her own and Markham's corner. Thrusting, ambitious young officers were not generally remarkable for unflinching integrity, but there was something genuine about Burton that compelled trust, he thought, surreptitiously observing her effect on the top brass.

She was the consummate professional while remaining true to herself, a combination that he found curiously winning. Despite the sordid and frequently depressing aspects of their work, she hadn't become jaded or cynical, which was remarkable in itself and perhaps explained why Doyle and Carruthers, for all that they called her a 'boff' and rolled their eyes at her culture vulture streak, would never hear a word against her. Noakes was equally protective, though it had taken some years before he and Burton appreciated each other's qualities and she relaxed sufficiently to let a surprisingly subversive mischievous wit flash out. Markham still cherished the recollection of Noakes's face the day they were interviewing a local thug about injuries allegedly inflicted by his wingman, when she informed the instructing solicitor in a deceptively saccharine tone that she 'supposed compensation had set in'. That was the day the tide turned and his friend began to view Burton in a whole new light.

The meeting with Hoxton Together passed off more easily than he had anticipated, a young black youth worker and reedy-voiced middle-aged woman seemingly anxious to prevent the housing estate becoming any sort of flashpoint for yobs bent on mischief. Hilary Probert looked strung-out and wretched, but she had an obvious rapport with the community representatives and was visibly pleased when he intimated, albeit in general terms, that James Daly was no longer on the police radar.

'James has got problems with impulse control,' she assured them earnestly, 'but we're addressing his issues through counselling and anger management.'

Markham would have given much to know exactly what had transpired, if anything, between Catherine Leckie and the teenager, but doubted they would ever get to the bottom of it, not least as her colleagues at Hope were bound to close ranks. 'Teaching's a minefield these days,' Burton said sadly afterwards. 'It's so easy to give out the wrong signals. Not that I'm saying she *did*, but he wouldn't be the first to have a schoolboy crush and then take stuff out of context . . .'

'*Hmm.* At least it sounds as if Ms Probert's on the case. And those community people seemed decent . . . keen to damp things down rather than stir them up.'

'Gavin Conors will be disappointed,' Burton observed sarcastically. 'A riot on the Hoxton would do wonders for circulation.'

Markham groaned. 'I'd forgotten about the press conference. We'd better get Barry Lynch down here. Don't worry,' he added hastily, remembering her distaste for the press liaison officer Noakes had christened Old Octopus Mitts, 'word has it his current fiancée doesn't stand for any nonsense, so you'll be safe . . . And anyway, he can earn his vastly inflated salary by coming up with something to buy us more time.'

'We should try and keep the press focused on the allotments and St Bruno's,' Burton suggested. Markham could literally see the cogs turning as she came up with a media-friendly pre-emptive strike. 'Victims embedded in local community, so we want to avoid unhelpful speculation that hurts the families . . . everyone coming together for Catherine's funeral on Friday . . . time to show respect . . . great response from public and new leads emerging all the time" etcetera etcetera.' With a weak smile she concluded, 'I can always chuck in some juicy stuff about BPD and sadism if they start getting impatient.'

He grinned. 'Let's keep that in reserve shall we . . . Don't want to be giving Conors ideas about how to start a mass panic.'

There was a knock at the door and Doyle came in looking shaken.

More bad news.

'The vicar at St Bruno's called about an accident,' the young sergeant told them. 'He said one of their sacristans went round this morning to sort the laundry or linen . . . something to do with vestments any road . . . She saw the door to the crypt was open and figured someone must've forgotten to lock up properly . . . but the lights down there were still on, which was a bit odd . . . she was halfway down the stairs when she saw a shape at the bottom and began screaming her head off.'

'The sacristan didn't check to see who it was?' Markham asked urgently.

'No . . . She made such a racket that people came running. But the vicar told everyone to stay back till we'd checked it out. He thinks one of their church helpers could've blacked out and taken a fall rather than it being anything sinister . . . But given that it's St Bruno's . . .'

'Quite.' A cold flush ran through Markham's body. Surely this couldn't be a fourth murder, could it? It seemed terrible in the circumstances to be busily assessing the chances of this poor soul, whoever they were, meeting their end by natural causes, but he knew the others were engaged in a similar calculation.

'Right, Doyle,' he rasped the words, feeling as if the tension he was holding in his neck and shoulders had suddenly migrated to his throat and was grappling with his voice box, 'I want you and Carruthers to liaise with SOCO and get round there right away. The vicar's done well to keep the gawkers away, but as soon as word spreads he'll have a job on his hands.' Especially once the *Gazette* got wind, he thought grimly.

Doyle promptly disappeared.

'That kind of thing *does* happen in churches,' Burton said tensely, 'especially when it's elderly parishioners.'

'Fair point, Kate. But it's an unsettling coincidence.'

And he didn't like coincidences.

'Let's not speculate till we know more,' he said getting to his feet. 'Once we've got an ID and Dimples's opinion, things will be clearer.'

If this *was* their killer, it was a major escalation which meant the entire situation was spiralling out of control. Despite his air of calm assurance, Markham's heart seemed to be lodged higher up in his chest than it should be and beating three times faster than normal.

Their faces taut with apprehension, he and Burton headed for the door.

* * *

'Everything points to accident, Markham,' Dimples said as they huddled in St Bruno's small crypt. 'There's no indication that she was manhandled or anything of that nature and I know for a fact there were issues with low blood pressure . . . it wasn't the first time she'd passed out.' Gently, he added, 'You can see from the way she's lying that her neck is broken. Death would have been instantaneous.'

Margaret Cresswell was indeed splayed at a very awkward angle. White-faced, Kate Burton fancied she could hear the sickening crack as the woman's head hit the stone floor.

Almost tenderly, the pathologist's gloved hands moved the incongruously thin sticklike legs together before positioning the sturdy body with the arms straight down by her sides. He had already wiped away a trickle of blood from the brittle grey crop and closed the wide shocked eyes before the detectives' arrival, motivated by an obscure (and no doubt old-fashioned) desire to prevent Markham's number two from being unnecessarily shaken by the unnerving spectacle. Of course he was familiar with Kate Burton's impressive career history and ruthless self-discipline but found she inspired a protective chivalrousness that was never aroused by other female detectives. He suspected that Markham felt much the same way, indeed had sometimes wondered if the extent of his feelings for Burton might take her handsome colleague by surprise some day or other . . .

Dimples recalled himself to the present.

'Margaret was assiduous about all her church duties,' he said quietly. 'Helped out here and at the cathedral . . . She was just getting over the flu, so it was probably too soon for her to be out and about doing jobs. But that's just the kind of woman she was.' Suddenly the medic looked years older: careworn and very sad. 'I knew Margaret when she was young,' he murmured. 'She was like a heroine out of Betjeman . . . Miss Joan Hunter Dunn or one of those home counties girls he fantasised about . . . a classic good egg.'

Markham met his eyes and recited softly: '*Around us are Rovers and Austins afar, Above us the intimate roof of the car, And here on the right is the girl of my choice, With the tilt of her nose and the chime of her voice . . . We sat in the car park till twenty to one, And now I'm engaged to Miss Joan Hunter Dunn.*'

Typical of Markham to get the reference, Dimples thought. There wasn't a detective on the force to touch him. Which was no doubt why he was admired and loathed in equal measure. Rarities always were.

'Only it was boring Henry Cresswell, dry-as-dust local solicitor, always dapper in his blasted wing collar, who snaffled Margaret,' he continued. 'My eldest brother Frank was quite devastated . . . really smitten with her . . . took him ages to get over it.'

Seeing that Burton looked slightly bewildered at these golden age reminiscences, as though she found it hard to imagine Margaret Cresswell as a tip-tilted charmer, he added kindly, 'Of course those were her glory days and she'd been widowed for years.'

'She seemed like a really good woman,' Burton said finally.

'Yes . . . a bit snobby and bossy but true blue.'

The medic regarded them shrewdly.

'You're wondering if the allotment killer did for her.'

'Presumably we can't rule out homicide, Doug?' Markham asked.

'No,' the other conceded. 'A shove from behind would have done it.' He looked down at the corpse. 'She's still warm, so it happened in the last couple of hours . . . All I can say at this stage is that there's no sign of a struggle or defensive injuries. Given her age and the medical history, a faint seems the most likely explanation . . . she was headed down here for some reason and then passed out at the top of the stairs. But,' his face was sombre, 'I can't rule out her having been surprised from behind.'

Noise from above alerted them to the arrival of paramedics.

'We'll leave you to it . . . and thanks.' Markham gestured to Kate to precede him up the stairs. As the sacristy began to fill up, they adjourned to a small anteroom where the Reverend Smeaton — the elderly clergyman whom Markham remembered from the Sunday service — was waiting. Diminutive and balding, with sparse white hair, he spoke in a husky tone which suggested that he was struggling with a bad cold. But he struck the two officers as eminently calm and sensible, his brief tribute to the dead woman warm and appreciative but without frills.

'Was it usual for the sacristans to come down into the crypt, sir, er sorry, Father?' Burton asked.

'Sir is fine,' he smiled at her kindly. 'There's nothing much to see down there. Just a couple of ledger markers in the floor covering interments of previous incumbents up until 1898 when burials shifted to the municipal cemetery. There's a few memorial lozenges of antiquarian interest, I believe, but that's pretty much it apart from the utility area at the back where we keep objects of worship like candlesticks, incense and altar vessels . . . oh and gifts from parishioners — holy pictures, icons, hanging lamps, the odd statue . . . the finer items are displayed in the church, but we catalogue everything and organise mini exhibitions from time to time.' With a touching anxiety not to be thought ungracious, he added, 'Some of the artwork is a bit sentimental and flowery for modern congregations, but it represents a wonderful legacy from parishioners down the ages.'

'No doubt,' Markham said courteously. 'So it's possible that Mrs Cresswell might have wanted to . . . look for an item she remembered.' He had nearly said 'rummage around' before realising that it carried overtones of snooping.

The clergyman snatched at this suggestion with an expression of relief.

'Quite so. Mrs Cresswell was always very interested in St Bruno's treasures,' he said eagerly. I wouldn't be at all surprised if there wasn't something she wanted to examine . . . or maybe she was undertaking some genealogical research — she helped with the parish archives, you see — in which case the various memorials might have a bearing.'

'What about access to the sacristy and crypt, how does that work?' Burton asked.

'Our helpers have their own keys . . . Miss Murphy who came in this morning, the lady who . . .' he faltered slightly, 'discovered Margaret, found the sacristy unlocked already, which is how she knew one of the team had been in.'

'You're not covered by CCTV?' Burton asked.

'There's a live feed so that we can stream services and protect the sanctuary,' the priest replied, 'but we never saw any need for a camera round the back.'

'So pretty much easy come, easy go then,' Burton said with a hint of censure in her tone.

The Reverend Smeaton looked distressed. 'The sacristans' rota is pinned up at the back of the church,' he said. 'It's also in the online newsletter, so anyone would know when Margaret was due in.'

'Don't torment yourself, Father,' Markham said gently. 'We appreciate the importance of parish helpers for your ministry. At this stage, there's nothing to indicate that Mrs Cresswell's death was suspicious. In light of an ongoing investigation, we just want to dot all the i's and cross the t's.'

Outside, he said to Burton, 'The vicar looked like a gust of wind would blow him away . . . No point in agitating him . . . not least as he's given us a clue.'

'*Guv?*' Burton was all ears.

'I think this is murder, Kate,' he said slowly as they stood in the church forecourt watching a procession of SOCOs and uniforms. 'Something was niggling Margaret Cresswell—'

'You mean she sussed the killer?'

'More likely, she was trying to get things straight in her own mind?'

'*What things?*' Burton was so eager that her tone uncharacteristically verged on belligerent.

'I don't know,' Markham admitted. 'I'm not sure *she* knew what was wrong . . . But I'm convinced something happened back there that made the killer flip.'

Burton screwed up her face in concentration, trying to visualise the sequence of events. 'So you reckon this was a chance encounter but then she pushed their buttons?'

'I think it was an impulse kill,' he said. 'Margaret Cresswell was recovering from the flu,' he went on. 'So she might not have been firing on all cylinders . . . in other words, blind to danger . . . And then her path crossed the killer's with fatal consequences . . . either because she revealed some latent mistrust or because she said something they found insupportable . . . It's possible the trigger was a combination of both but our murderer wouldn't normally have chosen to violate the precincts of a church — *that* would have offended their sense of propriety.'

Burton was watching him intently.

'You sound like you know who it is, guv.'

'I think finally I might have an inkling, Kate,' he answered.

Patiently, she waited. Virtually any other detective would have demanded a name, but she was content to follow his lead.

'I want you to check out that utility area in the crypt,' he instructed. 'Get Doyle and Carruthers to make a log of what's down there . . . you can cross-check with that catalogue the vicar mentioned.'

The brown eyes gleamed. Instinctively, she knew the contents of St Bruno's crypt was significant.

'If I'm right,' he said, 'we should be able to make an arrest after the funeral on Friday.'

At that moment, a little cavalcade — paramedics with their gurney followed by Dimples Davidson — came through the church porch. The two detectives bowed their heads as Margaret Cresswell passed by on her way to the waiting ambulance.

'There's no family to notify,' Burton said quietly. 'It was only her . . .' Softly she added, 'No wonder she was on every committee going . . . needed to feel she was still relevant, still *counted*.' Her voice dropped still further, so that Markham had to stoop down to catch what she said. 'It was the same with my mum after dad died . . . like she had to cling on to groups and clubs and guilds, otherwise she wouldn't know who she was.' Her gaze was misty as it followed the departing ambulance. But then, in typical fashion, she squared her shoulders ready for the task ahead.

'Do I need to sort surveillance on anyone, guv?' she asked.

Markham was about to answer when Doyle and Carruthers came up to join them, the former clearly excited.

'This woman who does the flowers is positive she saw Cresswell having an argy-bargy out by the Parish Hall on Tuesday afternoon.'

'Well, don't keep us in suspense, Sergeant,' Markham said drily. 'Who was the other party?'

'Hilary Probert, sir,' came the answer with considerable éclat.

Observing Markham closely, Burton felt sure this wasn't the name the guvnor expected to hear, though he gave no sign either of glee or disappointment.

Doyle looked crestfallen that his thunderbolt had failed to elicit much of a reaction. Of course, that was Markham all over, he reflected with exasperation. The chiselled aquiline features and dark eyes gave no clue to his thoughts. But Doyle had no doubt his keen brain was in overdrive. Burton was wearing her alert beagle look, which meant they were on to something.

'Once the crypt's been processed, let's bring Ms Probert in for questioning and see what she has to say for herself,' Markham said. 'No need to be discreet about it,' he added casually.

Doyle and Carruthers exchanged looks of the 'what's going on?' variety.

Whatever it was, DI Kate Burton appeared to be in on the secret.

'Come on,' she said tersely, jerking her head towards the church. 'Let's check it out, then we can pull Probert.'

'What's so special about the crypt?' Carruthers demanded before subsiding as the boss's cool gaze rested on him. *Ours not to reason why*, he thought crossly, stomping after Burton.

Left alone, Markham tried to marshal his racing thoughts.

The day had turned raw and sombre, a stiff breeze whipping up from nowhere and a cold, demoralising January rain starting to fall.

If he was right about what happened in that church, Margaret Cresswell had died because events overtook themselves too fast.

If his theories were accurate, the killer's rage would by now have abated.

He needed to confer with Eleanor Shaughnessy and draw up a battle plan.

CHAPTER 12

The rest of the day passed in something of a blur, but the various tasks were undertaken and uniforms dispatched to collect Hilary Probert. 'She's not under arrest,' Markham told them. 'You can say we just need to go through her statements again, clarify a few points . . . Make sure she's fed and watered . . . essentially keep her sweet until I've finished briefing my team.'

His colleagues duly assembled in the DI's office at 4 p.m., joined — to no one's particular surprise — by George Noakes.

Honestly, Kate Burton thought to herself in resigned exasperation, surely it would be simpler to bring him in as a full-time civilian consultant and have done with it. She half suspected this was Markham's ultimate objective, only he was proceeding incrementally — phasing Noakes back in, as it were — so the top brass wouldn't realise their *bête noire* had never really gone away. The cold case unit employed a number of former officers, of course, so why should the guvnor not have Noakes? Except, except . . . he was spectacularly persona non grata with the hierarchy who would be deeply suspicious of the prodigal's re-emergence amongst then. She couldn't help grinning as she recalled the cheerful self-deprecation with which he flummoxed Sidney at their last encounter: 'You can't fool me, I'm an idiot.' Nothing like disarming the enemy!

Now, watching as Rosemount's security manager happily slurped and wolfed his way through the delivery of drinks and pastries she'd organised from Costa, Burton was almost inclined to sympathise with Bromgrove's high command. *Almost*, she thought, as she observed his galvanising effect on Doyle and Carruthers. The Four Musketeers, that's us all right, she reflected dropping into her chair in front of Markham's desk.

It was already dark outside and rain was falling steadily. The office radiator was stone cold, needless to say, it being the depths of winter (baking hot in summer obviously), but she had brought the little electric heater from her own minuscule cubby-hole so they were reasonably cosy. And anyway, they were buoyed up by a feeling of suppressed excitement in the air which emanated from Markham himself, as if to say: *This Is It.*

The guvnor never postured or wasted time on flash parlour tricks, so after gulping down some black coffee, he came straight to the point.

'I want you to consider Peter Barlow for these murders,' he said quietly.

His colleagues' jaws hit the floor, even Burton clearly wrongfooted by this opening.

'*Barlow!*' burst from their mouths simultaneously.

'It was actually something *you* said, Sergeant, that triggered my eureka moment,' Markham told Doyle.

'*Me?*' Doyle was simultaneously pleased and confused.

The DI's dark eyes were intent on him. 'Do you remember when we discussed Elsie Parker's report about Dave Shipley having made a nuisance of himself with Rebecca Atherton?'

'*Ye-es.*' Doyle still didn't see where this was going.

'You said Ms Parker told you that Peter Barlow knew about it.'

Doyle was even more mystified. 'That's right, she quoted him as back up.'

'Your words about Mr Barlow stuck in my mind . . . You said, "The old gent was dead embarrassed when we asked him about it — almost like we were talking dirty about his favourite niece or something".'

'Yeah, but that was *Atherton* he was talking about, not Catherine Leckie.'

'True, but the reference to a favourite niece stayed with me.'

The DI turned to Burton. 'Then later on, we were discussing that lecture you went to at the university — the one about Richard III—'

'When that lecturer said Tricky Dicky had the hots for his niece,' Noakes interrupted eagerly as Doyle and Carruthers semaphored *WTF*.

'Well, it was a bit more *nuanced* than that,' Burton said helplessly. 'Dr Ashdown thought the stories about incest were most probably Tudor propaganda, but there *might* have been a sliver of truth in there somewhere because Richard lost his wife and son from TB and there was this beautiful niece floating around the place . . . Put it like this, you could see why he might have been desperate for a chance at happiness.'

'I was intrigued by what you said about Richard,' Markham told her. 'Almost as if he was trying to tell me something.'

Observing Noakes's consternation about having been excluded from this juicy confabulation, the DI explained, 'My knowledge of the Plantagenets and the Wars of the Roses is somewhat shaky and I'd always viewed Richard as the stereotypical hunchbacked villain, when in fact he was a far more complex character . . . something of a split personality really.'

That caught Carruthers's interest. 'How come?'

'Well, he was extremely devout to the point of being puritanical — even took his prayer book into battle—' Noakes's head come up on hearing this — 'so his religious streak must have been at war with those illicit feelings he had for his niece, Elizabeth of York. He was ultra-protective of her morals and chastity at the same time as he entertained hopes of marrying her. Of course, it all came to nothing because the public wouldn't wear it, but if he really *did* have less than avuncular feelings for Elizabeth, he was caught on the horns of a wretched dilemma.'

Carruthers frowned. 'Wasn't the stuff about him fancying her just a load of hot air?'

'Not entirely,' Burton said. 'His behaviour towards her gave rise to rumours, so there could've been something in it. And according to Dr Ashdown, Elizabeth gave out mixed signals . . . she may even have encouraged him.'

'Okay, okay. So where does *Barlow* fit in to all this?' Noakes demanded impatiently.

Markham took over. 'It set my mind running on the age-old theme of older men being vulnerable where young women are concerned—'

'You mean, being prats an' kidding themselves some bit of fluff fancies them when all the time she's jus' stringing 'em along,' Noakes interrupted trenchantly.

Nothing like the vernacular, Markham thought. 'Exactly.'

'Still ain't much to go on for a link between Leckie an' Barlow,' his old ally grunted morosely.

'You mentioned Peter Barlow was at that lecture, Kate?' Markham resumed. 'Something about him and Margaret Cresswell being ardent Ricardians . . . holding forth in the Q&A session about Richard's kingly qualities?'

'Yes, but quite a few other people from the allotments were there as well, guv.' It was clear that Burton didn't want to rain on the guvnor's parade but struggled to follow his drift.

Markham's gaze turned remote, his tone almost dreamy.

'Prissy, buttoned-up Peter Barlow whose wife succumbed to MS after a protracted, cruel decline . . . Pillar of his local church, school governor and long-standing allotmenteer,' he mused. 'A man perhaps more than usually susceptible to the charms of youth after years of marital sterility

'... who might easily have regarded Catherine Leckie almost in the light of a favourite niece . . . *or perhaps something more . . .*'

Burton's eyes sharpened while Doyle and Carruthers leaned in as though suddenly hooked.

'Peter Barlow who, according to the inventory of St Bruno's crypt, donated a print of *The Temptations of Saint Anthony* to his parish church—'

'*Whoa*, guv, you've lost me there,' Noakes protested. 'Who cares about some mouldy old painting?' he asked mutinously.

'Dr Ashdown talked about St Anthony in his lecture,' Burton recalled.

'That's right,' Markham continued. 'According to you, he said Richard III had a tremendous devotion to St Anthony who lived in the wilderness with a pet boar to ward off demons and sexual temptation, which was why his servants wore a boar badge.'

'So what if Barlow dug some weirdy saint?' Noakes wanted to know. ''S a bit creepy all right, but it don' mean he killed Leckie.'

The DI's face was calm as a limpid pool. 'Bear with me, Noakesy,' he said before opening a manila folder and withdrawing a photocopy that he laid down on the desk in front of them. 'The original painting is an oil by Van Aelst . . . As you can see, it shows a beautiful naked woman with a witch standing at her shoulder . . . In the background there's a burning city being looted or sacked and various strange monsters capering about.'

'Old Ant don' seem too happy about the youngster jiggling her bits,' Noakes chuckled. 'But looks like he's giving her a blessing or summat . . . s'pose being so holy, that's what you do.'

'She and the witch represent the lures of the Devil,' Markham pointed out. 'It's not so much a blessing as a gesture to ward off evil.'

Noakes peered closer, struck by something else.

'She's like the lass in that other picture,' he said slowly. 'The one we saw at the back of the church when we swung by on Sunday.'

Doyle and Carruthers exchanged bemused glances. Clearly the boss had dragged Noakes along on one of his churchy jaunts. But where did this sightseeing fit in?

Markham took another photocopy from the manila folder and set it down next to St Anthony.

'This is a copy of *The Three Ages of Man and Death*,' he told them. 'The one that hangs at the back of St Bruno's,' he added.

'*Yuck*,' was Noakes's forceful response. He was on the point of observing that Olivia had been with them and freaked out when she saw it, but something — some protective instinct towards the guvnor's highly strung partner — held him back. 'It's right depressing, it makes the other one look like a day out at Center Parcs.'

'The skeleton holding the broken spear and hourglass represents Death,' Markham informed them levelly. 'You'll see that he's holding the old woman by the arm, trying to lead her away. But she's grabbing on to the beautiful young girl next to her.'

'An allegory,' Burton piped up eagerly. 'About trying to hang on to youth and avoid dying.'

'Looks like the old woman, or witch or whoever she is, wants to drag the girl down with her,' Carruthers said. 'Perhaps she's jealous of her for being young and beautiful.'

'I agree with Sarge,' Doyle put in with a shudder. 'It's bloody depressing . . . quite anti-women too, if you ask me . . . even the young one looks scowly.'

'So would you if a witch had her claws into you,' Noakes retorted.

'What's with the baby on the ground?' Doyle asked.

'Allegorical again,' Burton said. 'To remind us that from the moment we're born, we begin to die.'

'"We were born to die, and we die to live." 2 Corinthians,' Noakes interjected with lip-smacking relish, 'so it ain't *all* bad news.'

Doyle and Carruthers didn't look as if they derived any particular comfort from this admonition.

Briefly, Markham wondered what the DCI would say if he could hear their earnest discussion of obscure medieval art. No doubt it would confirm his worst fears about 'Markham's talking shop'.

Carruthers pulled the two photocopies towards him and studied them hard.

'C'mon then, Melvyn Bragg, what've you spotted?' Noakes scoffed.

'The girls both look like Catherine Leckie,' the DS said flatly.

The silence suddenly became electric.

With grave deliberation, Markham removed a head and shoulders portrait of their first victim from his manila folder, lining it up next to the two photocopies. 'This is from Hope Academy's prospectus,' he said simply.

Noakes cleared his throat. 'You may be on to something there, mate,' he told Carruthers. 'That headshot . . . yeah, she's kind of pale an' transparent an' delicate same as them two in the paintings . . . like they could do with a decent meal . . . long brown hair an' all . . . *Hey*,' he said to Markham, making the others jump, 'what about that one of St Cecilia? The plaque thingy said the allotment folk donated it.'

Like a conjuror producing his rabbit, Markham took one last sheet of paper from the folder.

'Thass the one,' Noakes breathed. 'the droopy lass having a kip while the angel cops an eyeful.'

'Otherwise known as St Cecilia asleep at her organ,' Markham said ironically. 'Reproduction of a Victorian painting by Frederick Appleyard. Donated by Beauclair Drive Allotment Association.'

His colleagues examined it intently.

'Yeah, same hair and profile,' Carruthers said finally. 'And there's something about the pose . . . like how Leckie was when we found her.'

Silence fell once more.

Markham felt his nerves stretch.

'All right, guv,' Noakes said, 'seems to me like Barlow *could* have had some hang-up or obsession with that kind of look.' He scratched his bristly chin. 'Not everyone's idea of a pinup, granted,' cue vigorous head shaking by Doyle and Carruthers, 'but mebbe it were right up his street . . . jus' like ole Tricky Dicky fancying the niece,' he added with a happy flash of inspiration. 'If your wife's been sick for ever, that's *gotta* mess with your head so you don' think straight . . . mebbe start fancying your chances with pretty young lasses . . .'

'How long *was* Mr Barlow's wife sick for?' Markham asked Noakes. 'I know she had MS but there's not much else to go on.'

'Sheila were ill for yonks, guv,' Noakes informed him. 'In a wheelchair . . . an' I think they lost a baby when they were newlyweds. Pretty hard cheese all round.'

Markham hid a smile at the prosaic phraseology.

'An infatuation for young women and a dead baby,' Burton murmured. 'Just like Richard.'

'*One young woman*,' Markham corrected her. '*Catherine Leckie*. An obsession that took over his life.'

Doyle settled back comfortably, as if he was waiting for the guvnor to tell them a story, Noakes thought sardonically.

'How d'you reckon it happened then, boss?' the young DS asked. 'Did Barlow try it on with Leckie and get knocked back or what?'

'I doubt he did anything as overt as that, Sergeant,' Markham replied. 'I believe, however, that he *did* develop a romantic infatuation for Catherine Leckie who seemed to match this image of the ideal woman that he carried in his mind and clung to over the years as his wife declined.' He paused, marshalling his thoughts. 'With MS, it can be a long, lonely haul.'

Noakes's stubby fingers were drumming an impatient rat-a-tat on the table.

'Go on,' he urged.

'I believe that Mr Barlow could have had a schizoid ambivalence about these feelings for Catherine Leckie. On the one hand, he yearned, perhaps even lusted, after her. But on the other, he was constrained by his religious precepts and strict moral outlook.'

'Well, if she didn't knock him back, why'd he kill her?' Doyle persisted.

'When she started an affair with Raymond Cotter, that shattered the way Barlow saw her,' Carruthers replied. 'Spoiled his ideal image, so he began to *hate* her.'

Burton, a fellow psychology graduate, liked this theory. 'With a twisted mindset, he could have interpreted her liaison with Cotter as some kind of rejection of himself.'

Markham nodded. 'There might have been no "knock back" as such . . . But in light of his susceptibility — and there may well have been a degree of paranoia — Mr Barlow could also have misconstrued something Catherine said or did as amounting to disparagement.'

'Or Cotter might've had a go at him . . . said summat snide or picked up on how he felt about the lass an' made fun, so that set him off,' Noakes said as though he could well believe anything of the businessman. 'Pete's jus' this dry old stick — retired accountant for the council — while Cotter's your Slick Willie type,' he added knowingly.

Burton considered this, ramming her recalcitrant specs more firmly on her nose. 'Dr Shaughnessy thought there could have been some sort of trigger incident that happened in the allotments — some kind of humiliating experience for the killer — so maybe Barlow overheard them being unflattering about him, or perhaps they were just cavalier or insolent and it caught him on the raw.'

'I doubt we'll ever know the whole truth of it,' Markham said slowly, 'and certainly not from Mr Barlow . . . But Dr Shaughnessy's theory about sublimated sexual impulses leading to Catherine's belongings being stashed in that tree hole at the allotments definitely fits his profile as a repressed and confused individual.' He tried to picture the eruption of rage that led to the teacher being strangled. 'Mr Barlow might have turned up at Catherine's shed on New Year's Eve with a view to confronting her about the way she was carrying on. He might even have disclosed how he felt about her . . . If she displayed contempt or disgust or — still worse — tried to laugh it off, that would have been enough to light the fuse.'

'Was Barlow the one who was sending Leckie the poison pen notes then?' Doyle wanted to know.

'If I'm right about him, then yes, I think he could be the person who wrote the letters and spied on Catherine,' Markham confirmed.

'Okay, I can see him doing Leckie and Cotter,' Carruthers said. 'But what was his problem with Rebecca Atherton? Did *she* make fun of him too?'

'I think it's more likely he regarded her as a bad influence on Catherine . . . in his warped thinking, he might even have blamed her for throwing Catherine and Raymond Cotter together,' Markham replied. 'Bex and Catherine were apparently thick as thieves,' he went on. There was a slight hesitation before he added, 'Olivia told me that Elsie Parker was very put out by their close friendship — apparently she felt "squeezed out of the picture". But that could equally well have applied to Peter Barlow if he was possessive about Catherine. He and Margaret Cresswell were governors at the school, remember. "Old-fashioned and a bit officious" was how Olivia described them. She also said that Bex and Catherine used to "laugh themselves silly over some of the governors' meetings", which could suggest that Bex was encouraging Catherine to kick over the traces . . . maybe be a bit defiant and subversive.'

'Kind of like the bad girl of the class making the goody two-shoes put two fingers up,' Doyle mused.

'Well, I don't know if Catherine Leckie was ever a "goody two-shoes",' Markham laughed. 'But Mr Barlow undoubtedly held her professionalism in high regard to start with, so it's possible he resented anyone who encouraged a disrespectful attitude towards the governors.'

'Catherine was posed modestly on her side, like a child,' Burton recalled. 'Whereas with Bex it was different . . . sexualised and ugly . . . It wasn't just to send us looking in the wrong place, was it?' she asked Markham. 'It's like Doyle said before: in his mind, Bex was the bad lot, kind of the whore to Catherine's Madonna.'

It was interesting, Markham thought, how his colleagues echoed Dr Shaughnessy's analysis of the dynamic.

Doyle, highly gratified at being thus invoked, took up the story. 'Bex could've been in on whatever Leckie and Cotter got up to at the allotments . . . as in making fun of Barlow or just whooping it up.'

Seeing that Noakes was boggling at the idea of orgies amidst the onions, Carruthers said hastily, 'So you reckon Leckie, Cotter and Atherton were all premeditated, boss?'

'Mr Cotter and Ms Atherton undoubtedly — planning went into the poisoning and that ambush in Old Carton—'

'How'd he manage to lure Atherton out there?' Noakes interrupted. 'She had to have been on her guard after what happened to the other two.'

'Bex wouldn't have been suspicious of Barlow,' Burton said. 'He was an older man, respectable and a governor in the bargain . . . Easy for him to suggest a Sunday stroll out in the country . . . hint there was something damaging to Catherine's reputation that he didn't want coming out or he had suspicions about someone . . . or he wanted to take the heat off James Daly and the Hoxton . . . you know, appeal to her caring side.'

'Yeah, when we went to Hope, it was obvious the kids really liked her,' Doyle chipped in. 'Stands to reason she'd have been worried about Daly. Yeah,' he repeated with growing conviction, 'easy-peasy . . . and she never saw it coming.'

'But you're saying Cresswell were different, guv?' Noakes reverted to the final victim. 'An accident?'

Markham nodded confirmation.

'How come Barlow rocked up there when she were doing her sacristan bit?' Noakes continued, clearly baffled.

Rigid tension in his neck and shoulders was giving Markham the beginnings of a headache, but his attitude and voice remained calm as ever.

'I think Mrs Cresswell probably told him she wanted to have a look at some of the stuff in the crypt,' Markham answered.

'You mean cos she'd clocked there were summat iffy about the soppy girls an' him?' Noakes pressed. 'Or cos the Richard thing had got her wondering about him . . . the same way we did?'

'Maybe subconsciously she *was* uneasy about Mr Barlow,' Markham replied. 'Maybe something about him *was* bothering her . . . perhaps because she knew him so well, there was an alteration in his manner or other signs that she picked up on . . . something subtle that wouldn't have been obvious to other people.'

'But she still went ahead and met him?' Doyle asked incredulously.

'She might not even have admitted to herself that she had doubts about him,' Markham said. 'Remember they were old friends, which would have made her suppress any mistrust . . . But if something *was* niggling at her, then a chat about artwork meant a chance to put any fears to rest.'

'Yeah, the two of 'em went way back,' Noakes agreed thoughtfully. 'She were probl'y jus' thrashing round in the dark.'

Doyle tried to complete the scenario. 'But she let something out and that's when he panicked and whacked her?'

'She might just have said the wrong thing,' Markham surmised. 'Or he took some innocent comment the wrong way.'

'Something about Catherine?' Burton asked.

'Possibly . . . Or maybe it was something he found unbearable . . . a tactless remark or criticism that threatened his sense of self.'

'Some folk called her a bossy old bat,' Noakes commented, making Markham suspect he was echoing Muriel's verdict.

'There you are then,' the DI said. 'Having killed three people in quick succession, Mr Barlow would have been under considerable stress and liable to explode under provocation.' He let them absorb this before continuing, 'If they were standing by that unlocked door down to the crypt, one quick shove would have done it.'

The DI could see that at last he was bringing his colleagues with him.

'Let's just review Mr Barlow's alibis,' he suggested.

'He had his sister-in-law round for a sherry on New Year's Eve,' Carruthers recalled.

'Which means he could've gone round to the allotments once he'd got shot of her,' Doyle pointed out.

Carruthers moved on to the second victim. 'When Cotter was killed, Barlow had the flu or something,' he said. 'It was bad enough for the district nurse to come out with antibiotics.'

'And he couldn't make it to Cresswell's bridge shindig,' Doyle added. 'But that didn't matter in the end cos she came down with the same thing.'

Carruthers frowned. 'Are we saying he was never really sick in the first place?'

'He could've had an infection,' Burton reflected, 'but not been so sick that he wasn't able to meet Cotter and slip him the strychnine cocktail.'

'But the nurse did a call-out and gave him antibiotics,' Doyle protested. 'I mean, doesn't that mean he *had* to have been poorly?'

'Surgeries always err on the side of caution with older people,' Markham pointed out. 'I imagine he definitely had some sort of infection, but given his age and the fact that the lurgy was doing the rounds, he wouldn't have had to be Larry Olivier to convince the nurse he was very unwell and needed to be in bed.'

'He's not such an old crock,' Noakes weighed in judiciously. 'Quite steady on his pins an' all that.'

'Yes,' Markham concurred. 'He struck me as fairly hale and vigorous at our initial meeting, so it's not beyond the bounds of possibility that he played up his chest infection with a view to using it as cover for the murder of Raymond

Cotter. I think we'll find that he requested the house call on the basis that it would provide a useful alibi.'

'How'd he get Cotter to meet him at the allotments?' Doyle asked.

'Same trick as he used with Bex,' Burton replied grimly. 'Hinted that he knew something . . . came over all mysterious and secretive . . .'

Carruthers nodded. 'And Cotter was so grief-stricken, he never thought to wonder—'

'Yeah,' Doyle broke in eagerly. 'He'd never have suspected an older codger like Barlow, 'specially not if Barlow came the old soldier . . . snuffled and wheezed like he was on his last legs.' He broke off in confusion as Burton gave him one of her thousand-yard stares, clearly unimpressed by the pejorative language.

'Barlow was lucky that nobody spotted him,' Carruthers cut in smoothly, distracting Burton's attention from his hapless colleague.

'It was seven in the evening by Dimples's reckoning,' she said. 'So he timed it well . . . a winter's night, people down with the flu and hardly anybody around . . . couldn't have worked out better . . . though not for Mr Cotter, obviously,' she added hastily with a slight flush.

A thought struck Doyle 'Hey, do you think it was *Barlow* who put Gavin Conors onto James Daly?' he asked.

'Quite possibly,' Markham said, his expression darkening at the thought of that episode. 'An anonymous tip-off could never be traced back to him.' The DI's voice was taut as he added, 'I think Mr Barlow was probably also responsible for the fire at Beauclair Drive . . . As Dr Shaughnessy suggested, it seems likely that he was attempting some kind of symbolic eradication, though we can't know what was going on in his head at the time.'

Noakes shook his head sadly. 'Loony-tunes . . . totally round the twist.'

'Not so far round the twist that he didn't manage to take us all in,' was Burton's acid rejoinder. '*My* money was on Bernadette Farrelly after hearing she'd harassed Catherine Leckie and kept quiet about it.'

'I figured Dave Shipley was looking good for it,' Carruthers admitted. 'Or Donald Kemp, what with them being pervs. And the Creech bloke was well dodgy too.'

'I thought it might be one of the women,' Doyle joined in. 'Elsie Parker or Valerie Shipley . . . right little nest of vipers . . . I even wondered about Cresswell and Oddie cos they were both too good to be true . . .'

Noakes did the usual porcupine number on his hair, rumpling it wildly every which way.

'So what do we do now, guv?' he demanded. 'Sidney an' Bretherton won't be up for hearing about Richard III or them allegory wotsits.' An understatement if ever there was one.

Doyle and Carruthers exchanged broad grins at the very idea of broaching the Plantagenet king's passion for Elizabeth of York or attempting psychoanalysis of their prime suspect on the basis of some church paintings.

'Quite,' Markham said smoothly. 'Which is why we go ahead and speak to Hilary Probert while keeping Mr Barlow under surveillance.'

'You're sure he's our man, sir?' Burton asked softly.

You know what Sidney thinks about 'copper's hunch'.

The words hung in the air between them.

'It all came together for me when I read that entry in the crypt's inventory, Kate,' he replied. 'Suddenly I saw how it might have happened.' He stood up and flexed his shoulders, trying to loosen up, muscles rippling under the pinstripe. 'Thinking it through, I became increasingly certain Barlow was our killer. For all his respectability and established position in the community, it's been a case of famine in the man's personal life for many years.' Leaning with his back against the office window, he let that sink in before continuing. 'His wife was a former teacher, right?'

'Yeah, guv,' Noakes confirmed. 'Taught History at Hope back in the day . . . before she took sick. Only in her early thirties when it happened.'

'So I wondered if he harboured some resentment towards young teachers generally — the ones who blithely climbed the career ladder, sweeping all before them, while his invalid partner languished helplessly in a wheelchair watching her future go down the plughole.'

'Teachers like Catherine Leckie and Rebecca Atherton,' Burton said quietly.

'Such resentment could well have festered and turned dangerous over the years,' Markham pursued his argument. 'Along with his infatuation for Catherine Leckie, it led to his personality becoming misshapen and deformed.'

In that instant, her eyes irresistibly drawn to the St Anthony painting, Burton imagined Peter Barlow being dragged down by slithering demons into some shadowy abyss . . .

Registering Noakes's knowing, beady gaze, she recalled herself with a jolt. God, she thought, this room's overflowing with adrenaline and nerves, so no wonder I feel twitchy.

'I noticed the strange way he looked at some of the teachers during Catherine's memorial service at Hope,' she said. 'But I just put it down to the shock of the murders and him getting over the flu.'

'So far there's no forensics tying Barlow to any of the deaths, guv,' Doyle pointed out. 'Obviously he wore gloves or cleaned up after himself . . . And trace evidence won't incriminate him, seeing as him and the victims mixed at school or the allotments.'

'We won't be able to get a warrant for his medical records,' Burton said. 'Not based on what we've got . . . though I can speak to his GP . . .'

'We need a confession,' Noakes said flatly. '*A big fat confession.*'

'Let's find out what Ms Probert and Mrs Cresswell were quarrelling about when they had that "argy-bargy" outside the Parish Hall,' Markham suggested. 'It may be useful in giving us some leverage with Barlow.'

Noakes's piggy eyes narrowed. 'You're gonna let Probert in on this, guv?'

182

'Yes.'

'Bit of a risk, ain't it?' his friend said in a Jeremiah voice.

'I think it's one we have to take.' The DI exhaled surreptitiously. 'Hopefully we can use her to bait the trap.'

When you will spring it, guv?' Burton asked anxiously.

'After the funeral on Friday.'

Markham's expression was sphinx-like. 'At the allotments,' he said.

Noakes whistled. 'Does the trick cyclist know what you're planning?'

'I consulted with Dr Shaughnessy earlier,' the DI replied. 'She was very helpful.'

Easy on the eye too, Noakes thought warily, with a bat squeak of anxiety on Olivia's behalf as he registered the warmth in Markham's voice. It didn't escape his notice that Burton had picked up on it too, judging by her quick eye flick across the desk.

The guvnor and the university colleen . . . *That* would need watching . . .

Markham's voice interrupted his conjectures.

'I also took Dimples into my confidence. As Mr Barlow's fellow governor, it seemed to me his insights were worth having.'

'What did he think to it?' Noakes asked.

'Well, he was cautious, hindsight being a wonderful thing . . . But he *had* picked up on some signs of strain between Barlow, Mrs Cresswell and Catherine Leckie. He wasn't sure what was at the root of it — seemed to think differences over Elsie Parker played a part — but put it down to schools being such snake pits these days. Looking back, he noticed that Mr Barlow's temper had soured and he wasn't as genial, but assumed some of it was just the cantankerousness of old age . . . and maybe the strains imposed by his wife's long illness catching up with him . . . He *did* remember an uncharacteristically bilious outburst when someone — he can't be sure who — speculated about whether Catherine wanted to start a family with Raymond Cotter. But again, he explained it away as concern that the school might lose an outstanding teacher so soon after her appointment.'

'A possible pregnancy?' Burton breathed.

'Dimples had an impression it might have been on the cards. The PM showed no signs, but it may have been the case that Catherine believed she was pregnant.'

'Would that have tipped Barlow over the edge?' Carruthers asked.

'Who can say . . . Dimples knew about the Barlows having lost an infant and said there'd been several miscarriages as well . . . Given the family history, Dr Shaughnessy believes it's a feasible trigger.'

Outside the rain had almost stopped, subsiding to a soft quiet patter that matched Markham's thoughtful mood. Mercifully, his headache was easing and he now felt able to take on Hilary Probert.

'Right,' he said briskly, 'Kate's with me for this interview while you three watch from the observation window.'

The youngsters looked disappointed to be relegated to a supporting role, a fact which didn't escape their boss.

'Don't worry,' he assured them. 'You'll get your chance on Friday after Catherine Leckie's funeral.'

Friday 13 January, he thought.

Not the most auspicious of dates.

'The perfect tipping point,' was Dr Shaughnessy's prediction.

He hoped to God she was right.

* * *

'What did you and Margaret Cresswell argue about?'

'Who says we argued?' Hilary Probert sounded mulish. Despite bloodshot eyes, the social worker looked more groomed than previously, long hair tied in a ponytail and her eye make-up significantly toned down. The conservative black two-piece swamped her thin frame but was a vast improvement on dungarees and denim, Markham thought.

The uniforms had apparently tracked her down to a family case conference at the council offices, which presumably explained the formal attire, though her complexion was unhealthily sallow and he noticed her fingernails were bitten down to the quick.

'You were seen by someone from St Bruno's arguing with Mrs Cresswell outside the Parish Hall on Tuesday afternoon,' Markham told her.

As the other hesitated, clearly debating what she should tell them, Burton interjected urgently, 'Look Hilary, you're not under suspicion for the murders. Actually, we think we know who's responsible for them . . . and for what happened to Margaret.'

'Wasn't Margaret an accident?' the other said quickly. 'I heard she fainted and fell down some stairs.'

'We believe she may have been pushed,' Markham said calmly.

'Because she knew something?'

'Possibly . . . though it may just have been a case of her speaking out of turn . . . pressing the killer's buttons.'

A shaky laugh.

'Oh she was good at that,' Hilary Probert said bitterly. 'Told me to stop making an exhibition of myself over Cate . . . said it was melodramatic . . . *unseemly.*'

'She knew you had feelings for Catherine?' Burton prompted delicately.

'Oh, I'm pretty sure everyone knew . . . I suppose it was pathetic, the way I kept hoping that one day she'd decide to give women a try . . . always trying to please her . . . so abject and needy.' The note of self-recrimination was loud and clear.

'And Margaret was judgemental?' Burton pressed.

'*Not half!* A great one for inclusivity when it suited her — banged the anti-discrimination drum to show how *progressive* she was,' this was uttered in a hiss, 'but didn't care for homosexuality too close to home . . . It wasn't just that, though . . . I think she was quite possessive of Cate and didn't like the idea of me *contaminating* her.'

'An unattractive attitude,' Burton said sympathetically. 'That must have really hurt.'

'I'm used to it by now. Think she and the Beauclair committee only let me in to boost their diversity credentials. Apparently there were a couple of other stuffed shirts who didn't care for the way I "mooned over Catherine".'

'Who might they be?' Markham asked quickly.

'Peter Barlow for one. Which made me see red . . . I told her Barlow was just as bad . . . his fusspotting made Cate want to *scream*, even though she knew he meant well . . . The number of times she said, "There's no fool like an old fool".' The social worker bit her lip guiltily, oblivious to the look that passed between the two detectives. 'Perhaps I went a bit too far. But it served Margaret right for starting on me like that.'

'How did the conversation end?' Burton asked.

'She went red in the face like a turkeycock, drew herself up — all offended dignity — and flounced off.' Suddenly the social worker slumped in her seat, the indignation fading. 'If I had known that would be the last time I'd see her, I'd have played the whole scene differently.' Her voice thickened. 'Wish I could tell her I'm sorry and ask if we could start over.'

'Hilary,' Markham said gently, 'maybe there *is* something you can do for Margaret . . . For *all* of them.'

He nodded to Burton who, quietly and inexorably, disclosed the identity of their prime suspect and their need of her help.

The social worker sat up erectly, a surge of animation transforming her washed out appearance.

'Count me in,' she said.

CHAPTER 13

Friday 13 January, the day of Catherine Leckie's funeral dawned grey and monochrome, with a strange air of unreality hanging over everything.

Somehow it felt as if they were all characters in a play, Kate Burton thought as they slipped into the back of St Bruno's. People moving on and off stage.

The coffin, covered in flowers with a wreath from Hope, was already resting on a trestle in front of the communion rail.

She was glad of that. The memory of her dad being borne aloft into the church like some potentate in solemn procession for his funeral still haunted her dreams. It just didn't suit how he *was* — quiet, understated and self-effacing. Much better to have the coffin unobtrusively waiting. That way the wrench of parting wasn't so bad.

It was hard to know their killer was in the congregation, but Markham was adamant that everything had to go ahead just as normal so he wouldn't be alerted.

Churches always seemed colder when it was a funeral, she reflected, even though the heating was on and extra radiators had been brought in.

She just couldn't seem to get warm, and the sickly sweet smell of incense and flowers was making her nauseous.

Giving herself a little mental shake, she checked on the congregation.

Somehow on these occasions, the mourners always blended into one amorphous mass. Lots of smart black suits and poker faces. But she made out Hilary Probert across the nave with her elbows on the back of the seat in front and her forehead resting on her tightly clenched hands. She looked thin and lost and wretched, huddled inside a dark duffle coat. James Daly sat next to her looking equally miserable and subdued.

Burton's thoughts drifted to the post-funeral arrangements. There was to be a private burial, not a cremation. She was glad she wouldn't have to watch soil being shovelled into a great dark hole in the ground. Her dad's had looked far too big for him . . . She wasn't keen on crematoriums either, if it came to that . . . those weirdly leafy landscaped grounds designed so that you wouldn't notice the chimney amongst the trees . . .

There were quite a few children in school uniform near the front of the church. The order of service indicated that the senior choir from Hope Academy would sing 'The Lord's my Shepherd' and 'Amazing Grace'. Burton found this oddly comforting, as though it offered confirmation that Catherine Leckie's life was still somehow shaping her students' future and creating a pattern that no amount of evil could destroy.

She flinched as she spotted Peter Barlow standing next to Valerie Shipley in a tweed coat that was too tight for him, then steadied herself under Markham's quick, reassuring gaze. It was essential to behave as though their attendance was perfectly routine. Judging from some of the unfriendly sidelong glances directed at Hilary Probert, mourners were sizing *her* up as CID's prime suspect, with no inkling that the detectives would shortly be using the social worker to trap a killer.

Sidney, Bretherton and Ebury-Clarke stood together halfway down the church. Cynically, she supposed they wouldn't object to Gavin Conors door-stepping their exit from church. If this ambush in the allotments went according to plan, they would be swift to claim the credit (and, of course, the DI — who never jostled for laurels — would let them). If it backfired, they would be even swifter to cast themselves as champions of the community and Markham as a loose cannon, though he had received full authorisation for the operation. Which wasn't to say that Sidney was comfortable with the notion of Peter Barlow as a serial killer. It was Dr Shaughnessy who had fast-talked him into accepting that everything pointed to Barlow, cleverly stressing the markers for mental illness while avoiding any allusion to the strange sequence of coincidences behind Markham's conviction that this utterly respectable elderly citizen had committed four murders.

I am the Resurrection and the Life.

The funeral service had begun.

She was so tense, that it was difficult to concentrate. Glancing over at Doyle, Carruthers and Noakes (trussed up in a Sunday best outfit that was straining at the seams), she sensed they felt the same. The glories of the church's baroque interior — the paintings and statues of saints, the stained glass, woodwork and marble — were, unusually, largely wasted on her as she waited for the proceedings to come to an end. The plan required the team to slip out just before closing prayers and head for the allotments where Hilary would rendezvous with Peter Barlow.

The sermon began. She continued to dissociate until her attention was caught by the resounding declaration:

'We are born to meet God. Death is the end of school. Afterwards comes Paradise.'

The end of school. Pretty apt for a headteacher, Burton thought . . .

Now the vicar was quoting some saint — a young internet whiz — whom Catherine had apparently admired.

'"Everyone is born as an original, but many people end up dying as photocopies."'

Burton liked to think that the young headteacher was an original, liked to think she had written her own unique and unrepeatable story. The little group of students down there at the front eagerly waiting to sing were testament to that.

Noakes looked as though he was none too sure that stuff about photocopiers and the internet properly belonged in a sermon, but the vicar soon reverted to St Paul's Epistle to the Romans, so that was all right. He made no direct allusion to Catherine's fellow teacher and the other victims but, touchingly, spoke of recently deceased brethren who 'may have been totally unprepared to enter the Kingdom but will surely pass through the gates of eternity where the heavenly banquet awaits them.'

Talking of banquets, Burton wasn't disappointed that they would miss the buffet reception in the Parish Hall. While still on the force, Noakes had generally treated such occasions as some sort of All You Can Eat challenge, his unashamed gusto for the funeral baked meats invariably attracting official opprobrium. As he was unlikely to behave any differently on civvy street, all in all Burton figured this was a purgatorial experience she could well do without. To her intense mortification, Chris Carstairs had nicknamed their unit *Gannets 'R Us*. It was not an accolade to inspire a glow of pride.

Blissfully unaware of these dire reflections, Noakes was now bellowing his way through 'Thine Be The Glory', Sidney turning round to fix their pew with a baleful stare and terrible mouthful of teeth while Markham looked straight ahead and his subordinates affected a nonchalance they were far from feeling.

The closing prayers were at hand.

Trying to look as inconspicuous as possible, the detectives filed out.

* * *

Although it had grown colder, the weather was somewhat brighter, a wintry sun drenching the ceiling of cloud with a faint, moist light. Beauclair Drive allotments were deserted and peaceful, the rich, tangy scent of turned soil mingling with that of grass and things secretly sprouting and unfurling.

Hilary Probert's greenhouse stood over in a far corner at the end of a little line of flagstones. A pretty wild-rose tree grew next to it, while a small gravelled area in front contained raised vegetable beds. Next to this neat kitchen garden was a picturesquely untamed mini orchard which Markham figured was a bone of contention between Hilary and the Beauclair Drive committee. A forlornly empty chicken coop represented the triumph of hope over experience, since allotment rules stipulated that 'livestock' were not allowed on the site overnight. 'Chuffing ridiculous,' Noakes scoffed. Arguments about foxes and vandals cut no ice with him. 'Nowt wrong with a few hens,' he insisted. 'That's what happens when spoilsports rule the roost,' he pronounced, as Doyle and Carruthers groaned at the pun.

Hilary's derelict shed, which stood at the rear of her overgrown lawn, allowed space for Markham's team to squeeze in. The hut being at some distance from the greenhouse meant there was little risk of Barlow being alerted to their presence, though Markham had taken the precaution of installing acoustic panels to minimise the sounds of surveillance. Ideally he would have liked a position closer to the action, but Hilary was wired up and in no danger of being taken by surprise.

The script Eleanor Shaughnessy had devised was simple but squarely aimed at extracting that 'big fat confession'. Standing there, tense and silent, Markham's mind flew to the profiler's briefing . . .

'I suggest Hilary contacts Mr Barlow before the funeral — proposes that they skip the wake and meet in her greenhouse at the allotments because "she needs to speak to him,"' the profiler advised. 'Naturally he will press her for details. She then tells him that she's bothered by something Bex Atherton said . . . "it doesn't really add up, but she just wants to set her mind at rest". Once he turns up, she acts awkward and embarrassed, humming and hawing as though reluctant to get to the point. Eventually, however, she confides that Catherine Leckie apparently told Bex she thought *he* was the one who had been spying on her and sending the poison pen notes. "When Bex told her, she couldn't believe it, was sure it was all a big misunderstanding blah blah. And now the police have got it in for *her*, pulled her in for questioning just because she cared about Catherine.'"

'What if he jus' denies everything?' Noakes objected. 'Then it's game over.'

'Not if Hilary ratchets up his anxiety levels . . . gives the impression she's enjoying the drama of it all . . . an unstable attention-seeker who could give him real problems with the police . . . Then she turns over-familiar and insinuating — puts her social worker's hat on and starts explaining him to himself . . . mentions behavioural patterns and denial . . . says she knows about his "tragic" home life . . . tosses out words like "rejection" and "emptiness" and "hiding from one's feelings" . . . keeps coming back to his wife and how awful her illness must have been . . . commiserates with him about how Margaret Cresswell dominated the allotment association and bossed them all silly . . . slips in some snide observations about Catherine Leckie making fools of people including the two of them—'

'In other words, she makes him out to be pathetic and not a real bloke,' Noakes concluded.

'Exactly,' the psychologist replied. 'Hilary needs to come across like a neurotic busybody with the hide of a rhino . . . probing hidden wounds that have never healed.'

Noakes considered this. 'The way Cresswell did, you mean?'

'From what I've learned, it seems probable that Mrs Cresswell's tactless clumsiness, on top of everything else, could well have triggered an explosion. I was struck by that phrase Hilary flung at her—'

'You mean what Catherine Leckie said about there being no fool like an old fool?' Markham interjected.

'Yes . . . It seems to me that if Mrs Cresswell in turn used that against Mr Barlow — accused him of impropriety or *unseemliness* around a young woman — then the accusation might well have caused him to lash out and push her downstairs.'

'So if Hilary can build up to something similar, that should make him lose control?' the DI pressed.

'I believe so. Of course it depends on her acting skills.'

Noakes's countenance was eloquent in its conviction that Hilary Probert wouldn't have any trouble doing screwy and neurotic.

But all he said was, 'Won't he smell a rat? I mean, if she had doubts about Barlow, no way would she go anywhere with him by herself.'

'The idea is that she comes across as not believing for a minute that he could be the killer,' the psychologist replied, 'though her subconscious might be telling her different . . . He needs to see her as being all over the place — unbalanced and maudlin — which is why it might be an idea if she arrives swigging from a hipflask and prefaces their candid little chat by saying she needed something to help get through the funeral . . . If she's emotional and half-sloshed — swaying about and glassy-eyed — Mr Barlow will be disarmed.'

'Reckon she c'n do mellow as a newt all right,' was Noakes's verdict. Then, 'Happen this might work after all.'

'It had better,' was Markham's grim riposte . . .

Now suddenly, voices were audible through his headpiece.

Hilary and Peter Barlow.

Listening to the young social worker's crass and apparently half-cut monologue, it seemed almost as though she had missed her vocation, so compelling was her performance. She was pitch perfect: emotionally incontinent while making sure to target all Barlow's weak spots.

When the climax came, it was nevertheless a shock.

'You stupid little bitch.'

His words sliced through the babble, so icy cold that time seemed to stand still.

'Couldn't leave well alone, could you?' The voice was full of bile.

Hilary stammered, 'I'm sorry, *what?*'

'Using your big mouth to air other people's business when you know nothing about it. *Nothing.*'

'I'm sorry if I've offended you somehow. I was she only trying to help—'

'You and the rest weren't fit to wipe my Sheila's boots . . . And then madam decided to give me the run-around.'

'M-madam.'

And now they could hear genuine apprehension in Hilary's voice.

'You know who I mean. That's what you've been getting round to.'

'What?'

'That I killed her.'

'You're saying you killed Catherine?' Despite her fear, Hilary knew they needed it on the record.

'That's right.' And suddenly, unexpectedly, his voice cracked. 'Lovely, *lovely* Catherine letting that *creature* make free with her.'

Hilary was stuttering again.

'R-Raymond? You mean you killed him too?'

'Of course I did.' So matter of fact it was shocking. 'The great I Am who only had to crook his finger and they'd all come running like dogs on heat.' Again that strange clicking in his throat. 'Wasting herself on him . . . letting him crawl all over her when *I'd* have given her *everything.*'

'And Bex?' Hilary's voice was the merest thread.

'Oh she had to go too, Cotter's henchwoman. Between the two of them Catherine was *ruined.*' It was guttural, almost a growl. '*Ruined.*'

Four pairs of eyes were trained on his face, but Markham lifted up his hand in warning.

One more, he telegraphed silently. *We need Margaret Cresswell.* Hilary Probert knew it too.

'D-did Margaret guess?' she blurted out.

'That was a mistake.' His voice was flat again, almost bored. 'Thought she knew me better than I knew myself.' he added, malevolence creeping into his tone. 'Didn't understand the first thing about how it was between me and Catherine . . . made it into something ugly . . . *same as you* . . . stunted, sad little individuals spinning your nasty webs.'

Hilary Probert screamed and Markham gave the signal to his team. *Go!*

It took the four of them to detach Peter Barlow's hands from around her throat. The short, stocky man buttoned into his too tight coat seemed possessed of almost superhuman strength, foaming at the mouth and making a noise that sounded scarcely human. Loud, low and long, they continued to hear it even after the uniforms had burst onto the scene from Hollingrove Park.

As they hauled him out of the allotments, Peter Barlow looked back at Markham.

And smiled.

* * *

'I reckon in the end, he were glad we came for him,' Noakes said decisively.

The gang and Olivia were ensconced in the Grapes on a Saturday afternoon three weeks later, following their tradition of post-investigation drinks. Outside it was snowing, thick cottony flakes dancing and swirling in flurries past the pub windows.

It was the kind of hostelry that was shunned by the fashionable crowd, which suited Markham very well. Denise the landlady, a cross between Bet Lynch and Babs Windsor, had a fearsome reputation when it came to dealing with stroppy regulars but was 'soft as butter' (Noakes's words) when it came to the handsome inspector whose old-fashioned gallantry charmed her. Despite festooning the place with antique brasses and other knick-knacks that she couldn't find it in her heart to jettison, she attracted a loyal following.

''S'like being on the set of *Hornblower*,' Noakes muttered from time to time, but the team never thought of going anywhere else. Certainly the big screen television allayed any fears he and Doyle might have had about 'missing the footie'.

The Snug or back parlour, its walls lined with oak booths, was deliciously cosy in such weather, with an open fire blazing and the creaky floorboards sighing and settling like the heartbeat of the place.

Markham and Olivia were nursing glasses of Châteauneuf-du-Pape while Kate sipped a G&T and the others opted for Ruddles. Replete after the unpretentious house special of fish, chips and mushy peas (Noakes chuckling as usual over his favourite anecdote about how Peter Mandelson 'nearly got hisself duffed up when he asked for "some of that lovely guacamole"'), their talk had turned to the outcome of the allotment murders.

'Yeah, I reckon Barlow was almost glad the game was up,' Doyle said.

'He couldn't stop grinning,' Carruthers shuddered. 'Like Jack Nicholson in *The Shining* . . . lost it completely at the end . . . the way he kept shouting "It's a wrap" when we were booking him in . . .'

'Freaky,' Doyle said with feeling. 'Just as well the medicos decided to whip him into the Newman,' he added, referring to the mental health facility situated behind Bromgrove General on the outskirts of town. A disconcerting mix of redbrick gothic and submarine-like modernism, none of the team was ever keen to cross its portals.

'He's stopped talking now,' Burton said. 'Almost catatonic, apparently. I can't see him being fit to plead.'

'What a cop-out,' Noakes groused. 'Four dead cos he couldn't have what he wanted, an' he gets to do cushy time in the loony bin.'

'Special hospital,' Burton corrected him with a frown. 'And there's nothing cushy about spending the rest of your days in one of those.'

'It sounds as though he loved Catherine very much,' Olivia ventured. 'Well, it started out as a *crime passionnel*, didn't it?'

Noakes snorted but, noticing that she looked pale and tired despite the "I'm fine, thank you" signal she transmitted, didn't contradict her. He was relieved the guvnor hadn't included Eleanor Shaughnessy in their outing, jealous on Olivia's account of the way Markham and the psychologist had struck sparks off each other. There was no denying the woman was good at her job and nicer to look at than Shippers, but still . . . His mouth set in a hard narrow line just thinking about it. Then he saw Olivia watching him in consternation and twisted his pouchy features into a species of smile.

Carruthers, looking less Gestapo and more humanoid in off-duty chinos and sweater, said, 'I guess we'll never know now what was going on in Barlow's head.' It was clear the DS didn't like loose ends.

'That report from Marsh Lane Surgery makes interesting reading,' Markham observed. 'Clearly the sexual dysfunction and depression were of long standing, but his GP thought Mr Barlow had "come out the other side".'

'Cunning bastard,' Noakes muttered. 'Pulled the wool over their eyes good and proper.'

'I think we can conclude that the strain of his wife's long decline, on top of loneliness and grief, fed his paranoid delusions about Catherine Leckie,' Markham said thoughtfully.

'And nobody noticed what was happening,' Doyle said in wonder.

'Well, it's likely that Margaret Cresswell was uneasy about him,' Markham replied. 'She may have guessed that he was sighing after Catherine in a hopeless, ineffectual sort of way. But after that "no fool like an old fool" exchange with Hilary Probert, she took the bit between her teeth and decided to tackle him about it—'

'Not realising the danger,' Carruthers concluded.

'Exactly.' Markham's face was sad. 'She was a good-hearted, overbearing woman who got it horribly wrong.'

'D'you reckon Leckie *did* laugh in his face?' Doyle wanted to know.

'Perhaps she was annoyed Cotter wasn't able to meet up with her on New Year's Eve because of work,' Carruthers said, 'and then when Barlow turned up bleating about everlasting love, she just lost it with him.'

'If he did that and she suddenly twigged he was the phantom poison pen, she could've freaked out and screamed at him or something,' Doyle said. 'Then he laid his hands on her and everything changed.'

'It was too late to undo it,' Burton agreed. 'And,' very softly, 'maybe he found he liked it.'

Olivia swallowed hard at this.

Observing her reaction and hunched shoulders, Noakes said hastily, 'Well, the allotments are bound to get their chickens now that Hippy Hil's running for Chair.'

Doyle laughed. 'The Worzel Gummidge caretaker won't like it,' he said, thinking of Ninian Creech's dislike of the eco-mob. 'Shouldn't wonder if he decides it's time to move on.'

'No great loss,' Noakes grunted.

'Apparently Donald Kemp's giving up his veg patch,' Doyle continued.

'Very politic.' Wooden-faced, Markham added, 'Mr Kemp's had help from inside and I mean to know who.'

After an awkward silence, Carruthers said, 'What's the betting Dave Shipley brings an action against Beauclair for defamation of character or some such bollocks.'

Noakes grinned savagely. 'That'd be worth seeing.'

Eventually the others drifted away leaving Markham and Olivia with their old friend.

'In the end it was like that bloke Doggie told us about,' Noakes mused. 'Evie's brother Bill . . . the one who was making a fool of hisself over some young girl from the council.'

'Well, it may have been Richard III who put me on Peter Barlow's trail, Noakesy, but really it's just the old, old story—'

'Yeah, men being plonkers. Mind you,' with his head on one side, 'women can be daft too. The *Gazette* did a story the other day about some nun who walked out of her convent after this monk came to visit an' they brushed sleeves or sum-mat . . . she were struck all of a heap — ran off to marry him cos she felt this jolt of electricity . . . an' the two of 'em in their fifties!' Noakes hardly looked the type to hold any brief for an order of enclosed nuns, but as usual he confounded expectations. 'It were a bit mean doing that to the boss nun. She musta been proper hurt seeing as the one who eloped joined when she were nineteen.'

Eloped! But Olivia just smiled.

With a shake of the head, Noakes got to his feet.

'Any plans for tonight, George?' Olivia asked him.

'It's *Wives With Knives* night on CBS Reality,' he informed them solemnly. 'We don' want to miss that.'

'Bit of a busman's holiday for you, George.' She didn't think Muriel would be too pleased at having her penchant for ghoulish crime documentaries shared with DI Dreamboat.

'Well, Nat's coming round, so happen we'll get a takeaway.'

Nice uplifting viewing for the mother-to-be, she thought trying not to giggle.

Afterwards, walking home through a winter wonder-land, Olivia was still chuckling.

As they skirted the edge of the municipal cemetery, she turned meditative once more.

'I remember playing in the local RC graveyard with my friends back in the day,' she told Markham, peering through the railings. 'We got really possessive about the different tombs . . . I used to talk about such and such a one being *mine* . . . can you imagine?'

He found and squeezed the small gloved hand that bur-rowed into the pocket of his Crombie overcoat.

'Jon and I were just the same,' he smiled, surprised how naturally the name rose to his lips. 'Had our own particular favourites . . . spent ages making up backgrounds and stories for them . . . family trees, the lot . . .'

'Catherine won't ever see her children play in church-yards,' she whispered. 'And now she's gone.'

Looking up at the cemetery's heavy iron gates, he murmured, 'I like to think she's passed through the door to new vistas, Liv. So she can never truly make an exit.'

They were nearly home.

'I'm sorry about all that before,' she said.

'All what?'

'Driving you mad about babies . . . my harebrained scheme to adopt Natalie's child . . . I wasn't thinking straight.'

The instinct to challenge her with having confided in Noakes flared briefly but then died. Least said, soonest mended.

'*I'm* the one who should apologise for being selfish,' he told her. 'I should have realised what it meant to you.'

She turned round to face him and placed a gloved finger on his lips. Then she pivoted lightly, her arm through his, and they rounded the corner to the Sweepstakes, their apartment block transformed into a filigree confection, its balconies coated white.

'Probably best that we don't become George's in-laws,' she giggled. 'D'you know what he said, back there outside the church, before you disappeared on your stake-out?'

'Something utterly beyond the pale, no doubt.'

'He told me his dad George Senior always called the youngest child in their family "Little Pill Failure". How about that?'

'I have a feeling Muriel wouldn't care to have that piece of family lore do the rounds.'

Still laughing, banishing thoughts of the allotment ghosts, they passed into the building.

Into warmth and light and life.

THE END

THE JOFFE BOOKS STORY

We began in 2014 when Jasper agreed to publish his mum's much-rejected romance novel and it became a bestseller.

Since then we've grown into the largest independent publisher in the UK. We're extremely proud to publish some of the very best writers in the world, including Joy Ellis, Faith Martin, Caro Ramsay, Helen Forrester, Simon Brett and Robert Goddard. Everyone at Joffe Books loves reading and we never forget that it all begins with the magic of an author telling a story.

We are proud to publish talented first-time authors, as well as established writers whose books we love introducing to a new generation of readers.

We have been shortlisted for Independent Publisher of the Year at the British Book Awards three times, in 2020, 2021 and 2022, and for the Diversity and Inclusivity Award at the Independent Publishing Awards in 2022.

We built this company with your help, and we love to hear from you, so please email us about absolutely anything book-ish at feedback@joffebooks.com

If you want to receive free books every Friday and hear about all our new releases, join our mailing list: www.joffebooks.com/contact

And when you tell your friends about us, just remember: it's pronounced Joffe as in coffee or toffee!

ALSO BY CATHERINE MOLONEY